Built
on Bones

Greg Ried

In memory of Martha Eckman

~Mentor and Friend~

Acknowledgements

Thanks to my lovely wife, Eileen Ried, for her unwavering support and encouragement.

My son, Dan Ried, designed the beautiful and captivating cover by combining a keen artistic eye with graphic arts.

My father, Robert Ried, has patiently read and commented on numerous revisions.

Editorial assistance:
Robert Faherty, Publisher Emeritus at the Brookings Institution
Paul Krafin writer/editor
Ginger and Pete Eby, at PJEby@theebyco.com

Eric J. Mink and Mark Allen (US Department of the Interior, National Park Service) helped with the historical research.

Thanks to Dianne Gray for introducing me to the Chewning-Higgerson clan.

And special thanks to Mary Jane Fieser for sharing personal information about her great-great-grandmother, Permelia Higgerson.

A Note to Readers

On Christmas day 2001, my brother, Bill Ried, gave me a copy of Gordon C. Rhea's book, *The Battle of the Wilderness, May 5-6, 1864*. Rhea's book opened my eyes to Civil War history. I then became interested in a local Civil War civilian named Permelia Higgerson. Permelia was the courageous woman who chastised Union soldiers as they trampled her garden during The Battle of the Wilderness. Permelia Higgerson has inspired this historical fiction.

The American Civil War was a remarkably violent period in our nation's history, although love and human tenderness also thrived during those turbulent years. This novel deals with many of those aspects as seen through the eyes of civilians.

Most major characters in this novel are entirely fictional. Actual persons of public prominence have been included within the story in appropriate settings. The resemblance of any character to anyone, living or dead, is unintended.

The addendum includes an account of the actual life and times of Permelia Higgerson. Permelia's fifteen minutes of fame was only the beginning of her amazing story.

I live near Fredericksburg, Virginia on the border of the Wilderness Battlefield. Unlike the fictitious community of Scarborough Run, the good people of Fawn Lake have a great deal of respect for the Civil War and The Battle of the Wilderness.

None of the homes in Fawn Lake are actually

"Built on Bones"

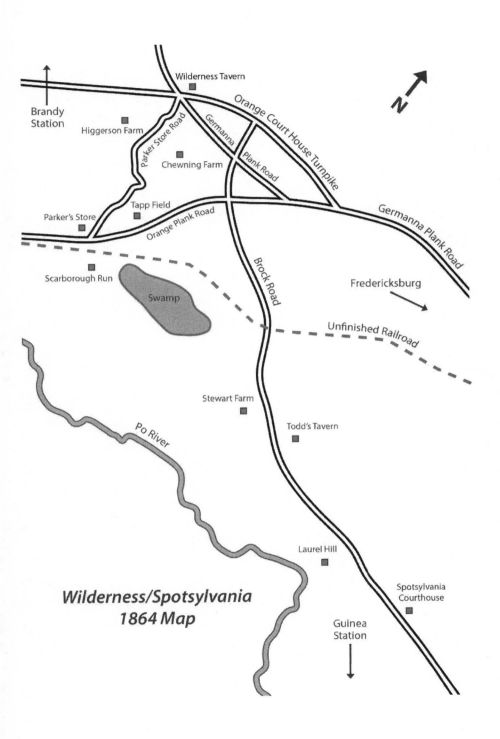

Brandy
Station

Wilderness Tavern

Higgerson Farm

Parker Store Road

Germanna

Orange Court House Turnpike

Plank Road

Chewning Farm

Tapp Field

Parker's Store

Orange Plank Road

Germanna Plank Road

Scarborough Run

Swamp

Brock Road

Fredericksburg

Unfinished Railroad

Po River

Stewart Farm

Todd's Tavern

Laurel Hill

Spotsylvania
Courthouse

N

*Wilderness/Spotsylvania
1864 Map*

Guinea
Station

Part One

~addiction~

1

The human shape in the fog seemed to glow as Jack floated nearer. The new moon could illuminate little else and the surrounding colorless trees waited for something to stir their leaves. As he drifted closer, the rant of agitated flies began to echo in his head and the pervasive smell of death filled the stagnant air. He wanted to turn away but glided closer to the phantasm like a cloud of smoke on an infinitesimal breeze.

The gruesome figure was hanging by the neck from a towering dead oak tree and a threadbare blanket was draped over its head. Compelled by something beyond curiosity or reason, Jack raised the blanket with a single finger and gazed at the distorted face that lived only in the sticky sweat of nightmares.

Hungry flies crawled over the dead man's extended purple tongue and scurried in and out of his wide-open mouth. A noose had been inserted into a gaping neck wound, which tilted the head of the corpse unnaturally and raised its protruding eyes to the heavens. More flies filled the gash in his neck forming a moving black ribbon and his nearly decapitated body hung below him as if on a thread.

As he began to rise from his cavernous nightmare, Jack sensed that he was lying face-up in a pool of water, gasping for air. He bolted up to a sitting position. As his horror began to subside, he recognized shapes, not of some pond or swamp but of the familiar things in his bedroom. He stared blankly, trying to make sense of it. Once his bleary mind assured him that he was safe and dry, he fell back into his soaking bed. The cool, sodden pillow and sheets woke him further although not completely.

He felt gnawing flies dancing on his neck and swatted the phantom insects as he rose further from his inebriated dream. The face of the corpse reappeared and then gradually morphed into a fern on his bed-side table. Still horrified, he sensed that he was lying next to the cadaver and his heart raced as he turned to face his nightmare.

2

To Jack's relief, he saw no swollen, infected flesh and heard no enraged insects. There was only Jill, and she was sleeping soundly. He listened to her slow rhythmic breathing and thought of a thousand things he had done to worry her—a long, pathetic list of selfish, alcohol-induced behavior that had left him awash in regret. His dream had disturbed him deeply and he longed for his wife as a child seeks his mother after a nightmare. He wanted to wake her gently and hold her in his arms but hesitated. Inviting her into the aftermath of his dreamscape would only add sparks to an already smoldering fire.

No, he'd keep his dream to himself, by God, and he wouldn't dare mention what he had seen, or *thought* he had seen, during his drive home from the airport. Jill was much too fragile when it came to nightmares and she was easily frightened. Telling her tales of strange apparitions on the foggy road would freak her out and undoubtedly stir up a discussion about his drinking. Those conversations never ended well, so he would keep his nightmare and his hair-raising encounters to himself.

Jill had few limitations and had always supported him in spite of the fact that, when it came to limitations, he had a truckload. He closed his eyes and remained facing his sleeping wife while the scent of her Estée Lauder began to elevate his desire. In spite of his nightmare and nagging hangover, he wanted her. Although the right half of Jill's face was compressed into her pillow, he could think only of her silky black hair, blue eyes, slender body, and the way she groaned when they made love. He missed her when he was away and he'd been missing her while at home as well.

Frustrated and exhausted, he tossed and turned while staring at the soft shadows on the bedroom ceiling. He finally accepted that sleep would not return and decided to trade his bed for his favorite chair on the screened porch. He stumbled clumsily out of bed, cursed himself for disturbing the stony silence, and looked at his reflection in the dim bathroom vanity light. His bloodshot eyes and haggard, alcohol-soaked reflection resembled the four a.m. mug shot of a strung-out movie star.

You look like crap, he thought.

His increasingly hollow, drained appearance worried him, but he dismissed his concern with a splash of water and a shot of mouthwash. He tiptoed into the kitchen, brewed strong coffee, and topped off the steaming mug with a generous amount of sweet-smelling cognac. With the coffee mug and cognac bottle in hand, he entered the screen porch and melted into the familiar cushions of his favorite wicker chair, which groaned under his weight. When the spiked coffee was nearly gone, he refilled the oversized mug to the brim with more cognac and drifted into the small hours of the warm, mellow night.

He planned to return to bed before dawn knowing that Jill would wake shortly after sunrise, work out, and then leave for school where she would teach important things to little people. She was more than qualified to teach in any graduate school but loved teaching young children and they adored her Disney-like manner. She referred to herself as "the queen of the pee-pee squeezers" because of the excited four-year-old boys in her classes. Year after year, the thrill and delight of Leprechaun traps, living volcanoes, and pup tent rocket ships would cause a few of the excited little guys to squeal with delight while squeezing their pee-pees. Every spring, in the predawn hours of registration day, dozens of Starbucks-toting parents wait patiently in line to secure positions for their children in Jill's class.

She was a "keeper" all right and Jack loved everything about her, including her sense of humor. Over the years, Jack and Jill had actually welcomed comments about "breaking their crowns" and so forth, although they agreed to avoid living on a hill of any kind—just in case.

Jill's positive support had been preventing his emotional collapse for years and he was determined to insulate her bright and blameless view of the world from his growing despair. He frequently thought of a quote from the Old Testament: "The merry heart doeth good like a medicine: but a broken spirit drieth the bones." Jack's broken spirit couldn't help dwelling on disturbing things such as the prior evening's harrowing flight home from Zürich. The alarming images he saw during his drive home and the impending economic failure of his airline had also increased his stress level. He would not, however, allow such things to taint Jill's merry heart.

Alone with his thoughts and demons, the tormented pilot sipped cognac and stared into the night as his dry bones and dark spirit replayed the previous day's events.

3

The intricate, slowly changing navigation and instrument displays on the Boeing 777 instrument panel were incredibly boring after six hours of flight. The tedious information is presented in high definition on numerous liquid crystal displays; Jack struggled to check and recheck every detail. Through his fatigue, his methodical pilot's mind was making every effort to ensure that the onboard computers were performing exactly as programmed. He was well aware that this particular flight from hell would end soon, with or without fuel in the tanks.

Things had begun to deteriorate ten hours earlier in Zürich when a commanding voice with a German accent bellowed instructions from the control tower. "Cancel takeoff clearance and proceed immediately to the bomb threat parking area!"

Tolerances used to determine credible threats had been exceeded for his flight and the aircraft was recalled for a thorough search. Since the 9/11 attacks, security issues were taken much more seriously; this one resulted in the removal of two passengers who were "suspected of being related to a known terrorist." Security personnel and bomb-sniffing dogs swarmed over the huge jet like maggots. Although the search proceeded with Swiss efficiency and speed, the delay was significant and the passengers became increasingly impatient.

Every twenty minutes, Captain Stewart pacified his passengers with reassuring cabin announcements. "Ladies and gentlemen, this is Captain Stewart again. Sorry for the delay. All is well and we will be under way shortly."

"Too bad my nose is the only thing that gets longer when I lie to the passengers," he said to his copilot, who was reading the *Wall Street Journal*.

Never looking up from his newspaper, his copilot said "More bad news, right?"

"Yep, sure is. Looks like liquidation may be our only option this time around."

Jack yawned and said, "Great...I'll read it on the way home if we ever get out of here."

The flight was finally cleared by security and they departed without further delay. Removal of questionable customers was a great idea but, instead of sharing those details with the remaining passengers, Captain Stewart told a few additional appeasing lies. "False alarm, folks. We'll be departing immediately. Thanks for your patience."

En route to Dulles Airport in Virginia, the transatlantic atmosphere was unstable and the aircraft bumped and jolted for many long, uncomfortable hours. A mere 1,000 feet separates flights within the congested transatlantic airway system; higher and smoother flight levels were unavailable. Worse, the delay in Zürich meant that Jack's flight was assigned to low flight level that was more turbulent and *always* burned more fuel.

At least it's bumpy, Jack thought sardonically as the aircraft's fuel burn increased by one, then two tons greater than planned.

Although Captain Stewart had left the seat belt sign on, he knew the passengers would eventually disregard the warning and wander back to the lavatories. If they flew through severe turbulence and some passengers were slammed against the cabin ceiling, the illuminated seat belt sign would lessen his liability. As always, however, the pilot in command would ultimately be held responsible. Jack called his premium flight attendant and asked that she supervise a quiet and discreet seat belt check. He also offered to make a general PA announcement about the seat belt sign, knowing that the flight attendants would rather die than risk waking sleeping passengers. Predictably, the flight attendant chose to check seat belts, which meant that Jack's ass remained covered as well as any pilot's posterior could be.

A relief pilot had been assigned to the flight and each pilot would receive a two-hour break. Jack sat in the first-class crew rest seat during his rest period but didn't rest at all as the aircraft bounced and lumbered along. He thought of flying throughout the Caribbean in the narrow-body Boeing 757. *Yeah, those were the days—flying by the seat of my pants in the good old Eastern time zone.* Instead, he found himself near the end of his career flying "long-haul" flights in a jumbo jet to enhance his retirement. *Doesn't seem fair, especially since I may be doing all of this for nothing if the airline fails.*

He couldn't sleep, so he reluctantly read about his airline in the newspaper. Twice, during the previous ten years, the airline had reorganized under Chapter 11 of the bankruptcy laws, which expunged large amounts of debt and left creditors and vendors holding the bag. The paper speculated that there would be no third chance and liquidation was now likely.

If the airline did liquidate, he would lose all of his income and most of his retirement nest egg. After twenty-five years of service, his last five years were to be his highest for pay and compensation. Retirement funds were based on those lucrative years. If the company dissolved, much of his retirement would be lost leaving him with a meager monthly sum from the government. In this economy, no airline would hire a fifty-five-year-old pilot. Even if he could find another flying job, he would lose all of his precious seniority.

"I'd rather be a greeter at Wal-Mart," he muttered.

"Did you say something, Jack?" his copilot asked.

"No, just daydreaming."

"The flight attendants are still complaining about the turbulence."

"Can't blame them," Jack replied. "It's pretty bad back there."

"Hey, Jack, how many flight attendants does it take to change a light bulb?"

Jack looked at him and shrugged his shoulders.

"Zero. They just sit in the dark and bitch about it."

"I'll be sure to pass that that on to them," Jack said with a grin.

Captain Stewart had returned from his break early, although he was still dealing with thoughts of gloom and doom. His son was a junior at Chapel Hill and, fortunately, money had been set aside for both undergraduate and graduate schools. Jill was over-educated and could certainly find a higher-paying teaching job, which would be more lucrative than anything he could find with an antiquated degree in pre-med.

He swallowed two Excedrin as his thoughts, dreams and concerns blended with those of his passengers and they pierced the starless sky, flying over the cold ocean at eighty-three percent of the speed of sound. He knew that even a small explosion in the pressurized aircraft could spell disaster. They were well beyond positive radar contact and the search for wreckage would be based upon their last known position. Flying the crippled aircraft to one of the distant alternate airports may not be possible. Chances of survival in the black, frigid Atlantic were slim, but Captain Stewart dismissed thoughts like that as most crewmembers do.

By the time they made landfall on the east coast of the United States, fuel and fatigue had become problematic. Stress levels were increasing and Jack's pain reliever was wearing off. Captain Stewart was blaming his sore head on the lack of sleep rather than the German beer he had consumed on the layover. His drinking problem had begun during the first bankruptcy and worsened considerably since. He was still unable to admit that his abuse of alcohol had become a serious a problem.

Twenty-four hours between bottle and throttle—close enough, he thought.

Flights like this were like a bad round of golf that continued to worsen. News of rapidly deteriorating weather conditions at Dulles Airport and a holding pattern delay seemed par for the course. The Traffic Collision Avoidance System or TCAS display indicated the relative positions of the other seven airliners stacked above and below them in the holding pattern. If one of the other airplanes unintentionally gained or lost altitude, its symbol on the TCAS would turn yellow, then red. A loud warning horn would erupt along with voice and visual instructions directing the pilot to avoid collision by taking manual control of the aircraft. The domino effect would follow and several half-million-pound turbojets would react to each other like lumbering whales in the sea.

After flying a fuel-hungry racetrack pattern for thirty minutes, an approach clearance was finally received. The clearance was timely because a diversion to Kennedy Airport had been planned and programmed and would have been executed if the delay had continued. The runway visibility at Dulles was a mere 300 feet and a completely automated, computerized approach and landing was required. Several aircraft diverted immediately because, unlike the "Triple Seven," they were not certified to accomplish the sophisticated "category three, autoland approach." Therefore, Jack's flight moved to the front of the line. He and his copilot had programmed the computers so that the huge machine would fly the approach and land itself automatically. It would be "hands off" for the pilots, who would not touch anything until after landing. The computers had one chance to complete the approach and landing precisely. It was Jack's responsibility to reject the approach if any error was detected. In that case, 200,000 pounds of raw thrust would push the uncomfortable passengers into their seats while hundreds of pounds of precious fuel fed the powerful engines during the "go around."

"I really don't want to scare the passengers tonight," Jack said to his crew. "Besides, if we go around, some of them will puke and puking is always contagious. That will really upset our flight attendants, who probably hate us already because of the delay and bumpy air. If we end up in "The Big Apple" rather than our nation's capital, we'll be on everyone's shit list."

Both copilots agreed and no one said a word as the computer inputs to the three independently powered autopilots were rechecked. Once every detail of the approach was thoroughly briefed, the crew settled in to watch the computers fly the two-hundred-ton machine. They were satisfied with the performance of the computers during the final approach segment as the ground rose at seven hundred feet per minute. Because they were reduced to computer babysitters, however, intense concentration was interrupted by milliseconds of mind roaming reprieve and each pilot had his own fleeting thoughts. Jack's most recent obsession was genealogy and the infinitesimal impulses that stabbed at *his* brain were all related to his family history.

4

If Jack hadn't abandoned history in favor of pre-med and then dropped out of medical school to become a pilot, he might have been writing pharmaceutical prescriptions rather than being hurled through the inky night in a half-million-pound computer. Because of his addictive personality, he was "easily obsessed" with one thing or another. Even the most compelling of his obsessions had ended abruptly because of boredom or a sudden fascination with something new.

Jack's father was a physician, who came from a long line of medical practitioners. He was disappointed when his son dropped out of medical school to become an Air National Guard fighter pilot. Jack had seemed genuinely excited about becoming a doctor, although Dr. Artie Stewart knew his only child well and feared that Jack would, eventually, lose interest in medical school. Artie knew that his son would be happier flying an F-16 "with his hair on fire" rather than learning "how the hip bone is connected to the backbone." To support his decision, Artie gave him a small, single engine airplane on his twenty-fifth birthday. He hoped that the Piper Cub would complement Jack's part-time Air National Guard position and further fuel his interest in flying.

Over time, barnstorming in the Cub at sixty knots and tactical flying hours in the F-16 at 600 knots, led to a pilot position with a major airline. After a few additional "fat, dumb, and happy years," he met and married his wife, Jill, and they started a family. Unlike flying the F-16, however, commercial flying proved to be rather boring. He then became obsessed with golf and moved his family from one golf course community to another. When he finally "checked out" as a captain, the Stewart family settled in an upscale community nestled among the Civil War Battlefields of Central Virginia.

There, he developed an interest in Civil War history and discovered that he was related to Major John (J.M.P.) Atkinson, who had been the president of Hampden-Sydney College and served as a Confederate surgeon during the Civil War. Jack quickly became preoccupied with genealogy and, after spending weeks on the internet, found Wilhelm Atkinson (J.M.P. Atkinson's great-grandfather) on a passenger manifest. The record revealed that Wilhelm had come from an area in western Zürich called Alstetten and arrived in America in 1748.

He was, once again, obsessed and began to fly his airline trips to Zürich in order to research his family history. He started with the Zürich State Achieves and then zeroed in on Canton Alstetten where he examined baptism records that served as birth records as far back as 1491. With the help of Rosetta Stone, he was able to communicate with librarians, who helped with written translations. He also spent time in the local pubs of the Alstetten Quarter, District 9 Zürich, which is a blue-collar, high crime area in the western part of that city. An open bar tab loosened the tongues of the locals, who would not have otherwise given him the time of day. His efforts paid off when he was introduced to a man named Lars Atkinson, who proved to be a living relative.

Lars was a jolly, blue-collar, back-slapping giant who loved to drink beer with his long-lost relative from America. Lars introduced dozens of thirsty kin to his American cousin and the pilot's celebrity grew quickly because of his liberal bar tab. After months of tedious interviews, extensive research, and gallons of beer, Jack was able to trace his family history all the way back to Scotland in 1066.

He recorded his European genealogy on a DVD and offered a copy to all of his new-found relatives who, in turn, decided that Jack would never buy another beer. He continued to fly to Zürich and the beer kept flowing. He then turned all of his attention to his American family history. There was a treasure trove of genealogical information available in America and he zeroed in on the life and times of his Civil War relative, J.M.P. Atkinson.

Jack's dad had told him about J.M.P. Atkinson though it meant little to him at the time. Now that he was helplessly obsessed with genealogy and living in the lap of the Civil War, he could think of nothing else. In 1861, Dr. Atkinson led an almost comical band of students into battle against General George McClellan's massive Union Army. The "Hampden-Sydney Boys" as they were known, fought at Big Bethel and were captured at The Battle of Rich Mountain and then released. That kind of information made Jack ache for more. What was the rest of J.M.P. Atkinson's story? How about his family? What did these people do during the Civil War? Those mysteries kept him preoccupied during the day and filled his dreams at night.

During the final approach at Dulles Airport, thick fog rushed past the windshield of his sterile cockpit as the runway rose to meet the airplane. Captain Stewart forced himself to concentrate while his ephemeral thoughts were of General McClellan's statement to the Hampden-Sydney Boys when he pardoned them:

"Boys, secession is dead in this region, go back to your college, take your books, and become wise men."[1]

5

If the computers operated correctly, the big Boeing would compensate for crosswinds, flare, touchdown precisely on the centerline of the runway, and apply the brakes with no input from either pilot. The pilots were trained to trust their instruments and simply allow the aircraft to land itself in a black hole. They were prepared to have absolutely no visual contact with the runway until after touchdown, which was both amazing and disconcerting. Although "blind landings" were rare, Jack had experienced several during his career and was a believer in the awe-inspiring technology.

Visibility? Computers don't need no stinking visibility, he thought.

"Thank God for computers," he said to his fellow pilots.

"Amen," one of the exhausted men said.

The dazzling landing lights reflected each molecule of the solid fog as a computer-generated voice called out decreasing heights above the ground: fifty feet, forty, thirty, twenty…An instant before touchdown, a ghostly white runway centerline stripe with embedded lights passed under the nose. After touchdown, the cockpit remained thirty-seven feet above the runway surface until the computers gently lowered the nose of the enormous machine to the ground.

"Perfect," Jack said as the aircraft automatically tracked down the centerline of the runway. Once they slowed to 100 knots, the weary Captain disconnected the autopilots and taxied clear of the runway.

"Piece of cake," he said to his copilot, who didn't hear him because of radio chatter. "Flying with our assholes the size of a BB," he continued as they approached the parking gate.

"Say again, Jack?"

Captain Stewart didn't answer as he parked the aircraft precisely at the gate; once all checklists were completed, the flight crew began to relax. Before leaving the cockpit, Jack shook hands with his fellow pilots and complimented their good work.

"I love this job," he said, receiving weary grins in response.

Pilots rarely say much to each other about approaches or landings, no matter how hair-raising they may be. "Any landing you walk away from is a good one." Pilots understand pilots like cops understand cops and incompetence is never tolerated—at least not for long. Jack had a good crew on this particular flight and appreciated their help.

Most passengers assume that the captain rather than the copilot or, heaven forbid, *a computer*, is at the controls of every landing. A successful touchdown in bad weather after many exhaustive delays meant that Captain Stewart would be a reluctant hero for at least a few minutes. To satisfy the marketing department, he straightened his tie, used eye drops to disguise his fatigue, and strolled into the cabin to say goodnight to his lucky passengers. He smiled, nodded, and bid farewell to each relieved customer while half-heartedly accepting credit for the computer's good landing.

With each bob of his aching head, he thought, *Thanks for flying with us, folks. Come back and see us when our sphincters are a little more relaxed.*

In truth, he didn't know if his airline would be operating when these people returned to the air.

6

Terrorist issues, low-visibility flying, and concerns about impending economic failure were stressful enough, but the two-hour ride home would take at least three because of the fog. Unlike the highly automated 777, his old Porsche had to be driven manually through the same inky night. Still, he was thankful that his job never came home with him and he was looking forward to six glorious days off as he strapped into his car and turned the key. He was headed home where he would catch up on much-needed sleep and forget about terrorism, delays, bad weather, and bad food.

He couldn't have known that this would be his last flight.

To his relief, his car started and he crept out of the employee parking lot as fast as he dared. He cracked open a window and reached into his cooler for a slightly chilled beer, hoping the mild night air would keep him awake and the beer would keep him steady. With the radio cranked up and beer in hand, he settled in for the last leg of his journey.

The anxious ride on winding Virginia roads seemed never to end and he strained to stay awake as he approached the dark, narrow streets near his rural home. The local roads resembled narrow English lanes with no streetlights or shoulders; the trees that met overhead darkened the route even on moonlit evenings. The fog thickened and he was forced to slow to a crawl, guided only by the worn centerline stripe on the road.

"Riders on the Storm" by The Doors was blasting from the radio when he turned onto historic Brock Road and into a solid wall of dense fog. Suddenly, in a heart-skipping flash, someone appeared right in front of him! There was no time to react as the murky figure filled the windshield and seemed to pass right through the car.

He completed the turn, stopped, and peered into the rearview mirror seeing only the red glow of his brake lights. With his mind racing and heart pounding, he realized that he could have or should have hit something or someone.

What the hell was that? he thought as he turned the music down, knowing he shouldn't remain stopped on the foggy road. The road offered no shoulder to pull over and he was not foolish enough to back up, so he accelerated slowly while trying to convince himself that he hadn't hit anything. *I didn't feel or hear anything, so how could I have hit someone?*

His brittle nerves were shattered.

"Someone?" he muttered. "That wasn't 'a someone'! You'd have to be crazy to stand around in the middle of the damn road on a night like this. What kind of idiot would be out here at all?"

He shifted his weight, shook his head and thought, *I don't know what that was but it wasn't a hit-and-run, that's for sure.* An awful smell filled the car and he coughed in disgust. *It was probably a big garbage bag blowing across the road and someone must have used it to bag a dead animal—that would explain this horrible smell.*

He opened the window wider and accelerated as fast as he dared, still trying to convince himself that nothing had happened. *The loud music and my tired imagination got the best me, that's all.* He cracked open the last can of beer and quickly gulped the contents. *I've got to get my sorry ass home and catch up on sleep.* He grinned weakly after driving another quarter mile and thought about going back. *Yo! Hop in. What up? Before I run into you again, how about standing a little closer to your deodorant can?* He tightened his grip on the wheel and accelerated on the wet, slender road. All he wanted was to relax with his dog and Jack Daniels, followed by sleep in his own beautiful bed.

"*If you give this man a ride, sweet memory will die.*" Those eerie lyrics from the Doors were rattling around in his head when he reached the four-way stop at Orange Plank Road and Brock Road, minutes from his home. He pictured the Union Army forming their lines here and facing the Confederates during the horrible Battle of the Wilderness. This was where hundreds of men and four general officers were killed or severely wounded. Confederate Lieutenant General James Longstreet, who was second-in-command of the Confederate Army, was seriously wounded by friendly fire near here.

The Union's Major General James S. Wadsworth died nearby. Wadsworth, at age fifty-six, was the oldest and wealthiest divisional commander, who had received his second star the day before he was wounded. His personal net worth was said to rival that of the entire Confederate Army.

The Civil War enthralled Jack and it was especially spine-chilling to see this intersection in the night's thick fog. In spite of his frazzled nerves and fatigue, he lingered to take it all in before looking in all directions for any sign of headlights. Seeing none, he slowly turned right and was startled again. A hooded man was standing a few feet from the road's edge with his head lowered. The new apparition appeared briefly in his headlights and then vanished into the gloom. With a rush of adrenaline, he slammed on his brakes, skidded, and narrowly missed a roadside ditch.

He remained in the swirling fog listening to the faint knock in his engine and looking into his rearview mirror. Suddenly, the hooded figure emerged from the fog bank and ran toward him! He floored the Porsche to gain distance. *Damn! That was no plastic bag. If this is someone's idea of a joke, it's not funny at all.* With his heart in his mouth, he continually glanced into his mirror before finally slowing down. *Who the hell was that and what's going on? What a lunatic. He's gonna get run over and I hope he does—stupid ass.*

The exhausted pilot drove another mile before settling down. *I could have run into him, which would have been my fault of course.* He sighed and thought that scaring people in the fog was pretty benign compared to some of the crazy stuff that went on in his area. Little kids had been abducted near his home and the terrorist cowards Muhammad and his little sniper buddy, Malvo, had chosen this area to murder innocent people at random, including the wife of a fellow pilot.

As he drove on, he remembered that some people blame the unusual behavior of the locals on ghosts. They think spirits from the Civil War are still roaming around. They claim that Fredericksburg is a hot bed of paranormal activity because 100,000 young soldiers and civilians died in a concentrated area. In addition to the Revolutionary War, there was an astounding loss of life during the four major Civil War battles, which were fought near his home:

Fredericksburg, Chancellorsville, Wilderness, and Spotsylvania Courthouse. Some believe that the spirits of many soldiers still linger. They also believe that the unnatural demise of so many has produced a kind of paranormal energy that agitates the living.

Jack had heard that nonsense more than once but didn't believe it. He dismissed notions of ghosts and the "dark side" and refused to dwell on such things.

Although a lot of people, including my next-door neighbors, believe every word, he thought.

He decided that the apparitions in the fog had enjoyed a little fun at his expense. He knew they couldn't have singled him out for their prank and chalked it off as "random entertainment for the feeble-minded." He was still thinking about the idiots in the fog as he drove through a National Battlefield Park and approached the security gates of his community. Scarborough Run was an upscale island in a sea of farms, trailer homes, and isolated country estates.

There are strange folks everywhere, he thought as he glanced at the peculiar-looking security guard. He didn't recognize the man and was much too tired to discuss his "encounters," so he drove by and smiled the same way he had smiled at his passengers.

Samantha, who was half golden retriever and half human, knew the sound of Jack's car and always greeted him enthusiastically. As he turned the doorknob that led from the garage to the kitchen, he could hear her tail banging against the mudroom wall and he was greeted with her smiling face, wet nose, and wagging body. As was the case with all Goldens, the tail really did wag the dog.

Sam loved it when the big cheese came home, stretched out on the living room floor, and drank whiskey. The more he drank, the more treats appeared and, when the whiskey and treats were gone, a belly rub was guaranteed. With the arrival of the big guy, she could relax because her master was home from another successful hunt and it was his turn to guard the house against the deer and the mail carrier.

"I'm exhausted," he said to the belly-up dog.

He collapsed into bed next to his quiescent wife and, the next thing he knew, he awoke from his nightmare.

7

It was 5:00 a.m. and the pilot's wicker chair squeaked as he stretched and gazed through a drunken haze into the lonely predawn. A three-foot layer of fog blanketed the open golf fairway and crept into the black woods, although the gloom had lifted enough to expose blurred shapes in his back yard. As he sipped his coffee-flavored cognac and watched the fog tumble, straighten, and flow, the bird feeder and individual trees began to emerge from the gloom. *Like Dracula, I'll have to return to bed before dawn.*

Abruptly, the chorus of crickets and peepers stopped as if they sensed a large animal passing by. Although the air was still and the insects were hushed, Jill's wind chime began to tingle illogically.

Then, someone appeared out on the golf course fairway, waist-deep in fog. The upper half of the figure seemed to be floating as if balanced on a cloud and Jack could feel its icy stare in spite of the cloak that kept its face hidden. The inebriated pilot rubbed his eyes, hoping the frightening vision would just disappear.

It didn't.

Instead, the vision continued to float on the fog like a buoy on the ocean and Jack felt a chill as drops of perspiration trickle down the back of his neck.

What now? he thought.

He could smell the cognac in his coffee cup and drank again, regretting his weakness. His dreams and visions would surely vanish when he put the bottle down; if he stopped hallucinating he could stop drinking. There was nothing he could do about it at the moment, however, so he watched and waited while the tingling wind chime serenaded another gulp of cognac.

Nothing happened.

"Hey!" Jack shouted.

Silence.

I'm okay…that guy is not really there, he thought.

He looked into his empty coffee cup, then back at the phantasm. He convinced himself that the figure was an illusion, but then it raised its hand and slowly gestured toward him. He rose unsteadily and switched the floodlights on, but the bright lights were defused in the fog. When he turned the lights off, the apparition had vanished.

Still sweating in the cool dawn air, he sat back down and rubbed his sore eyes. The fog had lifted and the morning was brightening, but his mind continued to play tricks on him. Then, he saw something moving on the far side of the fairway that looked like a massive herd of migrating deer. Hundreds of shapes and shadows were moving south within the misty forest like Tolkien's Middle-earth Ents and Elves. He stood and looked from left to the right, taking in the entire two hundred yards of visible woods and, sure enough, the whole area was moving. *Can't be deer—impossible.*

Nevertheless, there it was. The moving, almost shimmering motion looked like heat waves rising from a desert floor except that the motion was improbably horizontal. *What the hell is happening now?* He was beginning to doubt his ability to reason. The possibility of a brain tumor crossed his mind as he looked again into his empty mug. As quickly as the motion had started, it stopped, and the rhythmic songs of the insects returned.

Confused, tired, intoxicated, and a bit frightened, he watched the sun begin to rise. He decided to have one more drink, convincing himself that he would have no chance of returning to sleep without it. After a long gulp from the cognac bottle, he stumbled back into bed without waking Jill and managed to rationalize everything before drifting off to sleep. He assumed that the floating man was part of his alcohol-tainted imagination and he blamed the moving woods on the deer.

The last thing that moved through these woods like that was probably the Confederate Army on their way to fight in Spotsylvania, 150 years ago, he thought.

He reasoned that since the whole community is a "Posted-No-Hunting" nature preserve, he must have seen a heard of deer. Night and day, hundreds of deer roam around eating all the flowers in Scarborough Run—all except the purple ones.

"Maybe they can't see purple stuff," he mumbled as he pushed his face into the dry side of his pillow.

He and Jill had decided to develop an appreciation for purple flowers rather than wage war with the hungry deer-devils. He felt sorry for them. Besides, it was nice to see them wandering around the neighborhood as if in a petting zoo and he enjoyed pointing them out to visitors. It was also great fun to watch the deer eat his neighbor's flowers because Ralph Burnside was a major pain in the ass. Jack had considered tossing a few salt licks among the trees behind Ralph's house to lure the hungry shrub-eaters to his neighbor's yard.

He was high enough to find humor in that and, after nudging his soggy-bottomed pillow, he drifted into another bizarre dream.

8

In his dream, he was sitting in his golf cart in the middle of a fairway, peering through a hand-held laser to determine the distance to the flagstick on the green. It was exactly 179 yards.

"You should use your seven iron for this shot," said the man sitting next to him.

"It's almost 180 yards," Jack said skeptically.

"Use your seven iron," the man said from under a dark, thin blanket, which kept his face hidden.

"How do you know it's a seven iron and why are you here?" Jack mumbled as he peered through the laser device again, seeing only a hazy blur.

"I've been watching you because I need your help and I'm in a hurry."

When he glanced at the man again he was gone and his playing partner, Larry, had taken the hooded man's place.

Larry said, "What's up, Jack?"

"That guy told me to hit a seven iron from here and he said he was in a hurry."

Larry stared at him and said, "You should do what he said."

When he struck his seven iron, the ball seemed to hang in the air forever before landing softly next to the flagstick. Larry exploded into laughter and Jack was still laughing along with his old friend when he woke. He couldn't remember why he was laughing, but alcohol consumption had caused dehydration and his thirst forced him to rise shortly before 8:00 a.m. He ignored his headache, drank three glasses of water at the bathroom sink, and realized that sunlight had brightened the room enough to spoil his plans to "sleep in." Jill had refused to install blackout shades in their bedroom because she loved to wake in the dawn's light.

"Besides," she said, "I don't want you to think you're waking up in some lonely, dark hotel room."

To get much-needed sleep at odd hours, many pilots darken hotel rooms by duct-taping the curtains to the walls. Jack had threatened to do the same at home, but a heavy helping of "the look" quickly ended that discussion.

He crawled back into bed like a wounded animal, covered his head with his sticky pillow, and groaned when Samantha began to bark. Barking, especially incessant barking, was rare for Samantha.

Something must have spooked her, he thought.

The continuous barking accelerated Jack's headache and kick-started his brain. *I've never dreamed like that. Every detail was in full color and I could actually smell the grass on the golf course as well as the rotting flesh of that hideous corpse. I never dream in color and rarely remember my dreams, yet I remember every detail.*

Alcohol abuse had dominated his life and he became increasingly skilled at justifying his shortcomings and ignoring bad or confusing news. He also became an expert in mitigating all things, especially those over which he had no control. Flying airplanes offered complete control, even when computers were doing the job. If something in the day-to-day world became difficult to deal with, or if he was reminded of pure evil like the 9/11 attacks, he would file it away and refuse to deal with it. His encounters on the road and his crazy dreams were both confusing and disturbing. Alcohol and/or immersing himself in some other obsession usually kept such thoughts under lock and key—at least for a while.

He stretched and pulled himself out of bed. Jill wouldn't return until 3:00 p.m., giving him most of the day to sober up. He attempted to wash his hangover away by standing in a hot shower and singing mindless songs like, "How can I miss you if you don't leave?"

"I need coffee," he said to Samantha, who was still growling at something outside.

"Sam! Stop!"

When Samantha saw Jack, she wagged her body and followed happily while the big guy held his hand on his sore forehead and moved his six-foot frame into the kitchen. Jill had prepared a carafe of hot coffee for him, which made him think about her body again—it didn't take much. He added a generous amount of Bailey's Irish Cream to his coffee and sat in the living room. He yawned, scratched his dog, scratched himself, and looked through his tremendous picture window at the sixteenth fairway of "the best new private golf course in Virginia."

Several years earlier, a few bankers and a Congresswoman had become interested in developing this part of the Wilderness battlefield. With a wink and a smile, they transformed the area into Scarborough Run. Faster than bullets at Bull Run, a 300-acre lake and golf course were created along with several hundred one-acre building lots. The project was quickly sold to a large development company for a huge profit, which enabled the investors to go on winking and smiling elsewhere.

Early in the nineteenth century, most of the trees had been removed from the Wilderness to feed the many hungry iron furnaces. No thought was given to conservation. The violated land sprouted dense undergrowth and spawned huge swamps that transformed the area into a difficult place to live or farm and a terrible place to wage war.

War did come, however, and more than 25,000 soldiers died as a result of the two-day Wilderness battle alone. Tens of thousands of soldiers were killed or disfigured at the rate of nearly 1,000 per hour; many were incinerated when the brush was ignited by nineteenth-century weaponry. The earth swallowed what it could not burn and thousands of metallic items, such as bullets and belt buckles, remained buried and forgotten. Today, people with deep pockets and no history books come here to fish, golf, and build dream homes.

"Houses built on bones," Jack muttered. "Come on down! The golf is great and the fish are jumpin'."

He had intended to drive down to Hampden Sydney to do some research on J.M.P. Atkinson but decided to put that off until he felt a little better. Instead, he would hang around and wait for Jill to get home. *Maybe I'll take her out to dinner.* When his coffee was gone, he ate an energy bar, spiked another mug of coffee, and joined Samantha on the back lawn. Sam loved retrieving her tennis ball because it was her job to retrieve and she couldn't help herself. Carrying two tennis balls in her mouth simultaneously was something close to nirvana. She repeatedly dropped the ball at Jack's feet and enthusiastically asked him to toss it again, and again. When the coffee was gone, Jack offered a dog biscuit rather than the ball and Sam accepted the treat pretending that the subject had been successfully changed.

Samantha was really Jill's dog. She loved dogs as much as she loved children and, if Jack had not continuously objected, she would have adopted a dozen homeless strays by now. Her desire to fill the empty house increased dramatically when their son, Alex, left for college. She missed him terribly and decided that the company of a dog might help, especially when Jack was away. She found Samantha at the Gap View Farm in Broadway, Virginia. She had heard that local teenage girls rub the bellies and massage the toes of every Gap View puppy. For Jill, little Samantha was love at first sight.

Jill claimed that, "Good therapy dogs welcome human touch and they don't mind having their feet massaged."

Samantha had no trouble with her therapy dog final exams and quickly became known as "Wonder Dog" at the local hospital. Jack had promised to get involved with Sam's hospital visits. He regretted the fact that he couldn't seem to find his own ass with either hand lately and spent all of his time thinking about his dead Civil War relatives.

He looked out into the fairway and remembered driving through the tiny town of Brandy Station. He was halfway home from the airport, guzzling his second beer, when he reached the historic settlement. He slowed to a crawl because of a single-lane covered bridge at the south end of town. The intimidating road beyond the bridge continued to narrow and meander into the heart of one of the Civil War's bloodiest battlefields.

Jack was enamored of the Civil War and read a great deal of that time in history when life was hard for both soldiers and civilians. He loved the simplicity of that era and pictured himself living during those days. He was not a war reenactor but admired those who were, especially hard-core Confederate reenactors. They were passionate about mimicking the difficult life of Civil War soldiers. Hard-core reenactors would do just about anything to keep things as realistic as possible, to include "spooning" with their skinny buddies in the woods to stay authentically warm at night. They were known as "stitch counters" because of the meticulous attention given to every detail of their handmade uniforms.

The Southern reenactor purists would never bring fat guys along for body heat because there were few plump foot soldiers in the Confederate Army. Rebel soldiers had little to eat and were skin and bones by the end of the war. During the grisly Wilderness battle in 1864, a typical daily food ration for a Southern soldier was four ounces of meat and one pint of corn meal.

The unpleasant task of identifying bodies after each gruesome battle was a challenge because there were no dog tags; tens of thousands of uniforms were burned off or stolen. Body identification was not a happy thing to do, nor was it a priority. Some human remains baked in the sun for weeks, months, or even years, waiting to be recognized and buried. During the Wilderness battle, human skulls and bones from The Chancellorsville Battle, which had been fought nearby during the previous year, remained scattered throughout the woods.

Often, the body of a recovered soldier was labeled either North or South by the physical appearance of the corpse. The bodies of well-fed Northern soldiers swelled and bloated in the sun. The lack of nourishment prevented dead Southern soldiers from swelling much at all—a fat one here, a skinny one there and so on. Tossing a skinny Yankee or a rare fat Rebel on the wrong burial pile would have been the ultimate insult.

The fanatic Rebel hardcore reenactors probably eat all the fat guys, Jack thought. *Then again, "hard-cores" probably think golf is ridiculous, so who am I to criticize? At least I don't spoon with my golf buddies.*

He wondered if the battlefields had something to do with the apparitions standing around in the fog. It was May 1st, close to the 150th anniversary of The Battle of the Wilderness. *Maybe the lunatics in the fog were actually hard-core reenactors warming up for the big event.*

The spiked coffee was beginning to do its magic and he pictured the hardcore-garbage-bag reenactors playing a round of golf. *Nah, they wouldn't appreciate the dress code. Besides, spooning is frowned upon on the golf course.* He rubbed Sam's belly and considered that stress and beer might have had something to do with his visions, although a couple of beers couldn't have caused hallucinations. *Still, I know I saw something.*

Telling the police about his encounters was not an option because he didn't want to draw attention to himself. The airline frowned upon pilots who had vivid imaginations like the one who told his passengers that thunderstorm clouds were actually "mother ships" carrying fleets of UFOs. He was "asked to leave."

No, the airline had no sense of humor. Flying upside-down was fine in the military, but the airline pilot who decided to fly inverted was also asked to leave. He was ferrying an empty airplane and couldn't resist. He turned the airliner upside-down and got away with it until maintenance personnel discovered blue toilet water on the ceilings of the lavatories. Oops!

Jack never did anything stupid with company assets and he was not going to allow his imagination to jeopardize his career, bankruptcy or no bankruptcy. He would keep all this nonsense to himself and avoid that kind of attention, by God. After all, he had worked long and hard to qualify for his airline job. He and Jill struggled financially in the early years, but his airline career changed all of that. Although the fun and thrills of flying the F-16 and the Cub were gone, the money had eased the pain.

Other than terrorism, the thing he feared most about flying was the ride home from the airport, especially in nasty weather. While flying, his instruments told him where other airplanes were and what they were doing. Air Traffic Control kept things remarkably safe and everyone involved was highly trained. Earthbound drivers, however, launch themselves at you through steamy fog banks while drunk, stoned, or seriously preoccupied. That does a job on the old sphincter, especially when you are worried, preoccupied, and drinking yourself. *I'm just as bad as they are. I've got to stop drinking in the car.* He'd had that conversation with himself often but never did anything about it.

He didn't think of himself as an alcoholic. After all, alcoholism was an addictive disease and he had stopped drinking lots of times— no sweat.

I'll get help if I really need it, he thought.

He sighed and murmured, "Sure...fat chance now that the airline might dissolve into nothing."

9

"Incoming!" Jack had always said while throwing old golf balls into the empty lot next door, which was great fun especially after a couple of beers. He hoped that any potential buyer would be discouraged by the obvious bombardment from the tee box. Jack's house was out of range of most tee shots; the adjacent lot was closer to the threat and definitely in the line of fire. Jack and Jill had chosen an isolated building lot that was one-half mile down an unpaved road in a sparsely developed section of the community. Their "non-hill" lot was on the sixteenth fairway of the golf course, surrounded by thick woods. They enjoyed the isolation, although privacy-destroying neighbors were inevitable.

Once they realized they were living in a battlefield, they felt guilty about settling in Scarborough Run and playing golf on sacred ground. The joy of seclusion ended abruptly when Ralf and Charlotte Burnside broke ground next door and construction began on old golf balls and much older bones.

Ralph Burnside's great-great-grandfather was none other than Major General Ambrose E. Burnside, commander of the 9th Army Corps of the Army of the Potomac. Ralph loudly pointed out at every opportunity that his grandfather and the Union Army had won the Civil War. Ralph claimed to be a student of the war, who settled in Scarborough Run intentionally because he *wanted* to live in one of his grandfather's battlefields. Burnside's lack of respect served to define the fundamental difference between him and Jack.

Still, to make up for the golf balls he had scattered over Ralph's lot, Jack attempted to warn his neighbor about the hungry deer. Burnside knew better and planted dozens of azaleas anyway. The deer enjoyed Ralph's yummy flowers and Jack applauded the efforts of the hungry hordes.

Ralph's wife, Charlotte, didn't know anything about golf and Ralph didn't seem to care about the threat from the tee box, so the

Burnsides purchased the golf ball-infested lot and excavation began immediately. The day before the bulldozers arrived, Charlotte introduced herself with a basketful of old golf balls in hand. "I found all these golf balls on our property and wonder if you might be able to use them," she said cheerfully. "Ralph insists on buying expensive golf balls, but I can't tell the difference between one ball and another. Ralph says it makes all the difference in the world when you golf at his level."

Jill thanked Charlotte and glanced at her husband with "the look" that was usually reserved for his post-drinking episodes but not always.

Charlotte said, "Ralph and I haven't enjoyed dinner at the clubhouse yet and Ralph would like to treat you this evening."

"That would be lovely and thanks for the golf balls. If Jack can't use them, I certainly will," Jill said, still keeping her husband trapped within her peripheral vision.

"Good, then we'll see you at the club at about seven?"

If Jack had known Ralph better, he wouldn't have felt guilty about littering his property with golf balls or anything else for that matter. During dinner, Burnside announced that his golf scores were usually in the low seventies and referred to himself as a "scratch" golfer. Ralph had not officially join the club and the Stewarts were stuck with the bill for drinks and dinner.

Jack had learned the hard way that there is little relationship between physical appearance and one's ability in golf. Once, while playing golf in Florida, an old man limped up to him and said, "Hello, I'm Charley the snake killer. I kill the snakes on the golf course. Mind if I join you?" He was carrying an ancient golf bag and wearing old tennis shoes, but Jack was happy to have the company of someone who was familiar with the course. Charley suggested playing for "some friendly money" and Jack agreed to a bet he could easily win. He lost fifty dollars to the old hustler who shot one under par.

When Ralph said he was "scratch," Jack gave him the benefit of the doubt even though the lumpy man didn't look as if he knew which end a golf club to hold. Jill suggested that he and Ralph play golf together and they agreed to meet at the driving range the following morning. Ralph arrived wearing a straw hat, which did little to hide his bushy pork chop sideburns. Since Ralph was a Civil War reenactor, who loved playing the part of his grandfather, his funky sideburns made at least some ugly sense.

"Sideburns" came from Burnside like the idiom "hooker" was thought to have come from the womanizing General Fighting Joe Hooker. Jack wondered what Ralph would be wearing if he was related to Hooker rather than Burnside. Picturing Ralph in fishnet stockings and a thong was not a good pre-swing thought, so Jack concentrated on his warm-up routine while Ralph watched him and made irritating comments. "You didn't get all of that one," and "Whoa! Better leave that shot here on the range."

Jack moved to the practice putting green while the odd little man hit a few practice balls of his own. He talked to himself in the third person: "Ralph shouldn't hit a hook like that" and "Whoops! Ralph sliced that one." Burnside had no rear-end to keep his lime-green shorts in place. Thankfully, they remained miraculously perched above his knee-high black socks in defiance of gravity.

They moved to the first teeing area and Jack's drive was acceptable. Ralph lunged with one of the worst swings imaginable and his ball flew directly into the water hazard. Plunk! The ball splashed with no chance of retrieval. After a brief search, however, Ralph found a dry, mud-encrusted ball and claimed it as his own. It was as if a swamp creature had emerged from the marsh with the ball clutched in its jaws and placed it there after drying it with its great dragon breath. After that miracle, he struggled to reach the green in three additional shots, putted three times and said, "Give me a four on that hole."

Jack never drank while flying or playing golf but usually enjoyed a few beers afterward. To his amazement, however, the four beers in his cooler had disappeared. Somehow, Ralph had managed to drink all four beers secretly and without asking. *Incredible!* He swore he would never play golf with Burnside again and, as fate would have it, he would never again be faced with that dilemma.

He would have abandoned Ralph on the golf course if it hadn't been for Jill's budding friendship with Charlotte. "I'm glad you and Ralph are playing golf today," Jill said during breakfast. "It'll be nice to have neighbors, especially when you're on the road. Charlotte makes me laugh and I do need someone to fill your boots while you're away."

"Really? I didn't realize I amuse you so."

"Yep! You certainly do. Never a dull moment. But not to worry, you're a lot cuter than Charlotte."

"Come here," he said, pulling her near, "and I'll show you some significant other differences between Charlotte and me."

Golf with Ralph had ruined Jack's morning. Leaving him stranded on the golf course was not an option, especially since Jill and Charlotte had already appeared in each other's cell phone speed dial lists. He was determined to tolerate his obnoxious neighbor for Jill's sake.

Charlotte turned out to be a lovable woman and Jack could see why Jill liked her. She was a pleasant, plump, leftover flower child who dressed in colorful muumuus and wore huge gold-hoop earrings. She loved the deer, raccoons, geese and anything else that walked, crawled or slithered through the woods. When free-running guinea hens appeared in her back yard, she was thrilled and enticed the plump birds with food, water, and even a few songs. To Jack, the hens looked like a cross between a chicken and a bowling ball and he had seen them in his own yard a few times, but Samantha always chased them away. All the little bowling balls would gather around Charlotte's aluminum chair in the morning and wait for her to toss chicken feed from the ample pockets of her muumuu.

"Did you know that they eat ticks?" she said to Jill. "They eat all kinds of insects and they're so cute. I just can't stand it!"

Charlotte assigned names like Eggberta and Henrietta to each of her chubby chicken friends and spent hours watching them like a mother hen from her lawn-chair perch. Before long, she had attracted a dozen hens and came up with more names like Bertha, Henly, and for some reason, Bob. She insisted that her new friends were reincarnated and confided in her, which explained her long conversations with individual birds.

In addition to her free-running friends, Charlotte had an unusual relationship with the ghosts that haunted her house. She claimed to have regular contact with her harmless and amusing spirits. According to Ralph, Charlotte's ghost friends enjoyed her effervescent nature, although they never actually giggled along with her.

Inside her haunted house, Charlotte felt daily "puffs of cold air" on her face and neck. Each ticklish flirtation made her giggle like a schoolgirl. Somehow, she knew her guests were male spirits from a time when men had an outward respect for women.

"Why else would they amuse me and completely ignore Ralph?" she said to Jill, who humored her and then changed the subject.

She also claimed that her ghosts examined her daily as if they couldn't remember the prior day's analysis. She had no idea why she was being scrutinized, but she was sure they had good reasons. Her gloomy spirit friends were unhappy and wanted to leave but could not, so they amused themselves by playing with all things electronic, especially the Burnside's microwave.

Charlotte, a true believer in Atlantis, actually purchased an inexpensive microwave and placed it on one of the many empty cardboard boxes in her unfinished basement. This was an immediate success and the unit in the kitchen was left alone after that. Jill was sure she had heard the ding of the microwave bell during several of her visits, but Charlotte ignored it, so Jill did as well. Because of Charlotte's lack of concern about being haunted, the whole matter became nothing more than a lingering curiosity.

One day, Jill said, "I'm beginning to wonder about ghosts."

"What?" Jack said.

"Ghosts. I keep hearing about ghosts."

"From whom?"

"Well, Charlotte for one. She told me that she was reading a book in bed the other night and felt a "presence" in her bedroom. She remained wide-eyed for quite a while and then an indentation developed in the comforter on Ralph's side of the bed as if someone was sitting down. Ralph snored through the whole thing."

"What happened then?"

"Well...nothing. She just waited until the indentation disappeared and then went to sleep. It's almost as if she expects things like that to happen. Charlotte may be a little whacky, but she's pretty convincing."

"Did whacky woman tell Ralph about it?"

"No, but she couldn't wait to tell me."

"I wish she wouldn't do that."

"Me too," Jill said. "She's a sweet lady and that kind of thing doesn't seem to bother her, but it sure bothers me."

Jack said, "Why don't you mention it to her? Either that or just ignore it. I can't imagine that she would intentionally try to scare you. It's all nonsense anyway."

"I guess so...but there seem to be a lot of haunted buildings around here as well."

"Like what?"

"Well, there's Chatham Manor and Fall Hill Plantation," she said. "Then there's The Rising Sun Tavern and Aquia Church, and..."

"You believe that stuff?"

"I don't know. It's just that Charlotte insists she has ghosts in her house."

"I know," Jack said. "And I bet her spirits are watching you while you drink coffee in Charlotte's kitchen. And when you're in her *bathroom*..."

"Stop it," she said with a rare tone of insistence.

He realized he had upset her and said no more about ghosts.

10

After golfing with Ralph, Jack parked his golf cart in his garage under a poster of the Three Stooges that read "Golf with Your Friends."

"Never again," he said, reiterating his promise to avoid Ralph Burnside. He entered the house quietly, tiptoed across the kitchen, and lifted Jill off her feet.

"Whoo! What's gotten into you?" she asked

"Oh, just happy to see you," he said, setting her gently back down.

"How was golf with Ralph?"

"Well...let's see. How can I put this?"

"That bad, huh?"

"Yeah, I'm afraid so. Ralph is a true lunatic, all right."

"I kind of figured that, but thanks for trying, honey."

"Anything for you. I know Charlotte is a friend and all," he said. "Hey, how about we light some candles later and...you know..."

"Hold on, big guy, did you forget about the Burnside's barbecue tonight?"

Jack's heart sank. Spending part of his day with Ralph was bad enough and he would prefer poking a sharp stick in his eye to seeing him again, but he knew how much it meant to Jill. With a lame effort to hide his disappointment, he said, "Oh, that's right. Yeah...I almost forgot. Great...what time?"

"Are you sure you're up for this tonight?"

"Yeah, no problem. I mean...there are other things I'd rather be up for, but..."

She kissed him, rubbed the top of his head and said, "You've got about an hour to freshen up. By the way, you're awfully cute."

"I know," he said, grinning.

Jack sipped a large glass of Jack Daniels and waited for Jill to get ready. Talking to Ralph would take some effort so he sat in his wicker chair, drank and prepared himself. When Jill rang Charlotte's doorbell, Jack goosed her and she let out another classic "Whoo!" just as the door flew open. Charlotte Burnside was a loveable woman who couldn't help hugging everyone, including the mail carrier, for little or no reason.

Once they were thoroughly hugged, Charlotte escorted them to her lanai, which was full of muumuu chairs and muumuu cushions. It was unclear whether Charlotte had fashioned her muumuus from her furniture or if she designed the furniture with her tent-like dresses in mind, but the overstuffed chairs swallowed them and felt great. Ralph produced mega-margaritas served in huge glasses that looked like cactuses and refilled them before they were empty. Strange looking hors d'oeuvres appeared and Jack politely refused.

Ah, yes—nothing like dipping a happy-face cucumber into a bowl of delicious hummus and chasing it down with a tofu burger, he thought.

As the tofu burgers pretended to smolder on the grill, the margaritas began to return Jack to the fog from which he could not emerge. Then, Ralph resurrected his obnoxious banter about good old General Burnside.

"Come down to the basement with me, Jack. I want to show you the general's sword," he said.

"Maybe some other time, Ralph. I think we should pay attention to our dates this evening."

"Oh, they're fine, Jack. Look at them in there—yack, yack, yack. Those two won't run out of words anytime soon and they'll never miss us. Besides, I want to pick your brain about finishing my basement."

"Okay…sure, but let's make it quick so the ladies don't cut us off."

"Cut off what, Jack?" Ralph said with a repugnant laugh.

Jack shook his head and reluctantly followed him into a basement full of empty cardboard boxes, packaging paper, and a microwave oven sitting on a cardboard box in the middle of the room. He remembered the silly story about the microwave, but actually seeing it was bizarre.

"Sorry about the mess. I keep the general's stuff in that trunk," he said while pointing at a large black trunk in the corner of the room. "Give me a minute."

He kicked aside crumpled packing paper and slid empty boxes around until he reached the trunk. As he fumbled with the lock, he said, "I got this local hick to do the wiring down here and he was real cheap. He was quick too, which surprised me. I paid him nearly half what it should have cost and he was grateful for the work, dumb bastard."

Listening to Ralph hurt Jack's head, especially when the side-burned idiot claimed that the Smithsonian wanted him to donate his collection.

Ralph said, "The hell with the Smithsonian, do you know how much I can get for this stuff on eBay?"

Jack said nothing while Ralph cursed, struggled to open the heavy lid, and retrieved General Burnside's beautiful sword. Jack was dividing his attention between Ralph and the microwave, expecting to hear the little bell at any moment. He began to feel light-headed as Ralph approached him with the sword.

"Ain't she a beaut?" Ralph said while handing the sword to him.

As soon as Jack touched the sword, the room began to swim, his eyes rolled back, and he crumpled to the floor.

11

Jack was lying on the basement floor when he came to and he could hear Ralph pounding up the wooden steps, calling for help.

"Charlotte! Charlotte! Jack passed out!"

He got to his feet as quickly as he could, thinking that Ralph sounded as though he was possessed. He knew the whole gang would be rushing downstairs shortly and he wanted to be standing when they did. As they clamored down the noisy wooden stairs, he managed to stagger to his feet.

Jill rushed to him and said, "Oh, thank God! Are you okay?"

"Yeah...I'm okay. Too many margaritas, I guess. No big deal," he muttered while rubbing the back of his head.

"As soon as I handed the general's sword to him, he just passed out!" Ralph squeaked. Everyone looked at Ralph, who continued to elevate his voice, "He looked like a ghost!"

With a weak smile, Jack said, "Sorry, Ralph. I've been a little tired lately and I shouldn't have had so much to drink. I'm okay now."

Charlotte threatened to call 911. "I have it on speed dial," she said

"Oh, please, no. That's not necessary," Jack said, wondering why anyone would have 911 on speed dial.

Jill was worried. "I have to get you home," she said. "You really do need some rest. I'm *so* sorry, Charlotte. I'll call you tomorrow and we'll have you over as soon as we can."

"Oh, please don't give it another thought. We're just relieved that Jack is all right," Charlotte said.

During the next few awkward moments, Jack felt like an idiot, Jill apologized repeatedly, Ralph worried about a lawsuit, and Charlotte hugged everyone.

"My head is killing me," Jack said during the walk home.

Jill placed her arm around her husband's back and said nothing until they entered the kitchen. She turned to him and said, "Jack, we need to talk."

Those words from Jill had the same effect as hearing "Cancel takeoff clearance and proceed immediately to the bomb threat parking area!"

"I'm sorry, Jill," he said. "I don't know what happened. I'm sorry I ruined the evening."

"It's not that, honey. I'm *really* worried about you."

"I know. Believe me, I'm worried too."

"Maybe you're drinking a bit too much?"

"I didn't fall down because I had too much to drink." In truth, he didn't know why he passed out and it frightened him. "Ralph handed Burnside's sword to me and I blacked out. It was strange, but it had nothing to do with drinking. Maybe it was the ghost in the damn microwave."

He regretted saying that immediately. *Dumb shit*, he thought. He was embarrassed and frustrated, but that was no reason to scare Jill. "Hey, it's no big deal and I promise I'll stop falling down," he said with a silly grin.

Jill found no humor in that and gave him "the look."

"Just kidding, honey," he said. "I promise I'll stop drinking soon."

She put a kettle of water on the stove, hugged him from behind and said, "Please tell me what's bothering you."

"Oh, things are a little rough at work. You know…airline balance sheets and that kind of stuff. That's all. It'll be okay—no sweat."

Jill was wondering where to find a good neurologist. "I know you're worried about the airline, but is there something else bothering you? I mean…besides Ralph?"

"Will Rogers would have a difficult time with Ralph," he said. "No, really, I'm all right," he continued, knowing he would have to give her more. "I mean, I have been a little stressed out lately, but I'll be fine."

"You really need sleep and you've got to quit worrying about the airline. It'll be just fine. Meanwhile, Doc Goeden should check out that nasty bump on your head. I'm sure you're all right but just to be safe."

"I know I look pretty bad, but all I need is some rest. This whole thing is pretty silly," he said with some trepidation.

"It's just that you seem so stressed out and stress can mess you up physically and mentally. How about some exercise? Remember how good you used to feel after jogging a few miles?"

"I'm certain you're right about exercise," he stated, accepting the compromise. "Tell you what, I'll go for a nice long run tomorrow morning and then we'll both feel better."

"Promise?"

"Scout's honor."

"Good," she said. She knew he would never go to a doctor and admit to passing out, but he was going to get some exercise and that was good enough for now. She ruffled his hair and said, "Let's go to bed."

"You read my mind," he sighed with relief.

While holding hands in the dark bedroom, Jill searched for an explanation of the "sword thing." She said, "I know you're really interested in your family history, honey, but maybe you should relax about it. You may not find all the answers; some details are simply out of your control." She paused and said, "You've also been reading some pretty intense books about the Civil War lately, especially those by that…Gordon something."

"Gordon Rhea."

"Yeah. Perhaps it's a little too much for you right now."

"Gordon C. Rhea. He makes you feel like you were there, all right."

"Precisely," she said.

They lay in silence, each deep in thought until Jill fell asleep. Jack remained wide-awake and couldn't stop thinking about Burnside's sword. *Why did I pass out when Ralph handed the sword to me? What has General Burnside got to do with anything?* Finally, he got up and fumbled around in a bookcase until he found Gordon Rhea's book, *The Battle of the Wilderness, May 5-6, 1864.* He guiltily poured vodka into a tall glass of orange juice and settled in to read about General Ambrose E. Burnside. On May 6th, the second day of battle, Burnside was scheduled to attack at 5:30 a.m. Instead, he arrived hours late and stopped within earshot of the combat to enjoy a late-morning champagne brunch.

At that point, he must have heard and smelled the raging battle in the nearby woods, Jack thought.

At about 2:00 p.m., Burnside finally engaged the enemy in the thickets near the Higgerson Farm. The Union effort would have been much more productive if Burnside had left the Wilderness Tavern on schedule.

The apple didn't fall far from great-great-grandpa's tree, Jack realized.

Ambrose Burnside was arrogant and insisted on doing everything his own way. Later that year, in July of 1864, Burnside sent his men to their deaths after a prolonged stalemate in Petersburg, Virginia. His troops had excavated a tunnel under the Southern defenses and filled the cavern with explosives. When the big bang came, Burnside's men ran down into the huge crater where some were shot and others were captured. That lack of judgment was too much for President Lincoln and Burnside was finally "asked to leave."

In the morning, Jill found her husband sleeping in his chair next to an empty vodka bottle.

12

When Captain Stewart woke, he found a note next to the empty bottle:

> *I can't believe you have done this again.*
> *It's time to get some help.*
> *I have Samantha with me.*
> *I will be home later to talk about your problem.*
>   *Jill*

My problem? Damn! What an idiot I am. She's right, of course; I do need help. But not now! This can't be the right time. Then, in spite of his hangover, he had a truly inspirational thought. He would keep his promise to exercise and, at the same time, soften Jill up by dressing in the most ridiculous jogging outfit he could put together. If he could make her smile, even a little, maybe he could dodge at least some of her impending assault. He knew he needed help and he would accept it when he was ready—but not now. *I'll get Jill to crack a smile, jog down the road until out of sight, walk with Samantha for a while, and return to a hero's welcome. No, problemo.*

He rummaged through his dresser, revisited old things in the back of his closet, and emerged dressed like a jogging clown. He wore battery-operated jogging shoes with lights that blinked with each step like little kids wore at the shopping mall. He had worn the shoes in a charity event a couple of years earlier and the batteries were still good. He squeezed into skin-tight, black, Spandex shorts and, thinking of Ralph, chose knee-high black socks to complement his blinking sneakers. Printed on the front of his fluorescent-orange tee shirt was "Jog for Dravet Syndrome," and large wraparound sunglasses gave him the Arnold Schwarzenegger look. He topped it off with a bulky earphone radio that actually worked when the long metallic antenna was extended straight up in the air.

When Jill returned, she stood stoically with her arms folded and watched her husband dance around the room like Rocky Balboa. Finally, she revealed a hint of a smile and said, "Okay…all right… jog first, then we'll talk."

He headed out the kitchen door saying, "I'll be back!" in his best Schwarzenegger imitation. He then jogged down the street with Samantha, pumping the air with his fists and waving to Jill. She watched from the front porch with stubbornly folded arms.

I love that clown, she thought.

He jogged down the unpaved, uninhabited road for a quarter mile, turned into the sanctuary of the unfinished railroad bed, and stopped to catch his breath.

"Man! Am I out of shape," he said to Samantha.

He had always enjoyed jogging in the old railroad bed, which was nothing more than an overgrown, twenty-foot-wide gully, and he appreciated its rich history. The railroad was conceived in 1834 to serve Gordonsville, Orange and Fredericksburg but didn't operate until 1877.[2] The clearway was cut through the dense woods well before the Civil War, although the Union Army didn't seem to know about it. The South, however, knew it well and used the easy access for a surprise attack against General Wadsworth's left flank at the intersection of Brock Road and Orange Plank Road. The four Confederate brigades were "…like an army of ghosts rising out of the earth."[3]

The railroad cut had always given him a strong sense of something—history, maybe. As he and Sam walked through the unruly passage, he felt light-headed and his vision blurred. He stopped, shook his head, and continued forward while his mind drifted into history. He stopped again, closed his eyes and stood still. There was a crackling sound in his headphones followed by the sounds of continuous gunfire and men shouting in the distance. When he opened his eyes, he was standing ankle-deep in a puddle of murky water.

"What the hell?" he said as he removed his ridiculous headphones.

He turned and saw Samantha sitting about thirty yards away. "Here, Sam!" he repeated several times with no results. She stared at him and would not budge. "All right. You win," he said, as he sucked one foot from the muck.

With that, Sam bolted and ran back toward the main road. *Goofy dog*, he thought as he looked into the now silent gloom. With the little hairs raised on the back of his neck, he trudged through the water and stomped his mud-covered shoes on dry land. When he reached the road, he tried to dismiss what he had heard in the cut fearing that alcohol had finally gotten the best of him.

At home, he found the kitchen table covered with books, pamphlets, and DVDs that were all related to "drinking problems." Far worse, Jill still had her arms folded.

13

Two weeks later, while playing with Sam in the yard, he was at it again. *It's nine in the morning and here I am again, drinking Baileys with the same stupid look on my face.*

Then, he heard a startling female scream.

Ordinarily, it was quiet in his corner of Scarborough Run. The only sounds came from flocks of geese that honked as they flew overhead or the voices of frustrated golfers, but this was a real scream all right. Oddly, the cry sounded as though it had been amplified with a megaphone and the desperate shriek seemed to echo and reverberate. When a second, louder scream rocked the woods, Sam barked twice, pressed her body against Jack's leg, and sat on his foot.

"It's okay, Sam," he said while patting her trembling head.

She rarely trembled, so he continued to stroke her while peering across the fairway into the dark woods in the direction of the screams.

"Come on, girl. Let's go see what's going on."

The frantic female cries erased any sense of hesitation and he was drawn toward the foreboding woods. He quickly crossed the empty grass fairway and stopped at the edge of the woods to listen. 100 yards of thick, wet forest lay ahead, followed by the unfinished railroad bed, which separated Scarborough Run from parts of the Wilderness battlefield that were protected by the Parks Department.

This was the slicer's side of the fairway where most bad golf tee shots ended up and the nasty woods were filled with dozens of abandoned golf balls. "What's a four-dollar golf ball? I'm not going in there! Forget about it and play on." Jack and Samantha had been in the sticky woods once before while looking for golf balls, but Jack ended up with nasty thorns in his leg and a bad case of poison ivy.

He entered the woods carefully and sidestepped a thick patch of thorn-covered vines. Samantha stopped at the edge of the fairway and refused to enter. She was shivering and pacing nervously as if the mysterious sky was filled with thunder.

Although Jack would have liked Sam's company, he finally gave up. Then, another scream drew him into the quagmire alone. The woods were as dark and thick as a bamboo forest and the air was instantly stale and still. As he moved in the direction of the cries, he followed a narrow deer trail that meandered through the woods. He ducked under low branches and stepped gently on thorn-covered vines to avoid brushing his bare legs against them. Spider webs stuck to his face and naked arms as he swatted his way through the morass. Abruptly, he stopped within inches of the mother of all spiders. He had described these fat, hair-covered arachnids to Jill as "Jurassic Park spiders." That was all she wanted to hear about that—thank you very much.

"I can't believe you went into those creepy woods just to find some stupid golf balls," she had said.

He couldn't think of an explanation that didn't sound foolish, so he simply allowed her to bandage his thorn-torn leg and remained silent. In spite of that embarrassment, here he was again with his mouth zipped shut, smearing tacky webs from his neck, and trying to follow the now-silent trail. He was halfway through the quagmire when he stopped and cursed himself for not taking the longer fifteen-minute route around the woods via the old railroad bed.

I wish I had my cell phone, he thought.

He glanced at his topsiders that were sticking to the ground and threatening to come off and then bumped his head on a low-hanging tree limb. He didn't know it was possible to smell a dream, but the odor of the damp, rotting woods reminded him of the gruesome corpse in his nightmare.

He thought of the transcendentalist, Henry David Thoreau, who would have loved the natural woods and would have been proud of the perfect, decomposing and rejuvenating smell of decay. What Jack smelled was more than that though, and Henry would not have liked this unnatural odor one bit. Jack was reminded of the stale scent of mold that clings to unwashed elderly people who fry everything in fat and hibernate in stuffy apartments. Jack, Jill, and Wonder Dog had visited an elderly shut-in who smelled just like that. Raising his nose into the sticky air, he realized that the smell had evolved into the rotting cabbage-seafood odor that seeps from garbage dumpsters in the city.

His stomach began to cramp and he felt powerful gas building in his gut. He realized, with dread, that filling his pants was a real possibility. *I don't need this right now.* He was able to keep his gas or whatever it was to himself and had nearly reached the railroad cut when he heard a booming male voice shout "A-MAN-DA!" He turned quickly, lost his footing, slammed his knee into the ground, and impaled his calf on a hungry string of half-inch thorns.

"Damn!" he said as he watched his blood flow like water. The horrible odor intensified and he felt light-headed while his blood mixed with the yellow blob of spider guts on the side of his shoe. Heavy perspiration dripped from his brow and his stomach began to boil. *Keep your head lowered to stop the blood from flowing out of your stupid brain and whatever you do, don't pass out!*

He raised his knee and moved his hand toward his wounds while the embedded thorns moved further into his skin, ripping and tearing additional flesh. He was crouched down in the waist-high thicket, fighting nausea and dizziness. Breathing in rapid, shallow breaths, he realized that the woods had become completely silent. The constant chirping of crickets and all other sounds had abruptly stopped, leaving only the resonance of his own breathing that resembled the muffled inhalations of a scuba diver. He felt a chill followed by tremendous pressure in his ears as he reached to free his blood-soaked leg from the nasty thorns.

The girl screamed again, followed by another, "A-MAN-DA!"

Startled, Jack involuntarily jerked the vine in his hand. Blood poured down his leg, but he was free of the thorns and able to fight his way through the bulky undergrowth before stumbling into the bright sunlight of the railroad bed.

Part Two

~exodus~

1

Most men live lives of quiet desperation.

~Henry David Thoreau

An uncontrollable obsession with genealogy, job-related stress, financial concerns, and alcohol abuse had made Jack desperate indeed. He became increasingly frustrated with a world he could not control and his obsessions were beginning to ruin his life. He was simply going through the motions at work and spent a great deal of time sleeping on the couch at home. He stopped exercising and even golf seemed like a chore. Jill was worried and suggested everything from anti-depressants to Alcoholics Anonymous, all of which he refused because "the airline would not approve."

When the desperate pilot stumbled into the railroad clearing, his head was pounding, his sore leg was bleeding, and he was surprised to see a dog galloping toward him. Its long hound ears were flapping up and down and its muscular body rippled under a red-brown coat. Before he could brace himself, the animal slammed into him at full speed knocking him backward. As he left his feet, his adrenaline-soaked brain calculated that he had been airborne for an improbably long time. *I should have hit the ground or a tree something by now,* he thought, just before the back of his head collided with the earth. His last lucid thought was of a *New Yorker Magazine* cartoon. Ralph was standing in "The Ugly Clothing Store" with a small sign in the window—"Golfers Welcome."

His head contacted a root in the ground and the jolt masked the pain of the thorns while his world blazed bright white as if caught in a giant flash bulb. Thousands of chemical synapses in his brain malfunctioned and, once those little critters became confused, they shut things down. Sometimes the brain responds like a computer, which reboots itself, and sometimes it doesn't reboot at all.

During that piece of a second when everything went white, Jack's body remained where he had fallen and his consciousness was catapulted into history.

2

I am accustomed to sleep and in my dreams
to imagine the same things that lunatics imagine
when awake.

~René Descartes

When Jack opened his eyes, he was pain-free. In fact, he was clear-headed and felt as though he had awakened from deep, restful sleep. Most of the tall trees were gone, although the colors of the thick, rambling vegetation and vibrant blue sky were wildly vivid— almost surreal. He was floating, rather than standing, a few feet from a young girl who was lying on the ground and pointing an antique rifle into a small clearing. She was dressed in grey woolen trousers, an oversized indigo shirt, and a black felt hat that was turned up in the front. She was extremely attractive, yet adorable in a Paddington Bear sort of way.

"Excuse me," Jack said.

She ignored him.

He looked in the direction of her attention and saw a small deer standing forty yards away. It seemed odd that this lovely creature was about to shoot another lovely creature, but Jack had a euphoric sense of well-being and remained focused on events rather than consequences.

How can I be dreaming that I'm in a dream? he wondered.

The recoil from the huge rifle shook the girl's entire body and smoke from the Whitworth rifle stained the air. The deer jumped into the woods and someone shouted from the clearing.

"Don't shoot!"

Paddington was startled and stood quickly. "Damn!" she muttered.

A man's voice cried out again, "Hey! Stop shootin'!"

"Come out where I can see you," she shouted, trembling a bit.

As the figure slowly emerged from behind a tree, his size and age surprised Paddington. He was more than six feet tall and she was shocked to see that he was about her age. The young man approached and stopped awkwardly when he realized that Paddington was actually a girl dressed in men's clothing.

Neither of them noticed Jack, but he seemed to be able to read their thoughts.

"What are you doing on my aunt's property?" Paddington said.

"This isn't anybody's property. Besides, I hunt here all the time and I've never seen anyone else out here, especially not a girl dressed like a boy." He was already a prisoner of her eyes and said, "You're a girl, right?"

Suddenly embarrassed by her men's clothing and lack of grooming, she removed her hat allowing her long honey hair to topple to her shoulders. She shook her head and brushed the hair from her face with her fingers. Then, like one of Michelangelo's Cherubs gazing up into heaven, she looked up at the boy and said, "Who says girls can't hunt?"

The bewildered boy remained frozen in place.

With her heart pounding faster she squeaked, "What's your name?"

"I'm Luke Stewart. Who are you?" he said, finding it difficult to hold his stare.

His gorgeous brown eyes, curly black hair, and a boyish face softened his size, yet she felt small standing before him. She sensed his gentle nature in spite of his size and blushed when she noticed a dimple in his cheek. The pair stood facing each other at a loss for words, paralyzed by lovesick teenage awkwardness.

With her heart beating like a frightened rabbit's, she finally moved a step closer. She was convinced he could hear her heart hammering and the flush in her cheeks served to heighten her astounding natural beauty. Luke gawked at her, dumbfounded and amazed because she was the prettiest girl he had ever seen. He remembered a color picture of an angel in his mother's magazine, *Godey's Lady's Book,* and here she was standing right in front of him.

"Do you live around here?" she finally asked with a dry throat, embarrassed by her squeaky voice.

"Sure do," he said, unable to remember exactly where he lived or who he was. "I live, uh…a couple miles south," he said, gesturing over his shoulder with his thumb. "Where'd *you* come from?" he asked, thinking she might have floated down from heaven.

"Oh, I live near the Parker Store Road on the Higgerson Farm. Do you know the place?" she said, still trying to find some moisture in her throat.

"Sure, I've been by there but I've never seen you, that's for sure," he said. He thought about running away before saying something stupid.

"Well, I would have remembered you. I mean to say…if you came by my aunt's house…I would have remembered you," she said, as awkwardly as he felt.

Her clumsy answer made Luke smile and Paddington blushed. The boy found a sudden fascination with his dirty boots while Paddington rocked back and forth for several endless seconds, glancing alternately at Luke's downturned eyes and the sky above his head.

Jack glanced at his muddy topsiders, then back at the teens. He comically waved his hand in front of Paddington's face confirming his invisibility and pinched his arm in an effort to wake up. *Okay, so I'm either dreaming about trying to wake up or I'm dead. If I'm dead, this must be heaven, hell or somewhere in between. Since I'm vaguely worried about lots of things, this can't be heaven because angels don't worry about any shit at all. Hell, they don't even say shit!*

As Jack thought about that, he realized that cherub Paddington could easily pass for an angel, but the blissful ecstasy of paradise had to include more than one singular angel. *These two can't be playing parts in Dante's Inferno, so this can't be hell either.*

Luke was beginning to perspire, Paddington continued to rock back and forth, and the awkward silence was filled with a deafening lack of words.

Jack considered Limbo. *No, that was for unbaptized babies. Besides, Limbo turned out to be nothing but a head fake, which was good news for all those reassigned babies.* He pictured dozens of infants on the beach in the Caribbean dancing under a stick.

Luke wiped the moisture from his brow with the back of his sleeve.

If not Limbo, I must be in Purgatory, Jack considered. *I think Purgatory is still open for business.*

Jack recalled what George Carlin had said about "eating a beef jerky on Friday and doing eternity on the meat rap." Because questions of life and death were suddenly diminished to nothing more than amusing curiosities, he felt like a college kid with no responsibilities and an appreciation of recreational drugs. Nothing bothered him and he hadn't felt this good in a long time. He had no control over his purgatorial dream, however, and wasn't able to change the subject of his attention, so he simply floated, watched, and listened.

Finally, Paddington said, "Well, it's getting late and my aunt will be worried."

"Okay, goodbye then," Luke said, mostly because he couldn't think of anything else to say. He would have been happy to shoot himself in the foot rather than part company with her. Saying something like that might sound stupid, so he said nothing as the girl turned slowly and began to walk away. Luke wanted to call out to her and then he noticed her rifle lying on the ground.

"Hey! You forgot your gun."

"Oh!" she said, turning immediately.

She locked eyes with him and smiled. He didn't budge, so she walked toward him. When he handed the rifle to her and their hands touched, they both pretended to ignore the shock waves that followed.

Paddington accepted the heavy weapon without losing eye contact and said, "I hunt here every day."

"You do?" Luke said immediately.

"Yep," she said, walking backward, nodding her head, and stumbling a bit.

When she turned away again, he said, "What time?"

She spun around quickly and said, "Oh, about this time of day." She hesitated and said, "Will you be around here tomorrow?"

Luke didn't answer for what seemed like an eternity and finally said, "I'll be around here if you tell me your name."

"Oh! My name is Amanda. Amanda Atkinson."

Atkinson! Jack thought. *And did he say his last name was Stewart?*

"Okay, Amanda Atkinson, I promise I'll be here."

When he spoke her name, she felt a surge of warmth spread within her. The unusual sensation caused her to shudder slightly before saying, "Good. Then, um...I won't have to shoot you again."

She giggled and ran toward the railroad cut where her old horse, Star, was waiting. She mounted her horse and beamed with excitement when she heard Luke let out a yelp of joy from the woods behind her.

"Yee-ha!"

The smiling, dreamy teenager rode away forgetting all about her dog. As Jack floated along behind her, she injected Luke's name into happy little songs while bobbing her head from side to side. Then, a surge of euphoria passed through Jack like a drug and he felt like a child immersed in discovery. He consumed the beauty of every rock and tree and was astounded by the high-definition color of everything from Amanda's tiny waistline to Star's twitching ears. He whistled a cheerful tune of his own as they approached a farmhouse on a hill. Amanda stopped when she realized she had not seen her dog and turned in the saddle to call him.

"Zeus! Here, Zeus!"

Even after three years in the Wilderness, Zeus was still a city dog and the sound of gunfire terrified him. Whenever Amanda fired the Whitworth, Zeus would bolt and then return after a few minutes to examine the kill. *Where did he get to?* she thought, knowing that Zeus would eventually find his way home. He always did.

She turned back in the saddle and looked up to see her Aunt Permelia waving from her little house. The young beauty returned her aunt's greeting with a smile that brightened the entire Wilderness.

3

Most Scarborough Run residents enjoyed seeing the buxom blonde woman walking her small white Lhasa apso dog throughout the neighborhood. Melanie loved to bounce along and smile at everyone. Today, she chose the railroad cut for her walk because there, her dog could run free and she could frolic in true braless freedom.

Princess was sniffing something up ahead that looked like a deer carcass and she hurried to catch up, not wanting her dog to eat anything "yucky." She realized that the carcass was actually a human body and sprinted ahead repeating, "Oh my God! Oh my God!"

The crumpled man was lying on his back and she kept her distance while attempting to justify her unwillingness to administer first aid. She gawked at Jack with her hand over her mouth, then remembered her cell phone and dialed 911.

Maureen, the 911 operator, was dating a security guard at Scarborough Run named Ray Vance. Ray and Maureen had planned to drive down to the Richmond International Speedway that May evening for the Circuit City 250 NASCAR race, which was why they were both working the day shift. Maureen quickly dispatched an ambulance and called Ray's cell phone.

"Hi, hon. I just got a call from a homeowner in Scarborough Run. Looks like some guy collapsed in the railroad bed just east of your gatehouse. The ambulance is on its way."

"Oh! Okay. I can be there in a couple of minutes in the Jeep and I'll leave directions for the ambulance driver. Is he alive?" Ray asked while drawing a simple map for EMS.

"Well, yeah, I think so. The woman who called was pretty excited, but she thinks he's still breathing."

"Right. Okay then. I'll drive down there. Please tell the EMS folks that there will be a map taped to the security house window. I'll be sure to call your cell when I know something."

With the phone still pressed to his ear, he finished drawing the map and hung a sign on the door that read "Back in 10 Minutes."

"Okay, Ray. Be careful and I'll talk to you later. Love you."

"Okay. Bye for now," Ray said.

He drove a few hundred yards into the railroad bed and spotted Melanie bouncing toward him, spewing words.

"Oh, thank God you're here! I think he's breathing, but I didn't touch him or anything. He was just lying there where Princess found him and then I ran up and saw him just lying there. I hope he's all right. He looks okay, except for all the blood on his arms and legs, but that's not the reason I didn't want to touch him. Honest! I mean, that would be silly. I just want to help the poor man. Is the ambulance on its way? I hope so and I hope they hurry because he needs to go to the hospital right away, and..."

"Okay, Mrs. Pernice," Ray injected. "Calm down now. Everything will be just fine. The ambulance will be here any minute and they'll know what to do. Why don't you sit in my Jeep over there and I'll see about this fella."

"Well, okay. Sure. I'll wait here because they might want to talk to me about this poor man, and..."

Melanie's voice faded while Ray examined the unconscious man. He recognized Jack immediately and was greatly relieved when he found a pulse. EMS carried him by stretcher back to the road and then drove off, sirens blaring. Ray called Maureen and filled her in, drove Melanie and Princess home, and left a message on the Stewart's home phone. He followed up by driving out to the Stewart house where he saw Charlotte feeding her guinea hens.

"Hello, Mrs. Burnside," Ray said. He never forgot a name and the homeowners loved him for it.

"Oh, Ray! You startled me," she said as she walked toward him, wiping chicken feed on her blue muumuu.

"Sorry, Mrs. Burnside," Ray said, ignoring the hens. "Mr. Stewart has been in an accident and I'm trying to locate Mrs. Stewart."

"Oh, my God! Is he alright?"

"Looks like he passed out in the old railroad cut and they took him to the hospital. I'm trying to reach Mrs. Stewart to notify her."

"Oh no! I hope he's all right. Jill is probably teaching today. I have her cell phone number."

Ray dialed the number and Charlotte became increasingly upset while searching for Jill's school address. When she found it, she rushed outside, handed the address to Ray, and bounded toward her Cadillac with chicken feed flying from her muumuu pockets and mascara running on her face.

"I'm going to the hospital," she shouted while flooring the Cadillac and kicking up a cloud of dust on the unpaved road.

4

Amanda jumped from her horse and ran into the farmhouse. Jack, who was swept inside along with her, listened to the bubbling teenager jabber away about Luke Stewart. She darted around the kitchen filling soup bowls with a lumpy liquid that smelled like Ralph for some reason.

My sense of smell is incredible, Jack thought, although he had no appetite. He realized that most things were happening in real time while other things were skipping around like a dirty DVD. *All dreams jump around, don't they? Still, I shouldn't be aware of such things if I'm actually dreaming.*

He was forced to focus on Amanda's aunt and soon became transfixed. He recognized Permelia as the woman pictured on the roadside exhibit on Hill-Ewell Drive, near Scarborough Run. Permelia Higgerson was the feisty woman who had refused to leave her home when Union troops swarmed through the Wilderness. She greeted the hostile soldiers from Pennsylvania with her broom and a scolding.

So, I'm dreaming about the 1860s? he thought. *This is incredible…and I think I might be related to these people!*

As he stared at Permelia Higgerson, he realized he could read her mind and found that concentrating on her was revealing her deepest secrets. He couldn't wake up, however, even after pinching himself and slapping his face repeatedly. Instead, he plunged into Permelia's mind and discovered that Amanda was unerringly like her mother, Martha. Amanda had her mother's irresistible looks and personality and shared many of her mother's interests, including her general *lack* of interest in academic matters.

Permelia looked at her lovely niece absently, not hearing a word she was saying. *Even if Amanda knew nothing of academics, she would live well and flourish in this world based solely on her strong will and beauty—just like her mother,* she thought.

As Amanda jabbered on, Permelia's mind drifted back to her childhood. She had always been close to her younger sister, Martha, although they were complete opposites in personality and appearance. She and her sister grew up on the neighboring Chewning Plantation. As they began to mature, Permelia found that she was different from Martha and most other young women. Her younger sister was blessed with beauty that brought attention from men and women alike. Permelia was more intelligent, but that was of no real consequence in a society that viewed women as little more than ornaments. She did well in school while Martha was able "to do as well as a young lady was expected to do," and managed to complete most academic subjects with no emphasis on performance.

Permelia soon discovered that her intellect was useless, serving only to intimidate the opposite sex. Her unfortunate appearance became a source of amusement for other girls, who giggled about almost anything. Her mother did what she could for her daughter by grooming and encouraging her. As social pressures increased, however, the unhappy young woman chose to lock herself away from the society she had grown to hate.

When Martha entered her mid-teens, her beauty blossomed and one suitor after another called upon her. Permelia spent many hours in the background listening to her sister's conversations with young men who were dumbfounded and clumsy in her presence. Martha quickly learned all the techniques needed to enhance her "Southern Belle" status as Permelia continued to lose interest.

In spite of their differences, the sisters remained best of friends. Snuggled in their bedclothes late at night, they shared private thoughts in whispers. Martha described the silly things men did to impress her and Permelia feigned interest, although she considered such mindless behavior to be a meaningless waste of time.

By the age of twenty-six, Permelia had withdrawn from the mandates of nineteenth-century society. Instead, she lost herself in books. The unhappy girl read about places she would rather be and lives she would rather lead. She consumed everything from Homer to Hawthorne but cherished Charlotte Brontë's newly published *Jane Eyre,* in which Jane rejects both Puritanism and Libertinism in a search for her identity within a male-dominated society.

By the age of twenty-eight, attracting a man seemed hopeless. Martha had married a wealthy young man from Hampden Sydney named John Atkinson, who had completed medical training at Hampden-Sydney College. Martha joined her husband there, leaving Permelia alone and lonely.

Holly crap! Jack thought, realizing that *J.M.P.* Atkinson was Permelia's brother-in-law and that he was related to both of them. *Amanda could be my great-great-grandmother!* He was astonished as he involuntarily floated closer to the beautiful young girl. He looked into her bright eyes and considered how fleeting and fragile life really is.

Once Martha was gone, Permelia hid herself within her books and refused to leave home. Many lonely months had passed before she agreed to accompany her mother to Fredericksburg where she ignored the dress shops and shoe stores and headed, instead, for the apothecary shop. Old man Mercer was impressed with her questions and interest in his pharmacy and invited the inquisitive young woman to visit as often as she wished.

During the weeks that followed, Permelia returned to the pharmacy often and studied the delicate combinations of ingredients in the various potions and ointments. She absorbed the information in Mercer's library and learned how to make various ointments by boiling herbs in lard, straining the water, and adding melted wax to keep the remedies semi-solid. She examined the ingredients in the concoctions and taught herself basic Latin, which was used to write all inscriptions and subscriptions.

Eventually, applying live leeches to human skin to remove tainted blood from ailing patients seemed natural to Permelia and Mr. Mercer began to think of her as his apprentice. He began to pay the bright young lady a meager wage that boosted her self-esteem much more than her pocketbook.

The Land Grant Act provided for a college in each state after the Civil War. In 1848, however, there were few female pharmacists and women had limited access to higher education.

Permelia insisted upon working long hours at the apothecary and Mr. Mercer began to leave the shop early, trusting her to lock up. One spring evening, she lost track of time and left the shop just before sunset; most of her fifteen-mile journey home would be in total darkness. She departed quickly and raced against the clock.

In spite of her parent's objections, or perhaps *because* of their protests, Permelia had frequently ridden her horse on moonlit evenings. She loved to dress in black and ride like the wind over the dark but familiar roads near her home. Each exhilarating trip into the mysterious night strengthened her resolve and helped her believe that she would, one day, leave home for good. Following each ride in the moonlight, she slept soundly and dreamed of endless journeys into the unknown.

There would be no moonlight on tonight's ride, however. Thick, angry clouds smelled of rain as the terrified girl galloped west on the dark Germanna Plank Road. As she struggled against heavy gusts of swirling wind, three frightened deer leaped across the road and spooked her galloping stallion. The horse reared and threw her into the thick brush by the roadside.

As lightning ignited the atmosphere and thunder rolled, a wagon approached. A small, bearded man offered a calming hand to Star and then found the unconscious girl. He gently placed her in the back of his wagon and covered her with a blanket that smelled, to Jack, like the inside of an old chicken.

Wait a minute, how can I smell this woman's memory? Jack wondered.

When his skipping DVD drifted back to Permelia, she was sitting in a cabin with the man, who smelled like his nasty chicken blanket. Permelia had regained consciousness and the little guy was tending to her cuts and abrasions as the storm raged on. Chicken man offered some hot tea and they ate something that smelled delicious while Jack continued to linger in Permelia's memories.

Permelia paused and stared into her teacup as if in a trance, then slowly patted her mouth with a cloth napkin. Her lips began to move and she mumbled, "The more things change, the more they don't."

"What did you say, Aunt Permelia?"

"Oh, nothing, dear. I must have drifted off again. I..."

A coughing fit ended the conversation and Permelia expelled bloody phlegm into her handkerchief. Amanda was accustomed to her aunt's coughing episodes and paused only briefly before continuing an endless description of her encounter with Luke Stewart.

Great-great-grandpa Stewart? Jack wondered.

Permelia closed her tired eyes and pictured her beautiful dead sister describing yet another handsome young man from different lifetime. The weary and troubled woman decided not to ruin Amanda's jubilation with the news that would change everything.

5

Neither of them ate much supper because Permelia was too sick and Amanda was too excited. During Amanda's non-stop narrative about Luke, Permelia managed to mention that she had once met Luke's mother, who was the local schoolteacher before the war. Amanda was pleased that Luke came from an educated family and even more excited about her aunt's surprising interest in her new friend. She had been expecting some resistance. When Amanda finally ran out of words, Permelia offered no objections and sat quietly gazing at her wedding photograph on the fireplace mantel.

Amanda followed Permelia's gaze and said, "Please tell me more about Uncle Benjamin."

"Oh, Amanda, I've told you everything I can remember."

"But you haven't told me everything. I mean, well...how did you know you loved him?"

Permelia looked into the young girl's bright eyes and saw the same excitement she had felt about Benjamin so many years earlier. It was as if her sister had not died and somehow returned to Permelia's world only to be condemned to the lonely Wilderness. The broken woman felt sorry for her niece, but her news would free Amanda from this isolated prison. It would also take her away, just as Martha had been taken from her. The pensive, anxious woman feared that their destinies had already been determined.

"Can you hear me, Aunt Permelia?" Amanda said to regain her aunt's attention.

"Oh, did I wander off again? I'm sorry, dear. Let me see..." She struggled to compose her thoughts and said, "Well, Benjamin and I met here in the Wilderness as you know."

"Just like Luke and me," Amanda said with her eyes gleaming.

"That is true, dear."

Permelia controlled her emotions and continued, "As I've told you, Benjamin found me the night I fell from my horse. I was a long way from home and he was very kind. We talked for a long time while the storm raged outside and he was interested in what I had to say. He was also a perfect gentleman." Permelia smiled, leaned toward her niece and whispered, "You know, I secretly wanted him to kiss me."

The candid comment surprised and delighted Amanda and both women giggled, which stirred a deep rumbling cough within Permelia.

When she recovered, she said, "When the rain stopped, he carried me home in his wagon. My parents had been searching for me and they were more than grateful. They offered Benjamin a handsome reward, which he refused."

"What happened then?" Amanda asked excitedly.

"Benjamin told my parents that they had raised a remarkable young lady. I was embarrassed, thrilled, and hopelessly in love with him at that very moment. He tipped his hat to me and I had tears of joy in my eyes as I watched him ride away."

"When did you see him next?"

"The very next day I rode like the wind into Benjamin's arms and we were married six months later."

"And I came to your wedding?"

"Yes, you did, in your mother's belly."

They smiled at one another and Permelia continued.

"My father's wedding present was this farm and two slaves, Mr. Richard and his wife Evaleen, who helped build our house and worked as hard as ten men. We ate our meals with them and laughed and sang songs together." Permelia stared for a long moment and Amanda waited patiently for her aunt to continue. "Oh, those were good days. When the house was finished, I gave Mr. Richard and Evaleen each ten dollars of my own money. They were so grateful, you would have thought I was the Queen of England." Permelia drank from her teacup, which was laced with herbs. "Benjamin and I were married right here and we had a glorious celebration. I insisted on inviting Mr. Richard and Evaleen and your mother and father came all the way from Hampden Sydney."

Her damp eyes gleamed with melancholy joy as she continued to describe the man she loved. "Benjamin was so handsome in the suit of clothes he borrowed for the wedding and my mother purchased a beautiful wedding dress for me in Fredericksburg." She looked at the small photograph on the mantel and whispered, "I never told you that Benjamin was standing on a log when we posed for the photographer."

Amanda covered her mouth and giggled again, amazed that her aunt was revealing such personal and intimate memories. She looked carefully at the photograph and said, "You were so beautiful that day."

"Yes," Permelia said with swelling eyes. "I think I was."

Amanda hugged her aunt tenderly and said, "You're still beautiful."

Permelia began to cry and said, "I miss Benjamin so and I curse the typhoid fever that took him. If he hadn't insisted on caring for that sick Confederate soldier, he'd still be with us." She dried her eyes and continued, "I thank the Lord for the years we had together." Amanda gently patted her aunt's back and Permelia said, "As you know, I buried poor Benjamin in our little clearing down the hill."

"Yes I do," Amanda said. "It's a special place."

They sat in silence and Amanda said, "Do you know where Grandpa is buried? I know he helped rebuild the Catherine Iron Furnace for Jefferson Davis and died at the hands of the Yankees because he wouldn't surrender it to them."

"He was a brave and good man, but his body was never found."

"And when did Grandma begin her senility?"

"She hasn't been right for six or seven years, dear."

Permelia glanced through the window in the direction of her mother's neighboring farm. "She seems to have gotten worse since Grandpa's death."

"She asked me who I was again today," Amanda said.

Permelia shook her head. "She won't live here and she won't let us live there, so I guess it's up to Jeremiah to keep her company. Good thing she's not sick."

"Yes, ma'am. When I visited today, Jeremiah was sitting on the fence having his usual conversation with Lucy."

"I wonder what's going to happen if we have to slaughter that pig," Permelia said.

Amanda shook her head and said, "I never want to see that day and I hope this war ends soon. Lucy is Jeremiah's best friend."

"That old pig is his only friend. My brothers used to push Jeremiah around and tease him because he's stupid. Now they're all off fighting Yankees and Jeremiah is still talking to a pig."

Amanda grinned and said, "Grandma called *me* Lucy today."

Permelia crossed herself and said, "Ever since Jeremiah's parents died and Grandma took him in, he's been good company for her. Besides, he cares for her and cooks her meals."

"He's gentle, too," said Amanda.

"That he is," Permelia said. "When you carry vegetables to them tomorrow evening, be sure to tell them that I love'em. That probably won't mean a thing to either of them but you never know. I wish I could go myself, but I'm too weak."

"The good Lord knows you can't carry yourself there," Amanda said while patting her aunt's hand.

Permelia looked into her niece's eyes and saw her sister again. She could never hide her feelings from Martha and now Amanda could read her like a book. She cleared her throat and said, "I love you, Amanda, just like I loved your mother. You've suffered through your mother's death and you've been torn from your beautiful life in Hampden Sydney. Your father loves you dearly as well and he sent you here for your protection."

Amanda was deeply disturbed by her mother's death, although she kept the depth of her sorrow from Permelia. "Where do you suppose Father is now?" she said.

"I don't know, but I'm sure he's fine. No one knows what to believe about the direction of the war, but your father is certainly safe and I'm sure he misses you."

Amanda was comforted by that and said, "Did I ever show you the newspaper article that was written about Father when he was president of Hampden-Sydney College and led his students into war?"

"He told me about the Hampden-Sydney Boys, but I've never read the article."

Amanda disappeared into her room and returned with a book by Nathaniel Hawthorne called *The Blithedale Romance*, which had belonged to her mother. She removed a newspaper article that was neatly folded within the pages and read:

> *Once again, at the outset of the war the student body organized a company, with the president (J.M.P. Atkinson) as captain. The men were officially mustered as Company G, 20th Virginia Regiment, 'The Hampden-Sydney Boys,' saw action in the disaster of Rich Mountain 910 (July 1861), were captured, and then paroled by General George B. McClellan on the condition that they return to their studies.*[4]

"Father respected General McClellan and feared he would attack Richmond. He was convinced that the surrounding towns would fall into Union's hands, including Hampden Sydney. I know Father sent me here, far from the imminent siege, so he might continue to serve as a field hospital surgeon without concern for my safety." Amanda touched Permelia's arm and continued. "I also know he sent our family fortune with me to secure my future in case...in case something happens to him."

Permelia lowered her head and closed her eyes.

"And you've shown the hiding place to me in case something happens to you. I know more than you think and I'm stronger than you may believe," she added defiantly.

Both women sat in silence and then Amanda attempted to change the subject by saying, "Luke and I met in the Wilderness, just like you and Uncle Benjamin."

Permelia returned her niece's gaze and recalled how Amanda had refused to leave her father when he joined the Confederate Army. Amanda was an upper-class Southern Belle in training and she was grieving the recent loss of her mother, who had died of tetanus. The thought of being separated from her father was unacceptable, so she pleaded to become a nurse. She argued that she was already familiar with many modern medical procedures, having spent countless hours observing her father. Dr. Atkinson had taught her the same medical techniques he taught his students, such as the proper way to treat and bandage wounds and the correct way set broken bones. Amanda reasoned that, since she had witnessed the amputation of a woman's big toe, she was certainly qualified to become a war nurse.

Meanwhile, Jack was amazed. He was actually dreaming about his elusive family history. *Grandma Paddington Bear Atkinson is definitely not what she appears to be. Even though Mom is dead, Daddy is caring for the Confederate Army, and she's stuck in the Wilderness with a woman who is gravely ill, she has remained strong.*

Sending Amanda to friends in Richmond could not guarantee protection from McClellan's barbarous invading army. The consequences of that option gave Dr. Atkinson nightmares. He decided to send Amanda into the Wilderness, far from the tentacles of war. In spite of Amanda's endless tears, he did not waver. He sent his precious daughter to Permelia with everything from the family dog to the family jewels. One crate even contained a variety of stylish dresses, some of which had never been worn. Amanda was her mother's size and had modeled all of the clothes and accessories in the privacy of her little room. The teenager spent hours sampling the outfits, knowing she would have little opportunity to wear them in the backwoods.

Dr. Atkinson also sent his extensive gun collection in a dozen polished wooden boxes. The collection was exquisite and his beautifully scripted name, *J.M.P. ATKINSON*, was meticulously engraved on the barrel of each weapon.

The Atkinson family was well off and their slaves were loyal and well-treated. He entrusted them with the empty house in Hampden Sydney and the remainder of the family fortune was sent north with Amanda in the form of gold and jewels with little emphasis on Confederate currency. Permelia was asked to set aside what was needed and to bury the rest. Dr. Atkinson was then free to serve the Confederacy as a surgeon, confident that his daughter and his fortune were safe and well-hidden deep within the Wilderness.

Three years later, Permelia was not a bit surprised that Amanda had attracted the only eligible male within miles. Rather than seeing the young man as a threat, however, the sickly woman closed her eyes and thanked the Lord for Luke's timely arrival. She then assaulted her niece with questions about Luke's physical size, strength, and intellect.

Here it comes, Amanda thought.

Amanda, who remained confused about her aunt's interest and liberal attitude toward Luke, assured her that, "Luke is tall, healthy, and pleasant to look at. He's also intelligent—after all, his mother *was* a schoolteacher."

Permelia surprised her niece again by asking, with urgency, to meet Luke immediately. Amanda considered her aunt's surprising interest to be a form of acceptance and gladly promised to arrange a meeting as soon as possible. She then hugged her fragile aunt tenderly and retired to her bedroom with Jack in tow. The teenager was thrilled, nervous, and bubbling over with lovesick delight.

6

The light in Amanda's cramped room danced to a single oil lamp while she stared at her reflection in a hand-held mirror. She was rehearsing the kiss she so desperately wanted by moving the mirror close to her face and kissing it softly, trying to see what Luke might see. Frustrated by the need to keep her eyes open, she posed before a larger mirror in order to determine her best presentation. Every angle was stunning; poor Luke would have no chance to resist.

Grandma has not yet realized how truly irresistible she has become, Jack considered. *No wonder I'm so good looking,* he thought, grinning again.

Like her mother, Amanda's green eyes blended perfectly with her honey blonde hair that framed an angelic face with high cheekbones and full seductive lips. She brushed her long silky hair, reminding Jack of shampoo models. As she stroked her hair, she prayed that Luke would find her attractive and her aunt would continue to accept him. She could feel her mother's brush strokes and longed for her mother's touch. The frustrated débutant yearned for her long-gone lessons in etiquette, grooming, dancing, and piano but missed her mother's loving care and guidance most of all.

None of that matters. Mother is dead and I'm living like a pioneer in the Wilderness. What would she think if she could see me wandering around in the woods with a gun—dressed like a man! She ached for her mother and cursed her missed opportunities. *Forgive me for cursing and please help me to act like a lady when I meet Luke,* she thought as a tear began to form.

General McClellan had never actually attacked Richmond and she would have been safe at home after all. She didn't blame her father, who loved her and had her best interests in mind. Those young women who did remain in Richmond and Hampden Sydney, however, were continuing at least some of their education. She knew that once the North was defeated and gone, she would be far behind her peers.

By the age of sixteen, her mother had dozens of suitors and Amanda would have followed in her footsteps except that all eligible men were off fighting in the war. Her mother had explained that Permelia was not as "socially fortunate" as she was, so Amanda did not confide in her aunt regarding such matters. Today was the first time Permelia had opened up to her and Amanda was perplexed. In spite of her aunt's new attitude, she abhorred her fate as a prisoner in a lonely wasteland with no guidance, no mentor, no school, and no young men.

Luke Stewart was an opportunity she would not squander. *He may not be refined, but he is much more handsome than the men in Hampden Sydney and Richmond.* Southern gentlemen were polite participants in a rigid social structure that was condescending toward women. Amanda had recognized that folly even at the age of thirteen. Her ten-minute encounter with Luke, which the infatuated adolescent had poured over and analyzed, convinced her that Luke was not only different but somewhere between a demigod and Achilles himself. *Mother, I know you would appreciate Luke's beautiful smile, wavy black hair, and tremendous height.*

"Even taller than Father," she said aloud, which snapped Jack out of his dream within a dream.

He realized that Amanda was wearing one of her mother's dresses. *A dress rehearsal,* he thought, smiling again. She was attractive enough in her uncle's clothing—in a dress, she was stunning. The dress was a long, elegant, dark blue riding habit with long sleeves and a high neckline. Tiny white buttons began at the neckline and ended at her trim waist. She filled the upper part of the dress to capacity and wore a small feathered cowboy style hat. When she twirled around, he could see that she was wearing high leather riding boots.

As Amanda continued to spin in place, Jack wondered if any woman had ever worn a dress like this in the Wilderness. He understood that his great-great-grandmother had a strong will, but she was also a naïve, misguided teenager. She hadn't seen another person her age in more than three years and the former débutante was determined to impress Luke.

It seemed to Amanda that her aunt was almost encouraging her new relationship. If that were the case, she would not object to her fashionable riding habit. After all, she couldn't wear one of her old, grey dresses and Uncle Benjamin's clothing was out of the question.

"You're a girl right?"

Luke's words were stuck in her head and she suddenly feared that he might not show up at all! *Please, Mother, send him to me.*

If all went as planned, she would ride Star as far as the railroad cut, which ran west to east through the dense underbrush. The cut connected several north-south roads, such as Brock Road that rambled south toward Richmond. She dreamed of traveling to Richmond one day and what a fascinating journey it would be. The dreadful war would be over, her father would be safe at home, and Richmond would be the shining capital of the independent and peaceful South.

Close enough, Jack thought.

She planned to conceal some bread, cheese, and cider in one of Star's saddlebags and to tend to her last-minute grooming needs during the short walk from the railroad cut to the meeting place. She gazed into the mirror again and her heart skipped when she thought of Luke.

Because her reflection haunted her with thoughts of inadequacy, she fiddled with the delicate buttons at her neckline. As a young girl in Hampden Sydney, she had seen women entice men with a variety of techniques that females alone would recognize as significant. Southern Belles were taught to speak in soft flirtatious voices and to flaunt their frailty, appearing to suffer from both warm and cold weather with helpless desperation. That kind of behavior had impressed Amanda, although her tutoring and emotional development ended at a critical time. All that remained was an unedited collection of her mother's books. The collection had been hastily packed by an illiterate Atkinson slave and included several risqué novels such as *Adam Bebe,* by George Eliot and the controversial *Leaves of Grass,* by Walt Whitman.

Her mother had also enjoyed "romance novels." In 1856, she subscribed to *La Revue De Paris* magazine, which included serialized segments of *Madame Bovary*; a story about the moral degeneration of a middle-class French woman. Gustave Flaubert's novel had been attacked for obscenity by French public prosecutors and it left Amanda hopelessly confused. Thankfully, her mother's magazines did not include the entire story. Although Amanda was overwhelmed and embarrassed by the excerpts, she had read every word—repeatedly.

In a clumsy and confused adolescent attempt to distract attention from what she considered her "unattractive features," she playfully toyed with the little buttons at her neckline. Unhooking too many at first, she giggled before settling for just the right look. Amanda liked the unbuttoned look. Appropriate or not, she would not be denied the full attention of the only eligible male in the Wilderness.

Buttons or no buttons, she would quicken the pulse of any red-blooded male in any century, Jack thought. *Luke is toast.*

Amanda pictured walking through the woods with Luke, holding hands, and sitting on a little grassy knoll near a gentle stream as the perfume of lilacs drifted in the air. She could see him touching her face and kissing her tenderly and her heart raced when she thought of his long caress. She closed her eyes and felt giddy while hugging herself, pretending that Luke was holding her. The dreamy teen became convinced that sleep would fetch dreams of Luke, so she quickly changed into her nightclothes, snuggled into bed, and drifted off to the rhythm of ten thousand insects.

Jack was drawn closer to Amanda until his face was almost touching hers. She slowly parted her lips, quickly stuck out her tongue, and licked his cheek with a juicy slurp. He recoiled from his grandmother's affections and found himself face-to-face with the hound that had knocked him down in the railroad cut. He and the dog were outside Permelia's house in the moonlight and Jack realized that the dog could actually see him! "You can see me, can't you boy?" he said, thinking that this must be Amanda's dog, Zeus.

When he reached to pat the dog's head, Zeus licked Jack's hand and threw him into emotional overdrive. After another slurp,

Jack's eyes welled up and he was confused by his strong emotional response to Zeus. *Physical contact with Zeus must be increasing my awareness of the real world and eroding my euphoric dream!*

He began to drift farther away from the reverie of his fantasy until he had one foot in each world. The monitors in his hospital room surged momentarily and he felt physical pain. He realized that he could not escape the torment of reality, no matter how much he drank or dreamed.

He pulled away from Zeus and quickly regained his euphoria.

"Good boy!" he said. "I guess we're in this together and you're the lucky one because they can see you."

Zeus rolled over on his back and Jack wondered if they would be able to see him as well. He felt a little uneasy about that, although he was thrilled to have company in his fantasy as his feelings of exhilaration became even stronger. He couldn't move, so he studied the strange dog with the floppy ears and long tongue. Everything had returned to high-definition and, whether staggeringly beautiful or butt-ugly, each megapixel was clear and bright.

Am I a ghost? He didn't think he was dead, or nearly dead, but he was sure that contact with the dog had diminished his dispassionate trip into Wonderland. Zeus had bridged the gap between reality and fantasy. Jack was beginning to appreciate the latter because it was much more pleasant than blurry-eyed reality.

Zeus began to cry softly and Jack moved closer. The dog licked him again and then the face of the hound morphed into the terrified face of a young boy named Truitt Simms.

7

A casual stroll through the lunatic asylum
shows that faith does not prove anything.
~Friedrich Nietzsche

A shaft of sunlight reflected the terror in Truitt's spectacular coal-black eyes as Jack watched the frightened boy tremble in the darkest corner of his cot. Truitt considered the usefulness of prayer as he stared at the door where the monster would appear. His mother had always turned to prayer when the old man got like this and she was praying in earnest the night her husband pounded her to death with his fists.

Best he could figure, he was ten back then.

"Say a word 'bout this and I'll kill you too, boy," the old man said after he brutally murdered the boy's mother.

As time passed in the lonely Shenandoah Valley, physical and sexual abuse assured Truitt's silence. Dread and confusion destroyed the lad's emotional stability and he became increasingly passive. He said and did nothing about his father's cruelty until puberty began to erode his submissive attitude and a plan of retribution began to replace his debilitating fear.

Sunset came early in the shadow of Bryce Mountain and long autumn shadows were replacing the colors in Truitt's quilt with monotone gray and white. Individual items in the one-room cabin were fading and blending into the darkness—some had already vanished. He looked around at the pots, pans, and grease he had hastily spread on the floorboards and he could smell the animal fat that was smeared on his arms, neck, and bare chest. He wished that he could become one of the inanimate objects in the room so that his father could never find him.

No, he thought. *I'm fifteen and I got to make a stand.*

Five years earlier, his mother's blood had splattered on the colorful quilt she created for him while Truitt quivered and watched his father crush his mother to death. When the horrendous screaming ended, Truitt peeked out from under the quilt and saw his father kneeling by his dead mother, crying into his huge hands. The terrified child remained frozen underneath the blanket until he was sure his father was gone and then crawled to his dead mother's side. He cuddled with her cheek-to-cheek for the remainder of the night and swore to his mother's God that he would, someday, avenge her death.

That day had finally arrived. With blood rushing in his ears, he waited on the same cot, with the same quilt that was stained with his mother's precious blood. Each time his father attacked and sodomized him, the boy considered shooting him with the big Hawken rifle, but firing the long rifle inside the small cabin would be awkward. He didn't dare attack him with his knife while he slept because the old bastard always slept with one eye open.

No, he would make sure the old man was drunk and use himself as bait to lure him into the dark cabin where he would stab him to death. Truitt had confidence in that plan because he was lightning-fast and real handy with his oversized hunting knife.

Besides, he can't grab me 'cause I'll be all greased up, he thought.

The weeks, months and seasons passed slowly as Truitt lumbered through puberty and waited for the right moment. Finally, the time had come and he was huddled in the dark with a bleeding lip and pounding heart. The bastard was outside drinking, throwing things around, cursing his only son, and working himself into an uncontrollable rage. When his father's face appeared briefly in the dirty window, the cowering boy felt an adrenalin rush in his groin and twitched several times before diverting his eyes. His long, greasy strands of hair bobbed in front of his swollen face in concert with his thumping heart as he stared at the door and waited for the inevitable.

Jack could read Truitt's thoughts, although part of the boy's mind had "access denied" stamped on it. He hovered close to the strange-looking teenager and stared into his huge jet-black eyes; eyes that allowed him to see in the dark when other men couldn't. His thick, bushy eyelashes served to shield the sunlight, which gave him an advantage on bright days as well. When he blinked, it looked as though the inside of his eyelids somehow preceded his overweight eyelashes, much like the eyes of a lizard. His bulging, watering eyes were especially keen during twilight when he was able to see what his prey saw. During those tantalizing moments when all things were equal, he was transformed into a voracious, predatory animal like a werewolf staring at the moon.

The last glimmer of sunlight disappeared and Truitt wished again that he could vanish into a dark corner. Twenty minutes earlier, he had returned empty-handed from hunting. The old drunkard waited for him to get within arm's length and surprised him with a powerful backhand that knocked him down and opened his lip. Truitt was small like his mother, but he was also extremely quick and wiry. He dodged a vicious kick, which was intended for his head, and darted into the cabin to set the trap he had been rehearsing for months.

Jack could smell the stale grease and wet hardwood ashes in the stone fireplace, which permeated the stuffy air in the cabin. Truitt knew it was too late to run and lamented that, *if it's time to die, so be it.* The boy twitched just before the door crashed open and the silhouette of a huge man filled the opening. His father's uneven Scotch-Irish red beard, enormous body, and unnaturally small head made him look more like an ogre than a man.

The ogre snarled, peered through the darkness and shouted, "Where are you, damn it!"

Instinctively, Truitt pushed farther into the corner of his bunk and, to his disappointment, his tears blossomed.

"I told you to kill me a deer, boy. I'm hungry for some damned deer meat and you let me down!" the ogre barked. "Now I got to fix you right."

Truitt and Jack watched in silence as the beast staggered closer, swearing and kicking aside the pots and pans that lay strewn on the floor.

"What's all this shit?" he said as he staggered closer. "There you are. You can't hide from me, you little bastard," he slurred through clenched teeth. "And you ain't gettin' away neither."

The big man slipped on the greasy floor, clumsily fell to his knees, and continued to fall forward like a great tree. He landing short of Truitt's bunk and groped for the boy's legs in the darkness. Truitt quickly braced his Bowie knife on his low cot with the razor-sharp end pointed up. When the drunken ogre found his footing and lunged, he fell on the nine-inch blade. Both lower legs of Truitt's cot collapsed as the blade entered the ogre's upper stomach, just below his heart. After a sickening pop of the giant's skull against one of the wall timbers and several moments of violent shuddering, the monster lay dead and still.

As the sunset turned the cabin's gloom into complete darkness, both father and son lay motionless. Jack waited patiently, listening to Truitt's breathing and the melodious dripping of blood on the floorboards. Truitt remained wedged underneath his father for an unnaturally long time, praying the way his mother had taught him. He prayed that his mother would be happy now and that the old man wouldn't meet up with her in the afterlife. He doubted that there was an afterlife but "prayed on it just in case" while struggling to understand why his mother's God hadn't struck his father down long ago.

Still, the boy yearned for something more than residual body heat from his father. As the ogre's body cooled, however, only his sour odor and the lingering smell of stale whiskey remained. Truitt dismissed the idea of prayer and, for reasons that would haunt him, fell asleep while stroking his father's back.

Come on Truitt, wake up. I know you're under there because I can hear you breathing, Jack thought.

Hours later, Truitt woke, squirmed free, and slithered into a puddle of blood on the floor. He rose slowly, stood barefoot on the sticky floorboards, and stared at the grotesque corpse in the moonlight. Blood was matted in his hair, bare chest, and trousers; his quilt was covered with the stuff. He felt as though he had awakened from deep, refreshing sleep and that his dead parents and his entire life were nothing more than an illusions.

Jack realized that the boy was now completely empty, void of civility, and utterly insane. *One monster has begotten another*. Truitt knelt next to his father at the gruesome altar and began to critique his kill. He had pictured leaping on the clumsy drunkard once he fell and then stabbing him repeatedly in the neck and eyes "until the deed was done." The way it happened "so easy like," left him with a strange sense of failure, however, and he was uneasy because he feared he had missed something. He thought about that for a long time and then decided, *it don't matter none 'cause it's done anyhow.*

Truitt pulled the body from the broken bunk; the ogre landed with a wet thump and rolled face up. He felt the pre-dawn chill and covered himself with his blood-dampened quilt as sunlight crept through the small window. He felt empowered standing over to the body and became overwhelmed with an odd sense of righteousness. The smell of his old quilt and the peaceful silence in the cabin reminded him of waking to the sounds of his mother's gentle songs.

She was pure and had always tried to protect him from the old man. She comforted her son by reading aloud from the Bible or Hans Christian Anderson, although Truitt preferred the latter. His favorite tale was *The Little Mermaid,* and he knew the story well because she had always read that particular narrative with great enthusiasm. He could hardly read, but the remarkable semi-nude illustrations in the book told the stories well and enchanted him long after his mother's death. He treasured the mystical book and kept it well hidden from the ogre.

Beautiful images of mermaids and nymphs filled Truitt's mind as he pulled the knife from his father's chest and gutted the carcass. He found the liver, cut off a small piece, and studied it in his bloody hands—turning it repeatedly. His Indian friend Kuruk had taught him that a hunter could gain strength by eating the liver of a respected kill, but he dismissed the idea of obtaining anything of value from the dead coward before him.

Instead, he stuffed the liver into the mouth of the silent devil, spread oil lamp fuel throughout the room, and set the cabin on fire.

8

Jack was engulfed in smoke but not from Truitt's cabin. Instead, his dream had delivered him to the inside of Permelia's fireplace and the dying woman was staring directly at him in the smoldering fire. Her skeletal eyes were deep-set cavities and her bone-dry hair was tied in a tight knot. The sickening cup in her lap caused thoughts of death and dying to drift lightly through Jack's mind, like a butterfly flutters around a glass of sweet red wine. Those curiosities were then replaced by a fascination with the dying woman.

Permelia was hopelessly ill and the cancer had been sucking the moisture from her body. She coughed and hacked enough to fill her disgusting, ever-present tin cup several times each day. Jack was amazed that her lungs could produce so much liquid. He could feel life seeping from her body, which was like watching someone react to the receiving end of a stun gun—sure, you feel sorry for the victim but the process is fascinating. He watched for a while longer and realized, *none of this matters—I'm inside a fireplace and this is all a dream.*

Widow Higgerson was anxious and worried. She was responsible for her niece, her senile mother, and her simple-minded nephew, Jeremiah—but there was more. The mysterious letter, which was tucked deep within the folds of her black dress, weighed heavily on the poor woman. Jack emerged from the fireplace and moved uncomfortably close to the widow. He hovered inches from her face, but he could not "read" the letter in her mind.

Please don't lick me, he thought.

Instead of giving him a moist slurp, she fell asleep and the soft mantra of her snoring drew him into her psyche, allowing him to meander through her memories once again.

Permelia's husband, Benjamin, might have smelled like a spoiled chicken, but he was a noble and honest man. He was determined to do his part for the Confederacy and "took in" a feverish Confederate soldier. Permelia objected, mostly for Amanda's sake, so Benjamin cared for the man by himself. Permelia, Amanda, Mr. Richard and Evaleen moved into the large house on the neighboring Chewning Plantation where Permelia's mother lived. Unfortunately, Benjamin contracted typhoid from the soldier and died on Christmas Day, 1862, leaving Permelia and Amanda alone.

Shortly after Benjamin's death, Permelia's mother insisted that Permelia and Amanda leave her home. Permelia Chewning, who shared her daughter's first name, was suffering from dementia and had little control over her household and plantation. Her husband had perished while protecting the Catherine Furnace, most of her nine children were enlisted in the Confederate Army, and all of the Chewning slaves had abandoned her.

Permelia knew she could not support Mr. Richard and Evaleen, so she granted their freedom from slavery before returning to the Higgerson Farm with Amanda. Now alone, Amanda and Permelia became dependent upon each other for daily needs as well as for needs of the heart. Wartime life became a matter of survival; Amanda learned to hunt and both women tended to Permelia's garden. Eventually, Amanda was able to deliver fresh meat and vegetables to her grandmother on a regular basis.

In May of 1863, the inexorable war returned to the Fredericksburg area and The Battle of Chancellorsville raged within ten miles of the Higgerson Farm. During that battle, Stonewall Jackson was wounded, lost his arm, and died of pneumonia eight days later.

Hey, Jack thought, *maybe I'll dream about Stonewall Jackson, or maybe Robert E. Lee himself!* He lowered his head, squeezed his eyes closed and thought about Bobby Lee, hoping to join him in his dreamscape. It didn't work, so he tried to block Permelia from his mind completely but that didn't work either. He could hear Amanda singing softly, although he was forced to remain next to the snoring woman. Amanda was preparing breakfast, humming, and cheerfully twirling around the room.

Jack couldn't understand why he didn't have access to Permelia's mysterious letter. He knew, however, that it didn't contain any good news—at least not for Permelia.

Amanda floated around the small room like a bird and answered her aunt's muffled snores and snorts with cheerful singing. When she casually removed Permelia's nasty cup and dumped it outside, Jack realized how familiar she was with her aunt's sickness and to what extent the young woman had filled the role of caregiver and nurse.

Permelia stirred and Amanda said, "Good morning, Aunt Permelia. Are you in any less pain today?"

"Yes, dear, I'm fine," she lied as she shuffled outside to the privy.

To Jack's relief, he remained with Amanda until Permelia returned and said, "I want to hear more about your new friend."

"With your permission, I've agreed to meet Luke today," Amanda said, not knowing what her aunt's reaction would be. "I've, um…arranged a meeting with him and I'll invite him to visit if you like. I'm pleased that you're interested in meeting him and I'm sure you'll like him."

Permelia swallowed hard and controlled her emotions. Her mind was racing and her blood pressure was beginning to rise. With a great deal of restraint, she said, "That would be fine, dear."

Amanda questioned Permelia's tone and motives. *Why is she acting so strangely and why hasn't she objected to my new found relationship?* She challenged her aunt by saying, "Zeus found his way home and I'm sure he'll enjoy seeing Luke again."

Since Zeus was dedicated to Amanda and would protect her to his death, Permelia felt more relieved than confronted but said nothing. Because of Permelia's silence and because she had not objected to Amanda's intentions to meet a strange boy in the woods, the infatuated teen disappeared into her bedroom and donned her mother's dress. Then, she waited behind her bedroom door until mustering enough courage to reveal herself.

Permelia was quietly sipping tea when Amanda burst into the room and pirouetted around the kitchen table in her mother's elegant riding habit. When the ghost of Permelia's dead sister suddenly materialized, the fragile woman gasped and the vacillations within her heart nearly killed her.

Amanda noticed her aunt's ashen face and froze.

"Are you all right?" she said.

"I'm fine, dear," Permelia said weakly. "You surprised me, that's all."

Amanda fetched a glass of cool water and sat with her aunt. Permelia strongly but silently objected to Amanda's plans to meet a boy in the woods. *And dressed like this! Good Lord!* She knew she couldn't allow such a thing; what would her poor dead sister think of her? But she had no choice. She had to allow this unchaperoned meeting because she was too weak to go along. There is no time to waste and she couldn't risk losing the boy. Insisting on a meeting here at her farm would be far more appropriate but that might scare him off. *Lord help me, but I can voice no protest because we desperately need Luke Stewart.* She was mortified but knew damn well that the survival of her precious niece could depend on the strength and integrity of a newly-discovered, oversized teen. The unfamiliar young man might be Amanda's only hope.

As Amanda mounted Star, Permelia prayed that she was making the right decision. She knew Amanda, like her mother, could make any man dance on the tip of a pin. *Lord help me,* she thought as she stared up at her niece, who looked like a princess on her mount.

Riddled with guilt, Permelia reminded her niece again, "Make sure Luke visits us tomorrow," and Amanda agreed for the sixth time before riding off like a senseless débutante going to a Secessionist Ball. Permelia, who felt the weight of the earth upon her soul, watched her lovely niece ride down the hill in her beautiful dress until she disappeared into the distance.

The distraught woman knelt down in the grass and prayed for forgiveness.

9

It was nearly midnight and Jill couldn't keep her eyes open. She removed the warm towel from Jack's forehead and lowered the hospital bed guardrail. Then, she squeezed her small body into the bed, covered her head with the sheet, and prayed that her husband would return to her.

"Please come back to me. Please!" she whispered.

Her tears fell on the white sheets within her sanctuary and her thoughts drifted to the pure white snow in Maine. Two years earlier, on Valentine's Day, Jack had surprised her with a romantic weekend in Northeast Harbor on the coast of Maine. Six inches of new snow fell overnight. They ascended Cadillac Mountain on cross-country skis and glided between towering green pines on isolated carriage trails that led gently upward through the white stillness. The cold Atlantic surrounded the island like an endless blue desert and dark clouds gathered as they climbed the mountain trail.

Snow began to fall from the gunmetal sky as Jill turned to follow a narrow side trail that proved difficult to traverse. She stopped in a small clearing, turned to Jack, and removed her skis. As shafts of sunlight breached the icy clouds and huge snowflakes floated in the windless sky, she unpacked a small patchwork quilt and spread it on the snow-covered ground. She removed her shoes and quickly stepped out of her knickers, leaving only her woolen knee socks in place, and lay down on the quilt smiling impishly. The sweet scent of her perfume filled the cold air and their hearts pounded together while giant snowflakes covered them like feathers from a broken pillow.

The comatose pilot could sense the presence of his wife and he was vaguely aware that she was near. The pain in his body began to increase. Although he was unable to move, his remarkable sense of smell began to exaggerate the disinfected odor of hospital floors, used gauze in the waste can, and his own stagnant body odor. Then, as Jill's powerful memories of Maine began to surface within Jack's mind, the repugnant odors were replaced by the sweet scent of her Estée Lauder. He strained to move an eyelid while pain riddled his inert body but remained still and quiet. Jill fell asleep at his side in the dead hospital silence.

In the morning, a disheveled nurse sat down heavily at the nurse's station. Two smiley face stickers framed her nametag that read "Donna." She was tapping at her computer keyboard when another nurse arrived in quiet shoes and began to read the nightly reports from the hospital floor for "unresponsive patients."

"Hi, Lisa," Donna said.

"Good morning, Donna," the day nurse said. "Is Jill still here?"

"Yep. Jill and Samantha are both here. Last night there was a constant stream of visitors, all with flowers. Jill handled them well and patiently listened to their small talk. You know how that goes. When they finally left, she climbed into bed with Jack and fell asleep."

"Poor thing. She needs a break," Lisa said. "How's Samantha holding up?"

"Sam is such a sweet dog. It breaks my heart when she licks Jack's hand and rests her head on his bed. I'm glad the hospital is letting Samantha stay here."

"Yeah, me too. Sometimes therapy dogs can perform miracles."

"I hope so," Donna said. "You know, every time Jill takes Wonder Dog out to do her business, she visits Mrs. Shultz on the way back. It's so cute when Samantha nuzzles her snout under Ida's hand. You'd swear that the dog was praying."

"Maybe she is," said Lisa.

Wonder Dog heard Lisa's voice, pushed the partially closed door open, and padded out to say hello. Sam was always eager to receive affection from a dog lover who knew exactly where to scratch her.

"Hello, Samantha," Lisa said as she stroked the grateful dog.

Sam smiled at Lisa, enjoyed a healthy scratch, and returned to Jack's room. The nurses overlooked the fact that Sam was not always on a leash.

"Jill is exhausted," Donna said. "Dr. Huesgen is going to talk to her about going home."

"That's a good idea. She's been here too long already and she needs some rest," said Lisa.

"Yeah, but when she leaves it's going to be terribly quiet again. At least I can talk to Jill. Did you know that she went to Yale and has three degrees? I dragged that out of her yesterday and it wasn't easy. She teaches little children because she loves it and I'm sure the kids love her too. Must be nice. Anyway, I've enjoyed talking with someone who actually talks back." Donna sat back in her swivel chair and sighed, "I feel so sorry for her."

"It is sad but he might come back," Lisa said. "I'll spend some extra time with Jill until the doctor shows up. Meanwhile, I could use a little peace and quiet. My little one has been up with a cold. I'm on all day so my husband will have his hands full at home."

"Well, don't work too hard and I hope you're right about Jack. He sure is the cutest unresponsive male I've seen," Donna said, fiddling with her hair. "I'd take him in a coma over most of the men I've met in Fredericksburg," she continued, only half kidding.

"Go home and get some rest, Donna. I'll see you at six tonight, right?"

"That would be me," she said, waving goodbye over her shoulder.

Lisa fussed with Jack's tubes and bed sheets until Jill woke and forced a smile.

Lisa said, "You really need some rest, Jill. There is nothing you can do here; I promise we'll call if anything changes."

Jill looked at her husband and said nothing. She was exhausted and knew the nurse was right. She hadn't left Jack's side for thirty-six hours.

"You're right, of course. I'll go home after I speak to the doctor," Jill said while sitting up in Jack's bed and adjusting her ponytail clip.

She had already called Jack's father in Illinois and her mother in San Francisco. Jill's father had passed away when she was in her teens and she thought of Jack's dad as her own. Jack's father was due to arrive in two days and she had agreed to pick him up at the airport.

Their son, Alex, was in the middle of final exams; she didn't want to disturb him just yet, but she had added him to the list of phone calls yet to make.

Charlotte had arrived at the hospital before Jill. She greeted Jill with tears and hugs and spent hours sitting with her before driving home to get Samantha. She returned with Wonder Dog, a short list of toiletries, and healthy snacks. Jill had not left Jack's side even though he hadn't moved an eyebrow since "the accident" and she knew it was time to go home—at least for a while.

The doctor appeared shortly before noon. He mentioned that the latest CT scan showed nothing other than normal brain bruising caused by the concussion. He pointed out that the brain bruising was a concern, additional tests were needed, and that Jack appeared to be as healthy as a horse otherwise.

Even after speaking with the doctor, Jill couldn't force herself to leave the hospital. She spent another entire day and evening with him. The memory of her father's untimely death was burned into her heart and the thought of losing her husband was unbearable. When she finally went home, it was after 1:00 a.m. and she was exhausted. She drank a glass of wine and wandered around the empty house before swallowing a sleeping pill and drifting into dreamless sleep on the living room couch. No moonlight penetrated the thick clouds outside; the living room was darker still.

Shortly after 3:00 a.m., she woke to thumping sounds coming from the back deck and clumsily switched on the table lamp. She rose unsteadily, covered her shoulders with her blanket, and cautiously approached the sliding glass doors. Another loud thump startled her and Samantha began to bark. Her sleeping pill and wine cocktail had made her woozy, but she steadied herself and reached for the drape, which covered the door. When she pulled the drape aside, she saw two eerie yellow eyes that shredded all that remained of her fragile nerves. She screamed, released the drape, and Sam continued to bark and whine.

Exhausted and upset, she checked the door locks, switched on the floodlights, and went to bed with Samantha curled around her feet.

10

The next morning, Jill was staring into a cup of cold coffee when Charlotte appeared with a large Trader Joe's shopping bag in hand. After an exceptionally long hug, she surprised Jill with breakfast burritos, pre-mixed Bloody Marys, and a box of Godiva chocolate. She hugged Jill again and said, "Are you all right? Is there any news?"

"No change, although the doctor did say that Jack is in good health."

"He'll be just fine. I'm sure of it," Charlotte said. "It's time for you to relax."

Jill picked at her burrito while Charlotte poured two generous Bloody Marys and searched for something to say. Charlotte did not have many "filters" and usually said whatever came to mind.

"You'll never believe what happened yesterday," Charlotte said.

"What?" Jill said absently while gazing at an entire stalk of celery extending comically from her Bloody Mary.

"I was over at Carrie's house for lunch and her daughter, Shelby, was in the back yard playing on her swing set. You know little Shelby, don't you?"

"Oh, sure. She was in my class last year."

"Well, we were sitting in Carrie's kitchen—she sends her regards by the way. Anyway, Shelby came in from the yard claiming that a man was pushing her swing. Carrie bolted to the window and looked into the yard. Then, we both walked around to the front of the house and looked up and down the street, but we didn't see anyone."

"That must have been creepy."

"I know! According to Carrie, Shelby never makes things up or tells stories to get attention. She's a sweet little thing. Anyway, Carrie gently asked Shelby to describe the man. She said he had a beard and was wearing an old gray suit that had silver buttons on each side. Carrie asked if she had talked to him and Shelby said she did, but the man didn't smile or say anything."

Jill said, "I've had kids in my class with overactive imaginations and some, like Shelby, who don't exaggerate at all. She's not the kind of kid who would come up with something like that."

Charlotte, who had been unable to sleep because of her concern for Jack, had been testing and tasting her Bloody Marys and eating chocolate since dawn. She always turned to chocolate during stressful times. She gulped her second Bloody Mary, ate two more pieces of chocolate, adjusted her muumuu and said, "I'm pretty sure it was a ghost."

Here we go again, Jill thought. She knew Charlotte had been drinking and that her friend's comments were not meant to upset her, but her nerves were shattered and she didn't want to hear any more.

Charlotte continued to put her foot in her mouth. "I'm sorry, Jill. Silly me. I know you don't believe in ghosts the way I do. Many people don't. It's easy for me because I have a connection with the spirit world that others don't have."

Jill remained silent while Charlotte scolded herself for opening the subject. After a long hesitation, Charlotte said, "I also talk too much."

"That's okay, Charlotte. There may be something to that sort of thing, but I'm much too tired to think about it right now," Jill said, hoping Charlotte would decide to leave.

"I love you anyway," Charlotte said with a smile. "By the way, there's a dog under your deck."

"Oh! That must have been what I saw last night. I heard a noise on the deck and peeked out there. It scared the heck out of me."

"So, what did you do?"

"I turned the floodlights on and went to bed with Samantha."

"They're still on."

"What?"

"The flood lights. They're still on."

"Oh...okay. Thanks. Does the dog look friendly?"

"I really don't know. I walked over here yesterday because I was a worried about Henrietta getting too close, but I kept my distance because I was getting bad vibes."

"Bad what?"

"Bad vibes. You know, like creepy feelings. I mean the dog was all curled up and its yellow eyes gave me the creeps, that's all. I'll go with you if you want to take a look."

The dog turned out to be a relatively large, reddish-brown hound that seemed harmless enough. Charlotte, who was now hiccupping, kept her distance from the strange dog and seemed to be uncharacteristically wary of the helpless animal. The dog was curled up under the deck in a tight, frightened ball and there was blood-laced vomit on the lawn nearby. Jill approached slowly and stroked the traumatized hound gently.

She discovered a nametag that read "ZEUS."

Zeus was a conduit in time. He had emerged from the past, slammed into Jack, and found himself under the Stewart's deck with his stomach churning and his ears pinned back. He shivered through a terrifying red sunset while restless bones stirred in the ground beneath him.

"Charlotte, our vet's number is stuck on our fridge. It should be on one of those magnetic business cards. Will you call the number and let him know that I'm bringing this dog in? I'll take Samantha with me too."

"Okay. I'll call ahead," Charlotte said, relieved that she was not asked to go along. She couldn't ride in the car with Zeus, much less deliver him to the vet. "Are you sure you want to do this?" she slurred.

Jill had found her excuse to leave. "This poor dog is suffering and I have to run a couple of quick errands in town anyway. Jack is having all sorts of tests done this morning, so I'm not going to the hospital until this afternoon."

"Okay," Charlotte hiccuped. "Drive carefully, all right? I'll stop by the hospital later."

"Thanks, Charlotte. I'll see you there."

The bumper sticker on the back of Jill's SUV read "All Golden Retrievers Go to Heaven" and it had plenty of room for Zeus and

Samantha. Zeus had to be picked up and placed into the back of the SUV, which made him unhappy. To Zeus, the newly oiled macadam driveway and the engine exhaust smelled like dead animals. When the car began to move, "unhappy" quickly changed to doggy panic. The frantic dog leaped into the front seat and comically wedged his head behind Jill's back.

Off they went with Samantha's lips flapping in the breeze. Zeus, who had no interest in looking out the window, much less sticking anything out there, remained attached to Jill. Then, a wailing fire engine launched the quivering dog into a howling mode, although petting and baby talk calmed him enough to reach the vet's office safely.

Doc Weaver was an old man in an old house that served as his office in downtown Fredericksburg. He had no secretary or receptionist. Finding a seat in the waiting room was a challenge because of the antique junk that covered the walls and a good part of the floor. The vet collected anything that was old and related to animals; each dust-covered horse saddle, harness, branding iron and photograph had a dusty, yellowed description taped to it. As soon as Zeus entered the musty waiting room, he calmed down and went to sleep and the warm, pungent room put Jill to sleep as well. She had difficulty focusing when Doc Weaver woke her.

"Jill, are you okay? It's me, Doc Weaver. I had to wake you because I close at noon today."

Jill was the only one in the quiet room. She focused on the vet and said, "Oh...hi, Doc. Guess I fell asleep." She sat up, straightened her hair and looked at Zeus. "This dog showed up at our house and I think he's sick."

She didn't want to tell him about Jack.

"Well, thanks for bringing him in. Most folks wouldn't bother these days," he said while studying the dog's collar through the spectacles on the end of his nose. "I haven't seen a dog collar like this in a long time, but I remember seeing something similar when I was a boy in Fredericksburg. Rich folks had collars made for their dogs that looked like this. See how the brass plate is attached to the leather by carefully hammering the soft metal? Hardly anyone does this anymore."

"Hardly anyone?"

"Well, hard-core Civil War reenactors might do something like this for a dog. They pay attention to details like that. In fact, you might find Zeus' owner among them. Oddly enough, you can find them on the internet; I have a website you can try."

Zeus was sitting next to the vet and Samantha's chin was parked on the old man's lap. Samantha loved all humans and she was crazy about Doc Weaver, who was an animal lover with service dogs at the top of his list. Doc Weaver had actually offered to *rent* Samantha so that she could greet his patients. "She'd be much better than a receptionist," he said. Jack liked the idea but Jill didn't, so Samantha gracefully refused the job opportunity.

Zeus was panting softly and calmly staring at the gentle vet, who was stroking the dog's head. He massaged Zeus's neck while examining him and continued to feel the hound's entire body with no resistance. During the examination, Jill told Zeus' story, although the vet didn't seem to be listening.

When he completed the exam, he disappeared into his office and returned with a book called *Dog Breeds*. He found Zeus' breed and pointed out that he was a Red Irish Foxhound, a breed that was imported to the United States before the Civil War. By the late nineteenth century, the breed had generally disappeared, evolving into the Redbone Coonhound. He explained that Zeus was healthy and rare indeed. He prescribed stomach-stabilizing pills, a bland diet, and lots of drinking water.

"I'll have to give him a series of shots if you keep him," he said.

"Thanks," Jill said. "I haven't had a chance to look for his owner, but I'll ask around and try the internet."

Doc Weaver said, "May I borrow Zeus' collar? I'd like to show it to a friend of mine. He and I collect things like this you know."

Jill glanced around the waiting room and said, "Yeah, I know you do, Doc, and you're welcome to it. When I find his owner, I'll let you know."

Doc Weaver handed a bright pink nylon collar to her and said, "Here, let me replace it with this one and there's no charge for the exam."

"Thanks, Doc," Jill yawned. "I'll bring this pink one back when we swap collars again."

"You look tired, Jill. You ought to get some rest…and please don't bother to return the pink collar. I've been trying to get rid of that ugly thing for years," he said with a grin.

Jill gave the vet a little hug and he helped to get Zeus back into the SUV. She then stopped at the Scarborough Run guardhouse, hoping that Ray Vance was on duty because she wanted to thank him and tell him about Zeus. Ray was a jolly little man with white pork chop sideburns, a light-blue uniform, red baseball cap, and a red nose. Jack referred to the security guards as "Zouaves" because the red and blue colors of their outfits reminded him of the elaborate uniforms of the Civil War Zouave Regiments. Jill affectionately thought of them as Smurfs from the cartoon world.

Ray loved to talk, but Jill was ahead of schedule and prepared to listen. She had taken the time to introduce herself to Ray shortly after they moved in and stole Papa Smurf's heart with homemade cookies. Since then, she and Jack had gotten to know Ray fairly well and they all liked each other. Papa Smurf was on duty, so Jill left Zeus in the SUV and walked into the small, isolated security building with Wonder Dog.

"Well, Mrs. Stewart! Come on in. And there's Samantha. Hello, girl."

He patted Samantha's head and gave her a dog biscuit.

"Good to see you, Mrs. Stewart. How have you been?" he asked.

"Hey, Ray. How are you doing? And please call me Jill."

"Can't complain," Papa Smurf said, shaking his head from side to side. "How's Mr. Stewart? I mean…Jack. How's Jack doing? Everyone has been asking about him."

"He's still in a coma, although the doctor said he's healthy otherwise. Thanks for your help, Ray," she said, giving him a little hug.

Ray was instantly embarrassed and said, "Oh, please, just doing my job. Me and Maureen are praying for Jack and I'm sure he'll be just fine. If there's anything we can do…"

"Thanks for your prayers. I really appreciate it."

After an awkward pause, Jill said, "Did you notice the other dog in my car?"

Papa Smurf peered out the window and saw Zeus. "Good-looking hound. Now Sam has some company, eh?"

"His name is Zeus and he showed up at my house last night. Have you had any reports of a missing dog?"

"Not that I know of," he said, looking at the message board. "Nope. No calls but I'll make a note of it."

"Thanks, Ray. Zeus was the only thing written on his collar, but at least I know his name."

They sat down and Samantha installed her chin on Ray's lap.

"Ah, she's a pretty girl," Ray said.

"Yep and she loves everyone."

"Just like my ex-wife," Ray said with a grin.

Jill needed the laugh and said, "Sorry I brought it up."

They both laughed and Jill said, "How's Maureen?"

"Oh, she's okay. She's a 911 operator now."

"Really? That must be interesting."

"Oh yeah. Just the other night she got a call from a fella out in the county who was all upset because his girlfriend fell down and cracked her head open. He said he lived on Eucalyptus Street. When Maureen asked him to spell it, you know what he said?"

"No, what?"

"He says, 'How 'bout I drag her over to Oak Street?"

She wasn't sure he was kidding, but another laugh felt good.

Papa Smurf said, "I'm glad I was on duty when Jack, ah...fell the other day."

"I'm thankful for that too, Ray. I don't know what we'd do without you around here."

"Well, speaking of that, did you hear I'm retiring?"

"What? You can't do that!" she said, genuinely surprised. "What are you going to do?"

"Oh well...I guess I'll go fishing a lot," he said unenthusiastically.

"I thought you loved it here."

"Oh, yeah well, the thing is, I do love my job and all, but...well, I guess I can tell you."

"Tell me what?"

"I've been working a lot of nights lately because that's when Maureen works. For the last few weeks, I've seen some pretty unusual things out here," he said.

"Like what?"

"It might sound strange, but I've seen some crazy stuff in the woods." He hesitated and said, "The woods seem to move in peculiar ways. It happens most every night and it's not deer or anything like that. I thought it might be me at first—you know, seeing things in my old age. I guess it could be me, after all. Fact is, I've been too embarrassed to tell anyone about it except Maureen. She's been getting more and more 911 calls lately describing the same type of thing. Weird, huh?"

"Sure is," Jill said. "What's going on?"

"I don't know, but Maureen thinks we're haunted. She believes in stuff like that."

Uh-oh, Jill thought.

Papa Smurf continued, "She says we're sitting right on top of a place where thousands of young boys died during two horrible days of war. They died suddenly and violently, either by bullets or cannon balls or just because they were too mutilated to run from the battlefield fires—poor devils. Most of them never knew what hit them. Maureen is sure that thousands of restless souls are still trying to figure out what happened, like a bunch of hung-over sailors. She thinks the rivers of blood that oozed into the ground still stain the soil; she says some folks can actually smell it in the woods. Maureen insists that this nice-looking golf course doesn't hide a thing." He paused again and said, "No offense."

Tiny beads of sweat had formed on Jill's brow. "Don't be silly, no offense taken," she said.

Ray shook his head and continued. "Maureen has lived around here her whole life and she says the Wilderness ghosts are restless."

"Restless?" Jill said, trying to find a way to change the subject.

"People have been seeing ghosts around here for a long time. The locals still talk about an inventor named Mr. Wine, who settled here after the war. He was a descendant of a Union officer who fought and died in the Wilderness. Mr. Wine built a huge house that stood over near the soccer field and the locals thought the Wine house was haunted as hell—pardon my language."

"What do you mean by haunted?"

"They say no one wanted to work for Mr. Wine because of all the spirits in his house."

"Do you believe stories like that?"

"I never gave it much thought until I started seeing strange things myself."

"Did the Wine ghosts ever hurt anyone?"

"Don't know, but one night Mr. Wine's house burned to the ground for no reason."

"And the locals thought it was the ghosts?"

"That's what they say, all right."

"Why would ghosts do something like that?"

"Hard to say. Maureen says the Wilderness battle wasn't romantic like Fredericksburg, where the killing fields at Marye's Heights were lit up by northern lights, or Chancellorsville, where Stonewall Jackson lost his arm. Folks have always respected those battles and honored the memory of those lost men with lots of re-enactments and fancy exhibits."

Ray was looking out into the woods and Jill was looking at her SUV.

"Maureen says no one wants to remember the Wilderness battle because it was a gruesome, gut-wrenching slaughter fought on ugly land with no clear winner. Tens of thousands of brave soldiers died in a quagmire and it's difficult to reenact battles like that. Maureen says the spirits of those men need to be remembered but, since they're pretty much ignored, they're still here and still waiting."

Jill said nothing.

"Me and Maureen belong to a group called The Friends of the Wilderness Battlefield. They've been doing an excellent job of drawing attention to The Battle of the Wilderness.

Jill remained silent.

"I don't mean any offense, Jill, but instead of honoring them, we cover their remains with a golf course and big houses."

Jill thought of what Jack often said: "Houses built on bones."

Papa Smurf looked at her and said, "When I told Maureen about the things I've been seeing out here at night...well...she wants me out of here."

After a pause, Jill said, "I can't blame her, Ray. I can't say I'd be comfortable out here alone at night either."

She was spooked and wanted to leave, but Papa Smurf had just opened up to her and she didn't want to be rude. She said, "By the way, my neighbors think their house is haunted, although we haven't paid much attention."

"Jill, I'm not supposed to say anything, but lots of residents have called me about ghosts. Maureen receives calls from people all over the county who think they're being haunted in one way or another."

She said, "Maybe we should both go fishing."

Ray sensed that she was becoming uncomfortable. He squinted up at her and said, "I shouldn't be shooting my mouth off, Jill. I'm sorry. I don't want to scare you or anything. Maureen gets carried away with that kind of stuff. It's all pretty silly and you have nothing to worry about." He paused and said, "I've got to keep her happy... you know."

"That's probably a good idea," Jill said. "Hey, if there *are* ghosts around here, I'm sure they're harmless enough. Anyway, I hope you aren't leaving right away."

"Oh, no. I gave them my thirty-day notice yesterday so I'll be here for a few more weeks."

Jill stood and said, "Good. Maybe things will change soon and you'll decide to stay."

"I hope so Jill. Good talking to you. I'll let you know if anyone reports a missing dog and give my best to...I mean, take care of Jack."

"I sure will and thanks again, Ray. Give my best to Maureen."

Jill didn't want to hear any more about ghosts. Three days ago, she would have thought Papa Smurf and the 911 operator were crazy, but not now. Now, she was beginning to believe.

11

Jack watched Amanda dismount in the railroad clearing. She carefully unpacked her feathered hat and spoke sternly to Zeus, who had appeared from nowhere and followed her.

"Where have you been? Don't you wander off again, you hear!" she said while shaking the loose flesh of the dog's jowls.

Zeus shook his tail and smiled in agreement while Amanda giggled and affectionately patted the hound's chest. Then, Zeus sprang to his feet and ran back and forth from Amanda to the trail, as if excited about the impending rendezvous with Luke. She shook her head, smiled at her crazy dog, and followed him on the narrow path that led into the thickets.

Since arriving in the Wilderness, Amanda's menstrual cycle had begun, although she chose to keep questions regarding that confounding experience to herself. She was in mid-cycle now and felt small pains, which were not entirely unpleasant. She thought about the dimple in Luke's cheek while carefully negotiating the narrow path. Dizzy with anticipation, she guided her dress past thick brush, stopping frequently to remove sticky vegetation. When the footpath widened a bit, she stopped again, peered into her mother's small makeup mirror, and carefully applied rose lip salve—one of her mother's best-kept secrets. Permelia wouldn't think of wasting precious white wax, almond oil, and the root of alkanet tinctoria to make *lip salve*. Amanda didn't want to press her luck, knowing that Permelia would never allow her to actually use such a thing. She had decided to withhold this small cosmetic detail from her aunt as well.

With her lips gleaming, she turned her attention to the tiny buttons at her neckline. She looked skyward, trying to remember the button count from the prior evening's rehearsal. She fumbled with the closely spaced buttons, undid too many, then ripped the delicate threads of three additional mother-of-pearl fasteners. She looked on the ground for the elusive buttons and then impatiently dismissed the entire idea as unimportant, after all.

Unimportant! Jack thought, impressed by Amanda's exuberance and now as eager as Zeus. *Grandma is really hot and I can't wait till Grandpa sees her.*

It was early May. Spring had arrived in Central Virginia and the beauty of the automatic earth could be seen and felt, even in the Wilderness. Red bud, pear tree, and dogwoods had blossomed and wild flowers added blue and pink to an otherwise dismal landscape. Amanda, who was "anticipating the kiss," was filled with the fragrances of the season. Like Jack, the love-sick teenager saw only beauty in every rock, briar, and bramble.

When Luke spotted Amanda, he thought his imagination had produced a princess in the Wilderness, or that his mind's eye summoned the vision of an angel. Amanda saw him, smiled broadly and struggled to control her speeding heart. Luke rushed to her and offered his hand to cross a tiny stream. When she didn't let go of his hand, his oversized palm became instantly moist with embarrassing perspiration, although Amanda didn't seem to notice. She held his hand tightly and led him through the broken woods, glancing back frequently. Luke held on, willing his hand to stop perspiring and trying not to step on her dress.

They arrived at Amanda's magical place where she had spent many dreamy afternoons and time became meaningless as their hormones erupted. Unable to eat, they talked when they could think of something to say while Amanda played with her hair and absently plucked one daisy after another.

She forgot about her "silly buttons." Each time she reached for a fresh daisy, the hint of her bosom became the absolute center of Luke's universe. That, and the warm sun stirred a powerful arousal within the boy, which prevented him from standing in her presence. *No, sir! That would be embarrassing beyond anything I can imagine!* He remained as rigid as a barn door and tried, unsuccessfully, to divert his attention from Amanda's bosom. She slid her hand into his and flushed with excitement every time he moved his fingers, which further enhanced her powerful beauty. They continually glanced toward, then away from one another, while searching for conversation.

Impetuously, Amanda tossed a bouquet of daisies into Luke's face. She laughed, rolled down the slope of the hill, and he tumbled after her. She giggled like a child when he tossed a handful of grass in her face. The giddy teen crimped her nose in mock displeasure while brushing the grass from her hair. They lay still with their faces inches apart and the kiss that followed proved far more spectacular than any anticipation could have been. The thrill they felt would never again be as exquisite, nor as wonderful.

The innocent young lovers remained tied together as if infatuation could replace the racing clock and passion could freeze time in the Wilderness. They lay together for endless moments, exhilarated and slightly embarrassed. Amanda's warm breath tickled Luke's ear and he became more excited than any seventeen-year-old boy had ever been. They lingered there, avoiding direct eye contact until he found the courage to kiss her again. Although the kiss was clumsy and brief, it erased any remaining hint of ugliness in the Wilderness.

Luke was enthralled and Amanda was deeply in love, but the lovesick pair could not have guessed that the strength of their infant love would become the key to their survival. When they parted and walked in opposite directions, he was determined to marry her as soon as possible and she swore she would love him until her dying day.

The enchanted boy was preoccupied and chose a few wrong turns on the gnarly trail. As he walked deeper into the Wilderness, however, he was undaunted by the damp swamps and haunting trees. He was in love with a beautiful girl and nothing else mattered—not the approaching war and not even his promise to meet Amanda's aunt the next day.

12

Jack's dreamscape returned to Truitt, who was wading in a slow-moving river. The unholy baptismal flow washed the naked boy and the waist-high water made him look small and child-like.

Two years earlier, the ogre had wounded himself in the leg after mixing alcohol with hunting. He gave his Hawken rifle and Bowie knife to his thirteen-year-old son with instructions to "keep meat on the table, or else." His father had lost everything of value at the card table except for one sturdy horse, the huge knife, and a deadly, fifteen-pound Hawken rifle. The powerful rifle featured a hair trigger and a distinctive octagonal-shaped barrel. Truitt became one with the rifle that was accurate up to two hundred yards and, before long, he could outshoot anyone in the Shenandoah Valley. He quickly understood how wind, temperature, and elevation affected the trajectory of his .50 caliber rifle shots and rarely missed any target.

Truitt's only companion was an Indian boy named Kuruk, who was a descendant of the Catawba Tribe, or "People of the River." The boy was Truitt's age and lived with his mother in the nearby hills. Truitt taught the young Indian how to use the Hawken and Kuruk passed on ancient techniques used to track and kill animals. Truitt also learned Catawba customs, such as eating the liver of a fresh kill. The boys painted their bodies to blend with the woods and quietly hunted like brothers without the use of spoken language. Kuruk marveled at his friend's eyesight and ability to silently stalk his prey, even on moonless nights. Truitt became so skilled that he was able to kill several deer with nothing more than his knife and bare hands. Gnawing on the warm, bloody livers of those particular deer empowered him and gave him the confidence and desire to crawl through the dark woods like a visceral animal.

Truitt also became unnaturally attached to Kuruk and wanted to be like him in every way. He learned a great deal from the young

Indian and spent so many hours with Kuruk and his mother that he felt like part of their family. He wanted to run away from his brutal father and live with Kuruk like a twin brother, but he knew his father would find him and kill everyone.

Better still, he thought many times, *I could be Kuruk. I know what he knows and we're the same size and all. I could paint my body and his mother would never know. The old man would never find me.*

Sounds like a plan, Jack thought.

The boy provided for his father only after the Catawba family had what they needed. On several occasions, he had suffered the consequences of arriving at home with "no damn meat."

As he swayed in the river water, he considered the great strength he would gain by eating Kuruk's innards. As the lad's peculiar mind considered that option, his troubled psyche could not connect the dots. He finally decided to run, rather than kill the only person he loved.

Truitt washed his father's blood from his body, closed his eyes, and continued to sway gently in the soothing flow of the river. Black smoke from his burning cabin rose from the tree line behind him. Jack gave the newly conceived lunatic credit for two things: he had destroyed the evidence of his gruesome deed and he wasn't going to murder his only friend.

Jack considered his *own* sanity as he stared with fascination into the dark mind of the young killer. Once inside Truitt's intricately septic head, however, he lost his sense of will and almost became trapped within the dismal void. He fought the urge to linger in the darkness that all addicts seek. When he finally emerged from the madness within the boy's head and floated close to him in the river, he was both fascinated and enthralled by the bottomless pit of despair within Truitt's mind.

13

After speaking with Papa Smurf, Jill drove home with Zeus and then went back to the hospital with Samantha. There were no changes, so she went home before midnight to get some sleep. In the morning, she planned to pick Jack's father up at the airport. She bedded Zeus down in the kitchen next to a bowl of rice, took another sleeping pill, and went to bed with Samantha.

She woke to the ringing telephone and immediately thought of Jack. Her heart was racing when she raised the phone, expecting to hear Dr. Huesgen's voice. She was surprised and confused when she heard Doc Weaver instead.

She said, "Oh, Dr. Weaver! Yes...hello, how can I help you?"

"Good morning, Jill. I know it's early, but I have some interesting information for you."

Her image of Doc Weaver always included her feather duster because the man looked as though he needed dusting. She said, "Oh? What is it?"

"Well, um...it's about Zeus's collar. You see, I gave it to a colleague of mine at the Smithsonian and he actually did a carbon test on it."

Jill said nothing, although her uncomfortable feelings about Zeus were being fueled by this new information. Still light-headed from her drug-induced sleep and at a loss for words, she ran her fingers through her hair and struggled to understand what the vet was trying to say.

"My apologies again for waking you, Jill, but the test indicated that the collar is more than 150 years old!"

"Carbon test?" Jill managed. "I don't understand, Doctor. How can that be? Why would Zeus have a collar like that?"

"The Smithsonian is asking the same question, especially since the leather looks relatively new. It's a mystery for sure, but I thought you and Jack would want to know. Oh, and one more thing. Zeus is a rare breed that I've never seen before and I'd love to know where he came from if you find his owner."

So would I, Jill thought.

"I haven't had time to look for his owner yet, but I'll call if I hear anything," she said through a yawn.

"Thank you. My friend wants to show the collar to a few people and I'll let you know what they think. That is if it's all right to keep it for a while longer."

"Certainly, Doc. Take your time and please let us know what they have to say."

"Sure will, Jill, and thanks again. Please give my best to Jack."

Jill hung up and stared at the phone as if it had caused the confusion. Then her eyes settled on Zeus, who was staring back with great interest.

"Where did you really come from, boy?" she asked, sensing that something about the strange dog was just not right.

Zeus tilted his head, thumped to the floor, and licked himself enthusiastically.

Jill smiled and said, "Well, maybe you're a typical male after all."

After breakfast, Jill left for the airport wearing blue jeans that fit her trim body perfectly, white pearls that Jack had given her, and a white silk blouse. She absently reverted to her old habit of keeping part of the pearl strand in her mouth as she drove, which helped her think. On this bright, sunny morning, however, she could think only of losing her husband. *What if he never comes out of his coma? What then?* She felt helpless and prayed for answers. *I hope Dad can help. Having him here will be such a relief. Maybe he'll be able to reach Jack somehow. He's a good man.*

During the rest of the ride to the airport, Artie became the focus of her hope. He had always been the central figure of the family and she needed his strength now, more than ever. The moment she hugged him, she felt better and resisted the urge to break down right there in baggage claim. His real name was John, but he insisted on being called Artie. Like thousands of World War II Veterans, he was both humble and proud. While driving home, Artie patted Jill's shoulder and said, "Jack will be okay, honey—don't worry. I'm here to help and I'm sure everything will be just fine."

Jill's sudden tears embarrassed her.

"Tell you what. Why don't you pull over and let me drive; then you can collect your thoughts and fill me in."

When they walked around the car to switch drivers, she hugged him again and said, "I'm so glad you're here, Dad."

Once they were back on the road, Artie said, "All right, now tell me everything."

Jill updated him on everything from Jack's medical reports to Zeus. "Artie, I think you know that Jack has been worried about the airline and he's been drinking a little too much lately—not to mention his latest obsessions with genealogy and the Civil War."

"Jack and I talk every week and I know he's been worried. I didn't know drinking had become a problem."

"I hate to say *problem*...or maybe that's exactly what it is. It has been getting pretty bad lately," she said. "And it seems as though the more he drinks, the more obsessed he becomes. Sometimes, he stays up all night drinking and reading about that ugly war."

Artie said, "I understand they found him in the unfinished railroad bed."

"That damned railroad bed is certainly one of the things he's been obsessed with. It's just an overgrown ditch full of mud, but he was actually jogging in there the other day." Her tension headache had returned and she paused to message the bridge of her nose. She knew Jack had been jogging to please her. "The morning they found him, he must have had a tremendous hangover because he had been drinking all night. In fact, I doubt the effects of the alcohol had worn off," she said, slightly embarrassed. "He must have gotten home from his trip real late because of the fog. When I left for school, he was sleeping in. I found an empty bottle of cognac on the screen porch and I know the bottle was nearly full before he came home."

Artie shook his head and said nothing.

"I love him so much," Jill said as she blotted her tears with her last tissue, which was now a soggy cotton ball.

"I love him too," Artie said, holding back his tears.

They drove directly to the hospital and Artie spoke with Dr. Wexler from radiology for quite a while. When they arrived at Jill's house, Artie attempted to befriend Zeus while Jill poured some wine and joined him and the dogs in the living room. Sam rested her chin on Artie's lap and Zeus sat stoically, staring at the newcomer.

"I guess Zeus doesn't know what to think of me," Artie said.

"What do you mean?"

"He seems a little skittish and he won't come near me, but he sure loves to stare."

"My next-door neighbor, Charlotte, has the same problem with Zeus. She also thinks there are ghosts in her basement. In fact, Jack passed out in Charlotte's basement last week when he touched General Burnside's sword—long story."

Artie merely nodded and then surprised her by saying, "Jack told me about that and I haven't been able to think of anything else."

"What do you mean?"

"Jill, I don't want to sound crazy or anything, but have other strange things been happening lately?"

"Like what?"

"Well, unexplained things or other stories about ghosts in basements and such."

Jill's stomach turned and she said, "Well, yeah. There's been a lot of that now that you mention it." She told him about Papa Smurf, his 911 girlfriend, four-year-old Shelby, and Charlotte's encounters. "Zeus is supposed to be extinct and he showed up wearing a 150-year-old collar," she said. "Pretty strange, huh?"

"Yes, it certainly is," he said. "Listen, Jill, I have something to tell you."

14

Artie poured more wine and said, "As you know, Jack grew up in Manassas. We lived near the Manassas battlefield until Jack was about seven or eight and then we moved Illinois, which was the home of Jack's mother. What you don't know is why we moved and what led to Barbara's...problem."

"Please go on," Jill said.

"Jack's mother, God bless her soul, had a few problems that you and Jack never knew about. Like Jack, she had an addictive personality, but she also suffered from paranoia. She could not always separate what was real from what was imagined because of her delusional disorder."

He sipped some wine and continued. "When we lived in Manassas, Barbara discovered a letter among her mother's things that had been written during the Civil War by her great-grandmother's brother, a Union soldier named Henry Mueller. Henry fought at Manassas and later became a scout for the Union Army. Just before his last assignment, he wrote a letter to his wife in Illinois and was never heard from again. After the war, Henry's wife actually visited this area to search for her husband. She never found any sign of him, but she left a tombstone alongside Orange Plank Road in his memory. For some reason, Barbara became obsessed with Henry. She wouldn't let it go and became paranoid when I suggested destroying the letter. She went to great lengths to hide the letter from everyone. It got pretty bad and I suggested professional help, but she refused." Artie paused and said, "This is hard to talk about, but it may be significant."

Jill could not imagine how any of this could help her husband, but she had a great deal respect for Artie. She said, "I understand, please continue."

Artie took a deep breath and exhaled. "Barbara became delusional and began to see things."

"Like what?" Jill asked, dreading the answer she might hear.

"Well, like ghosts. Particularly Henry's ghost. She claimed that many other people were seeing ghosts as well."

Jill said nothing.

"That's when we moved to Illinois and things seemed to improve after that."

They both sipped wine in silence. Jill knew what was coming.

"Barbara's suicide was sudden and unexpected," Artie said.

"I'm so sorry, Artie."

"I did everything I could. She was normal most of the time, so no one had a clue. She left no note, although Henry's letter was clutched in her hand."

Jill patted Artie's back and he excused himself. When he returned, he said, "I never told Jack about Henry and the effect he seemed to have on Barbara. I bring this up now because of Jack's behavior lately. He's been calling me quite often asking about our family history. I've never told anyone about Henry because it upsets me to think about it, but Jack got me to spill the beans. He already knew about Dr. Atkinson, but hearing Henry's story seemed to change his attitude toward his genealogy dramatically."

"How do you mean?"

"It's complicated and maybe a little strange," he said, raising an eyebrow.

"Okay," she said, thinking that everything else was strange and praying that Artie was not. She had every confidence in him though, and knew he wanted to help Jack.

"Look, I'm not trying to scare you. Jack doesn't share Barbara's disorder or anything like that," he said, although he wasn't really sure. "It's just that Jack began to sound a little like his mother."

Jill was silent and he continued, "I never dreamed that you and Jack would move close to another Civil War Battlefield, especially not this one."

"Why is this one any different?"

"This is where Henry disappeared. He was sent into the Wilderness by General Meade and then vanished."

Jill headache was getting worse. She said, "We have felt a little guilty about living here. Jack was particularly uneasy about it and he even brought up the subject of moving again. He's been restless lately and totally obsessed with this genealogy thing."

"Jill, you've done all the right things. I'm the one who hasn't."

"What do you mean?"

"Well, I should not have mentioned Henry Mueller and I should never have allowed him to touch Henry's letter."

"When did that happen?"

"After Barbara passed I let him read it. I don't know why, I just did."

"What happened?"

"Oh, he was pretty young and didn't seem interested, although he became lethargic for a couple of days, which was not like him. I thought it was the flu, but all tests were negative."

"Where is the letter now?"

"I have it with me. I just couldn't destroy it."

"May I read it?"

"I think you should."

He reached into his jacket pocket and produced Henry's letter. Jill removed it from a Ziploc bag and read:

May 2nd, 1864

My Dearest Caroline,

 I've been missing you and I'll be home soon. My heart is not here in these lonely Virginia woods because I'm already home with you in my mind and heart. I want to hold you and our son in my arms and live our lives away from this horrible war.

 I suppose my campaign is almost over, but General Meade gave me my last orders and I'll be going into the Wilderness to scout for him. I wish to God I could come home now but in all things I must see His will be done. The good general thanked me for my service and filled my heart with pride, but my real joy is back home with you.

> *I've got to leave camp soon and I suppose you might worry about not hearing from me for a while, but my work will be done soon enough and I'll return to you straight on. I'll be home before summer comes, for sure.*
>
> *I love you always and I can't wait to hold you and our new child.*
>
> *Love,*
> *Henry*

Jill began to cry.

"Are you all right?" Artie said.

"I'm fine. The letter was touching, that's all. I'm all right—really."

Artie watched her carefully and then excused himself and poured another glass of wine for each of them. When he returned, Jill said, "Artie, do you really believe in the supernatural?"

"You mean ghosts and such?"

"Well, yeah...ghosts and all that sort of thing."

"Barbara was convincing. Because she was right as rain most of the time her claims seemed more believable. Let's just say I have an open mind about such things."

Jill said nothing and stared out at the golf course.

"As I mentioned, Jack told me about the incident with Burnside's sword at your neighbor's house. He has always had a vivid imagination; alcohol may have over-stimulated his mind, making him more receptive to things...metaphysical. Jack is not paranoid or delusional like Barbara was, but he *may* have had a traumatic reaction to something he imagined in the woods."

Jill sat quietly and considered that. *Jack's active imagination and his decision to enter the ugly woods with a hangover could have triggered an unusual reaction, but why did he go in there to begin with? Last time it was for golf balls, although he swore he'd never do that again. Then again, he'd made lots of empty promises lately. The cuts and abrasions on his body were a clear indication that he had been in the quagmire, but he had no golf balls in his pockets so he must have had another reason to reenter the woods. He could have fallen down in there, gotten tangled in the thorny mess, and panicked, although he had always kept a cool head during stressful situations. Then again, General Burnside's sword was enough to knock him out in Ralph's basement. Maybe stress, drinking, filling his head with too much Civil War genealogy, and his wild imagination were all in play.*

"Maybe he saw a ghost," Jill said.

Artie pursed his lips and swallowed some wine.

"It sounds ridiculous to me, but what if Charlotte, Maureen, and poor Barbara were right? What if battlefields *are* haunted? I'd pass out if I saw a ghost, hungover or not. Is that why so many people are reporting supernatural activity lately? Is it because the Wilderness battle started 150 years ago? Do the people around here freak out every year at this time? What the hell is going on, Artie?"

"I don't know, hon, but we'll get to the bottom of it—and Jack will recover. Let's get some sleep and tackle this tomorrow with clear heads."

15

Jack's dream drew him back to Permelia's cabin where three uncomfortable people were huddled around a small circular table. In her perpetual black dress, Permelia looked like a life-sized dung beetle sitting between Amanda and Luke. Nervous energy had made it impossible for Amanda to stifle her giggling; everything was extremely humorous. With her hand over her mouth, she tried not to look at Luke, who was dressed in ill-fitting Sunday clothes with a tight collar. He was repeatedly smoothing his unruly hair that refused to behave and stuck out in odd directions. Each uncontrollable curl was hilarious to Amanda, who fought to control herself while allowing little squeaks and odd sounds to escape into the room. Luke, however, was extremely uncomfortable and found no humor in any of it.

Permelia sat quietly, ignoring her niece's silly nonsense. The broken matriarch lowered her teacup, began to cough, and then rose and scurried outside. The teens stared at her until she was out of sight and then Amanda released a pent-up laugh, lunged across the table, and kissed Luke on the cheek. Luke was wide-eyed and embarrassed long after the giggling girl returned to her seat and he was still dripping with nervous perspiration when Permelia returned.

Even though the crumpled woman badgered Luke with questions, he recognized that she was distressed and sensed her anxiety. Her trepidation, in fact, was much greater than his. Permelia fell silent and began to cough softly into her handkerchief while Luke looked into her dry eyes.

She has a greater purpose than mere harassment, he thought. *Her suffering is not just physical but in her mind too. She's desperate for something. I wonder what she wants.*

Luke felt sorry for her and wanted to cooperate. He tried to relax and then explained that his father was away at war and he lived with his mother, aunt, and younger brother, Adam. His mother was the only schoolteacher in the area and his aunt was a war widow. He and his brother were about the same age and their small farm was productive because of the rare manpower. Their farm was two miles north of Todd's Tavern, a mere eight miles south of the Higgerson Farm as the crow flies.

As her inquisition proceeded, the skeptical widow began to trust the nervous but honest boy, although she was not yet convinced that he was the answer to her prayers. *He's certainly not stupid and I believe I can trust him,* she thought while trying not to stare at the fidgeting youngster.

Permelia prayed that her perceptions of Luke were accurate and became lost in her own thoughts. During the awkward silence, Amanda stared at the tabletop and poor perspiring Luke could not help glancing at the door. He wanted nothing more than to squirm out of his sticky shirt and run all the way home.

Finally, Permelia reached into her apron and unfolded the enigmatic letter that would change everything.

16

"Amanda, we've received an urgent letter from your father. His concern is so great that he agreed to pay a courier well for a swift delivery. Although the courier was two days later than planned, he will be paid fairly when your father receives my return letter written in Latin, noting his arrival date." She realized she was rambling and said, "The delay has made your father's concerns grave indeed and I want to read this so you'll both understand his alarm."

Luke and Amanda glanced at each other while Permelia cleared her throat and began to read:

April 28, 1864

My Dearest Permelia and my Precious Amanda,

As I continue to serve and protect our cherished home, I am compelled to keep you far from this war and its cruel heartlessness. Because I am a surgeon, I see the horrible results of the war. I am not involved with combat operations and have little knowledge of military planning. I have, however, obtained information from high-ranking combat officers that is alarming.

Based on this information, I fear the path of this dreaded conflict will soon be upon you. The course of the war, although unpredictable, should not be underestimated in breadth or severity.

General Grant has assembled a massive force of more than 100,000 men, north of the Rapidan River between Culpeper and Brady Station. It is his intention to march to Richmond. The Federal supply line is said to stretch twenty miles toward the port at Aquia, then on toward Washington. This is the largest and best-equipped army that has ever been assembled.

> *Persecution of civilians and the ruin of their property is*
> *common in the wake of Union Army. As the war has*
> *worsened, the number of atrocities has increased. No*
> *one presumes that General Grant will be foolish*
> *enough to face General Lee in the tangled Wilderness,*
> *although that venue would, apparently, please our*
> *leaders. However, all agree that Union troops will*
> *traverse the Wilderness during their march south, like*
> *a swarm of locusts, and you must not be trapped in their*
> *destructive path.*

Permelia's cough returned; the lumps in her breast had spread
their tentacles into her lungs and her life was ending. It was Luke's
turn to stare at the tabletop while she regained control and continued
to read:

> *The massive Union Army may be a threat to*
> *you within weeks, or perhaps days. You must,*
> *therefore, leave the Wilderness immediately for the*
> *protection of Richmond and let nothing impede your*
> *decision nor haste in this matter. Carry with you a*
> *sufficient amount of the hidden gold reserves and leave*
> *the rest safely buried. I have enclosed a separate letter*
> *of introduction that should ensure your safe passage*
> *with the Army of Northern Virginia, although that*
> *cannot be guaranteed.*
> *Therefore, you must not make contact with*
> *either army, for your own protection!*
> *I have made arrangements for you in Richmond*
> *and those details are enclosed. Once you arrive in*
> *Richmond, you will be safe and well-cared-for by*
> *trusted friends.*
> *In spite of overwhelming odds, we have the will*
> *to protect our homeland and our sacred way of life*
> *from the invaders and we will win our independence.*
> *This, I fear, will be at great cost to both sides in this*

conflict, but Richmond will not fall and the South will prevail.

You are both dear to my heart and your safety must not be compromised. Please depart as soon as you are provisioned and I will join you in Richmond shortly.

Please destroy this letter once you have read it.
In your Dear Mother and Sister's memory,
—with my Love,

John Atkinson

It was Permelia's turn to stare at the table while Amanda's emotional cocktail bubbled over and tears streamed down her face. *Am I leaving the Wilderness? Will I finally return to my home in Hampden Sydney?* Her eyes swelled as she looked at Luke's blank stare. She couldn't leave Luke behind in the path of the Union Army! She knew he was planning to enlist and he would fight the Yankees. She might never see him again. She feared Yankees and she was deeply concerned for her father's safety, but the added concern for Luke would be too much. She also knew that Permelia could not survive such a journey—the whole idea was impossible.

Amanda was crying and holding her aunt's hand while Permelia continued to ramble on. Luke looked back and forth between Amanda's tears and Permelia's sunken face. *What is this strange woman saying?* He knew they would be in great danger—they would never make it to Richmond. He could not let Amanda go and he was becoming enraged.

Suddenly, he pounded his fist on the table and shouted, "No!"

Both women were startled by his outburst and turned to him.

"If Amanda is going to Richmond, then so am I!" he declared decisively.

Amanda's heart leaped and Permelia surprised them by smiling broadly and saying, "Thank God!"

17

Permelia's odd reaction was met with startled stares from the teens. Earlier that day, the tormented woman had been talking to herself while stumbling around in her garden.

"Lord, I hate Yankees," she muttered. "They'll never force me to leave my home—never!"

In truth, she was too weak to travel to Richmond and the burden on Amanda would be unbearable. Such a journey would end in disaster and Amanda would be left alone to find her way through the hostile landscape. Nevertheless, she had to honor her brother-in-law's wishes and protect her precious niece above all else.

"Good, graceful Lord Almighty, I won't leave my home! I'll stay and Amanda must go!" She cursed her frailty and bemoaned her poor niece.

"Aunt Permelia?" Amanda said. "Can you hear me?"

Permelia's mind returned to the table and she said to Luke, "I have prayed for your will in this matter and I welcome your eagerness to help."

Luke stared back at her, thinking that the old woman must be crazy.

Then, she turned perfunctorily to Amanda and surprised them again by saying, "This fine young man will escort you to Richmond because I am too weak to make the journey, and..."

"No!" Amanda cried. "You must come with us! We'll carry you with us and we'll care for you. We won't leave you behind!"

"Amanda, dear, we have no wagon and we have no time to find one. I would need a wagon for such a journey and that could very well expose us to unthinkable danger. I'll be comfortable here where I belong and you'll be safe in Richmond where you belong. I don't have the strength to walk or ride and I would slow your progress. Your father wants you to leave immediately and I've thought this through. You *must* hide from both armies and you might have to move quickly to stay out of sight. I could never keep up with you. Instead of wasting time, I've prepared some of Benjamin's clothing for you to wear and gathered supplies for your journey."

"But, Aunt Permelia, how will you stand up to the entire army by yourself?" Amanda said sardonically.

"Enough!" the crumpled woman said with impatience. "I've already made arrangements with our neighbor, Mrs. Tapp, who will join me here," Permelia lied. "We'll be fine! The Yankees will have no interest in two old women who present no threat and they'll leave your grandmother and Jeremiah alone as well. We'll bury ample food to survive. After they're gone, Mrs. Tapp and I...we'll help each other."

"When did you make these arrangements?" Amanda asked suspiciously.

"Mrs. Tapp came by yesterday while you were... picnicking."

The teens glanced at each other guiltily.

"Poor Mrs. Tapp has almost nothing," she continued. "And she's all alone in her dreadful little cabin. I asked her to go home, gather her things, and return tomorrow morning. Mrs. Tapp agreed to look in on your grandmother on the way—she was so grateful, poor woman."

Amanda began to accept Permelia's logic. She knew her aunt couldn't travel to her mother's farm, much less all the way to Richmond. Permelia's lie about Widow Tapp had given her some solace as well, but her tears streamed and she hugged her precious aunt as tightly as she dared.

"I can't leave you here," she moaned.

The fragile woman felt the physical pain of Amanda's embrace and returned her caress with all the strength she could muster. Luke was left staring at the table while everyone calmed down. Then, Permelia produced a detailed list of supplies that would be loaded on Star. She had thought of everything from food, water, and medical supplies to a map, compass, weapons—and, of course, a Bible. She included the .45-caliber Whitworth rifle and a LaMat twin-barrel revolver from Major Atkinson's beautifully engraved collection.

Amanda would also carry her father's small derringer. The pistol would be carefully concealed within her clothing along with gold coins, although Luke would know nothing of those hidden items. Permelia trusted Luke, but she was no fool. Since the well-being of her niece could not be compromised and because Amanda had to be prepared for anything, she planned to explain the necessity for such secrets once she and her niece were alone.

Permelia asked Luke to "hurry on home" and tell his family about the approaching army and of his intention to travel to Richmond with Amanda. "I'm sure your younger brother will escort your family to safety," she said, hoping Luke would agree.

He had only this night to prepare his family for their exodus and to convince them to leave. Luke assured her that his family would go to the coast of Virginia where they could "put up with kin." His brother was capable and would protect them during the journey. Luke offered to take Amanda and Permelia with his family, but Permelia politely refused. She reiterated that she was too weak to travel and they were compelled to honor Major Atkinson's wishes. Amanda had to be delivered to Richmond as planned.

Luke agreed to meet Amanda at dawn in the unfinished railroad bed near Parker's Store, a place they knew well. From there, they would travel east within the cover of the railroad cut to Brock Road, then south toward Richmond. Finally, Zeus was sent along with Luke so that locating Amanda in the morning would be assured.

The two women spent the remainder of the dismal night preparing and carefully packing Star's saddlebags, reviewing each home remedy, and studying a map. Supplies were packed on Star and Amanda was dressed in Benjamin's clothing to disguise her gender. Although she had worn Benjamin's things many times, she didn't want to be dressed as a man while traveling with Luke and complained vehemently.

"You might get separated from Luke. If that happens, you'll have a much better chance traveling as a man," Permelia said. "Dressed as a woman, you would not be able to move as quickly and you would certainly attract more attention."

Permelia didn't want Amanda to attract anyone's attention, including Luke's, but Amanda would not acquiesce until Permelia allowed her to carry a single day dress in one of Star's packs.

"You may change into your dress when you reach Richmond safely and not until then." She hesitated until Amanda looked at her and said, "Do you understand?"

"Yes, ma'am."

Amanda was overwhelmed and Permelia knew it, so she kept her niece busy with packing and lifting. She hid coins within Benjamin's clothing and sewed a pocket into the outer thigh of Benjamin's one-piece underwear. The pocket was designed to conceal a derringer and Permelia carefully explained that the gold and pistol were being hidden for her protection. She insisted that the items remain hidden from Luke and Amanda reluctantly agreed once she saw the urgency and sincerity in her poor aunt's eyes.

Amanda examined the Philadelphia Derringer and ran her finger over her father's tiny initials, *J.M.P. ATKINSON*. She felt butterflies in her stomach while thinking about her father and the terrible burden he had placed upon her. *Will he forgive me for leaving Permelia behind? Will my precious aunt be safe?*

"Once the Yankees are defeated and gone, I will return with a wagon and carry you to Richmond," Amanda promised.

Permelia promised that she and Widow Tapp would hide and offer no resistance to the Union Army. "We'll be safe and I'll be waiting for your return," she said, knowing that she would never see her dear niece again.

Amanda had learned to respect firearms. She removed the tiny derringer from its elegant wooden box and read the directions carefully. She ensured that the hammer was in the half-cocked-notch, which acted as a safety in case the pistol was bumped accidentally. Then, she rammed a lead ball into twenty grains of black powder, leaving no air gaps that could cause the handgun to explode when used. After placing a percussion cap on the tube, she fully cocked the hammer and test fired it into the night.

She was not impressed with the miniature weapon but humored her aunt and thanked her for her thoughtfulness. The loaded pistol would be cleverly hidden in the pocket at Amanda's upper right thigh making it accessible in an emergency.

When all was readied, the women sat together in the small room and talked until they fell into restless sleep. Permelia drooped in her rocking chair, Amanda stretched out on the floor, and Jack gave thanks because they had finally stopped talking.

Jack watched Permelia sleep; just before she dissolved, he thought, *she is beautiful after all.*

18

Truitt had been hiding in the Shenandoah Valley for more than a year. On May 25, 1862, during Stonewall Jackson's successful Valley Campaign, he witnessed The First Battle of Winchester. The newly conceived lunatic was impressed with the death and destruction of the war machine. He followed the South until the Union retreated into Maryland and then showed up at the headquarters of General Richard Taylor's "Louisiana Tigers" and volunteered for service. They accepted him without question. Truitt knew the army would hide him from the law and all they asked in return was "some killin' and such." No problem.

Truitt's shooting accuracy drew the attention of an officer, who then evaluated the recruit's skills on horseback. He was far more accurate when shooting from horseback than any man who took aim from solid ground. His extraordinary evaluation was delivered to Regimental Commander, Colonel George O'Brian, who decided to pass the peculiar-looking volunteer on to his good friend, Major John Singleton Mosby.

Jack knew all about Mosby. He was small like Truitt and weighed less than 120 pounds when fully dressed for battle. "The Gray Ghost" was the most effective guerilla leader of the Civil War, who struck fear into the hearts of Union soldiers. Mosby was intense and his intimidating blue eyes could look right through a man.

Mosby was frail and sickly as a child and other boys bullied him regularly. At the University of Virginia, he finally stood up to a bully named George R. Turbin. He shot the unarmed student in the jaw at close range, severely wounding him. During sentencing in court, "Court clerk Ira Garrett directed Mosby to stand, and Mosby looked at the jury, eyes bright and clear, showing no sign of penitence or regret."[5] He was sentenced to months in jail to atone for his unnecessary violence and lack of remorse.

Mosby joined the Confederate Army as a private and fought at Bull Run with the Virginia Volunteers. He impressed J.E.B. Stuart with his scouting abilities and was quickly promoted to lieutenant. After being captured and exchanged, Stuart arranged for Mosby to command the 43rd Battalion Virginia Cavalry that became known as "Mosby's Raiders" or "Mosby's Rangers."

He and his band of 350 men disrupted the operations of the Northern army. It was the most effective force of its kind and they cut and slashed at the very core of the Union. Mosby's Raiders robbed military payroll trains, destroyed railroad lines, and even managed to abduct Brigadier General Edwin Stoughton from his Fairfax headquarters.

The spoils of war were shared equally among Mosby's men like a band of pirates. Mosby, who was promoted to the rank of major in March of 1863, always refused his share. His men loved him and, as the war progressed and the romantic reputation of Mosby's Rangers grew, more than 2,000 men volunteered to join his battalion eliminating the need for recruitment. Mosby's Raiders were part of the most romantic fraternity in the Civil War. When they rode through small towns in Virginia, they were greeted as heroes, especially by women.

The tough, seasoned men scoffed at Truitt when he and Jack were escorted into camp. They were surprised when the strange-looking child was escorted directly to the major's tent. The boy stood in front of Mosby with his eyes lowered and Jack watched while the major read Truitt's evaluation report. As he studied O'Neal's letter, he sensed incredible malevolence oozing from the lad. He was sure the boy had been bullied as he had been, or perhaps abused in some way.

If Colonel O'Neal's reports are accurate, Mosby thought, *this young soldier's strength, incredible skills, and anger could be useful.*

He waited patiently for Truitt to answer any of his numerous questions or to look him in the eye. Truitt would not speak or raise his bushy eyelashes that looked like black charcoal smudges on his cheeks. The Gray Ghost was an incredible judge of character and used his intuitive insight to handpick his men. His intense stare always disarmed other men, leaving them unable to deceive or challenge him. He waited patiently for the boy to look at him.

He could feel the cruel nature of the peculiar-looking lad and he was tempted to poke him from a safe distance as he might nudge a poisonous snake. Indeed, sharp pointed teeth and a forked tongue would not have been a total surprise as he waited patiently for Truitt to raise his eyes. Each reticent moment that passed in the stuffy tent compounded the major's curiosity.

"Did your Pappy hit you around some?" he finally asked while moving closer to the boy.

I can't wait to hear this one, Jack thought.

Truitt began to twitch and then slowly met Mosby's stare. The major gasped and looked away because the boy's bottomless, glimmering eyes looked through *him* as if looking through a thin membrane! Mosby had never before lost his intimidating advantage, but eye contact with Truitt instantly disarmed him and left him both surprised and icily uneasy. In that brief moment, the failed intimidator felt his energy being drained by the boy's kindred spirit. He suddenly thought of Truitt as a manifestation of himself.

Meanwhile, Truitt bonded with Mosby during the momentary eye contact and he impulsively swore allegiance to him. He instantly decided that he would do anything for his commander. He would die for him without question because he suddenly loved the Gray Ghost even more than he loved his Indian brother.

Then, to Mosby's relief, Truitt bolted from the tent.

The following day, Truitt's shooting performance was extraordinary and the men began to accept him as one of their own, although he did not respond. He said nothing and looked directly at no one. The curious boy moved his tent away from the others, as close to Mosby as possible, and blended into his surroundings like a chameleon.

When chow and chores were done, Mosby's men always gathered around a communal fire to drink and tell lies as soldiers have always done. Sunset, however, was Truitt's "happy hour." He would either creep through the woods in semi-darkness, exploring creative ways to stalk and strangle his prey or sit by his tent in almost complete darkness and thumb through his book of fairytales.

His mother's *Hans Christian Anderson* book was always neatly folded within his blood-stained quilt, which he carried in his standard issue fifteen-by-thirteen-inch backpack. Like his razor-sharp Bowie knife, the blanket and book never left his side. He struggled to read the tales "like how my mother done" but usually ended up paging through the pictures, remembering the words she had read—or *how* she read them.

Weeks passed and then Truitt was told that he would go along on a raid of a Union train.

Mosby's Raiders worked as a unit. They all seemed to know what to do without much guidance and they were given a great deal of freedom to act and react on their own. Once the train was commandeered, Mosby oversaw the operation from horseback but failed to notice that a railroad passenger had him in the sights of his long-barreled rifle. Truitt quickly killed the potential assassin with one quick shot, which impressed everyone—especially Mosby.

The Gray Ghost was well aware that the success of great people depends upon the effectual delegation of authority as well as the ability to surround yourself with those who are both trusted and highly proficient. The major continued to evaluate Truitt's skills and soon accepted him as a kind of bodyguard. The boy had incredible eyesight, shooting skills, and an uncanny ability to anticipate any threat. Mosby appreciated the fact that the lad was dedicated to him beyond reason and he kept the born killer by his side.

During fire-lit evening briefings, Truitt and Jack sat close to Mosby. The men thought of Truitt's eerie, glistening coal-black eyes as those of Satan. They began to think of Truitt as the dark side of their commander and kept their distance from him, not wanting to provoke the devil. Embellished stories about "Mosby's fiend" began to spread throughout the battalion.

Whether Mosby's Raiders slept in someone's barn or camped in the woods, they extended their courtesies and performed mundane duties without being ordered to do so. Everyone, that is, except Truitt. Newcomers to the camp resented the boy's lack of manners and participation until they were warned about him and his "peculiar" relationship with Mosby. Newcomers eventually decided that Truitt's icy stare alone was reason enough to "leave him be."

On April Fool's Day in 1863, Mosby and sixty-nine of his men woke to a cold morning at the Miskel Farm near Herndon Station, Virginia. The Potomac River and Broad River surrounded the farm on two sides and the only approach to the farmhouse was also the only exit. Mosby had often accepted the hospitality of Southern sympathizers, although he had never before boxed himself in. Jack knew that Truitt was uneasy about the compromising circumstances and hovered next to the boy all night as Truitt's huge lizard-like eyes scanned the darkness.

Meanwhile, Captain Benjamin Flint was leading 150 men of the First Vermont Cavalry in fevered pursuit of the Gray Ghost. During the prior month, Mosby had captured General Stoughton and his entire staff at the Union's General's headquarters in Fairfax Courthouse. He personally delivered the prize to Robert E. Lee, who was annoyed because Mosby had embarrassed a fellow West Pointer. The Union, however, was more than annoyed and sent the cavalry to put an end to the Gray Ghost's reign of terror.

Before dawn, Captain Flint had learned that Mosby was camped at the Miskel Farm. He organized a surprise, early-morning attack, but lizard boy was able to warn his boss at the last moment. Before he was able to wake his commander, however, Captain Flint and his men had silently entered the Miskel Farm and shut the gates to their rear.

The owner of the farm looked out his window and said, "They've got old Mosby this time sure."[6]

Mosby was surprised and outnumbered but decided to go on the offensive. He ordered his men to saddle up but not to shoot. He told them to direct their fire at Captain Flint, who led the cavalry's saber charge. Concentrating lethal force to remove the head of the snake was a shrewd tactic and Mosby's men promptly killed Flint with six shots. When Flint fell, confusion spread through his ranks. Without a leader, the First Vermont Cavalry panicked and tried to run, but they were trapped by the closed gates.

"With about twenty of his men mounted, Mosby, still on foot, ordered, Follow me! Charge'em! Charge'em! And go right through 'em!"[7]

Truitt remained at Mosby's side and ran with him, marveling at the courage and valor of the man he idolized. His hero was leading a cavalry charge *on foot!* Truitt was flooded with pride and overwhelmed with excitement. Mosby's men emptied their revolvers at close range, killing dozens of Yankees. Truitt killed three men with three shots and clubbed another to death with the butt end of his revolver before the rear gates flew open and the Union Cavalry ran.

The elated Rebels hollered and chased the Vermonters on horseback. Mosby mounted a horse and caught up to a retreating rider who "...jumped off his horse and sat down on the roadside."[8] Mosby accepted his surrender and rode on, but Truitt was exhilarated and eager to please, so he stabbed the defenseless soldier in the neck and dragged him into the woods.

The decision to stop pursuing the enemy rested with each individual man in Mosby's democratic army. One of Mosby's most trusted men, Sam Underwood, was "...wounded in the left foot and riding with crutches tied to his saddle."[9] When Underwood could not keep up, he rode back to the Miskel Farm and discovered the obvious signs of a struggle in the road. With a crutch in one hand and his revolver in the other, he moved slowly into the woods where he saw Truitt squatting over a dead soldier. To Underwood's horror, the boy drew his huge knife, gutted the man and stuffed something into his mouth! He smeared blood on his face and bare chest and murmured foreign gibberish into the morning sky. Underwood was sickened but managed to slip back to the road without being seen or heard.

That's my boy, Jack thought, as he and Underwood returned to camp to celebrate the victory.

Truitt was missing until the following morning when he reappeared, clean and scrubbed. News of what the vicious boy had done moved through the battalion like lightning and Sergeant Underwood spent most of the day riddled with nervous apprehension. *I know Mosby favors the boy and holds him in high regard. Still, I have to say something 'bout the atrocity I witnessed,* he thought.

He finally gathered enough nerve to speak to the major. "It's like this, sir," Underwood explained. "The men are pretty much spooked by Private Simms. During the action yesterday, I followed him and...well, sir, he gutted a poor Yankee and..." Underwood stopped and stared at the ground.

"What, Sergeant? Please go on."

"Well, sir, he gutted the man, ate his innards, rubbed the man's blood over his bare chest, and howled like a dog."

Mosby stared at the sergeant, attempting to digest the information while Underwood diverted his eyes, feeling ashamed for some reason.

"Are you certain of this? Those woods are thick and the terrain is rough."

"Yes, sir. I'm sure, all right, and that's God's truth. Some of the men are superstitious and they believe this boy Simms is the devil himself. As I said, they been uneasy 'bout Simms, but eatin' that poor man's innards is too much for'em."

Mosby turned his back to Underwood and clenched his fists in rage, knowing that the sergeant had told the other men and the damage was done. The boy had to go and he felt a deep sense of loss. His almost cosmic attraction to Truitt captivated him, although he knew the odd youngster was insane and that he would eventually be discovered.

Truitt was delivered to Mosby, who stood with his back to him. He and Jack waited for the major to face them. After an uneasy pause, Mosby told the psychotic killer that he was pleased with his performance and considered him to be the best soldier in his charge.

"I wish I had more men like you, Private Simms. If I did, we could whip the Yankees all by ourselves."

History loves Mosby's Raiders, but "Mosby's Lunatics" just doesn't sound right, Jack mused.

"As much as I need you, General Lee needs you more," he lied. "General Lee himself has asked me to give my best man a special assignment. It's General Lee's opinion that we should do everything in our power to demoralize Yankee soldiers. I agree with him and I know you do too." Mosby cleared his throat, looked up at the ceiling of the tent, and said, "Do you know what demoralize means?" He didn't expect an answer and shifted his gaze to a hanging map, wary of eye contact and fearing that his lie would be recognized. "Most Northern soldiers are city boys, who were drafted into service and don't know which end of a rifle to hold," he continued. "It's our job to send those boys back home to their mamas and leave the South alone. We're protecting our homes and our way of life. The Yankees want to destroy us and we can't let that happen." He looked up at the ceiling of his tent and continued. "General Lee wants me to send my best man out between our two armies to scare the britches off those Northern boys. I need a brave man like you to do that."

Truitt glanced up briefly when the Gray Ghost referred to him as a "man." He saw Mosby's back and lowered his eyes again, but Jack could see that he was grinning. Suddenly, the major spun around, relieved to see that Truitt's eyes were still lowered. With a commanding voice he said, "I want you to kill Yankees anywhere you find them. Kill them one at a time or any way you want. Then, I want those dead men to scare the sense out of other Yankees. I want you to make scarecrows out of them and hang their bodies where their army will see them. I know you can do this. You'll be on your own and well supplied. I'll give you an advance on your pay and hold the rest for you. I know you'll do more for the South on your own than ten of my men can do here."

An adrenalin rush passed through Truitt and his left eye began to twitch, but he didn't look up until Mosby turned and moved away. The major opened a crate in the corner of his tent and removed a Henry Repeater rifle. He placed the rifle on the table without looking directly at the boy and said, "This is the newest and finest rifle in the world and I want you to kill Yankees with it. We captured twelve of these repeaters and I'm entrusting one to you, son, along with one hundred rounds and more when you need them."

The troubled boy felt lightheaded when his commander called him "son." He was enamored of Mosby and, if the major ordered him to turn the Henry rifle on himself, he would do so immediately.

"I want you to leave right now and do me proud, soldier. After you kill one hundred Yankees, return to my camp and I'll salute you."

Jack the Ripper with a license, Jack thought. *This should be interesting.*

The state-of-the-art Henry Repeater rifle was one of the Civil War's first semi-automatic weapons. It could shoot up to fifteen rounds at a rate of more than one round per second. It was nine pounds of rapid killing power and, in Truitt's hands, it may have been the most deadly rifle in the Civil War.

Still, Jack thought, *it's not the arrow, it's the Indian.*

"I know you understand me, Private Simms, and I'll accept your nod as your promise to do your duty." To Mosby's relief, Truitt didn't raise his eyes and simply nodded. He dismissed him saying, "Go kill us some Yankees, son."

The boy snatched the rifle from the table and ran from the tent because his eye was twitching uncontrollably and he had an erection.

Talk about a pee-pee squeezer, Jack mused.

19

Mosby began to dissolve and Jack became increasingly anxious. He thought he might be waking from his bizarre dream and he didn't know what to expect. He could be lying in the railroad bed where he had collided with Zeus or stuffed into a morphine-deprived hospital bed. Of course, there was a chance he'd wake up in his own bed with another regrettable hangover and nothing but a foggy recollection of his dream. *Maybe I won't wake up at all because I'm actually dead.*

As he considered that possibility, he began to feel a sense of relief because Mosby's face was changing into the unmistakable, thin, baggy-eyed face of General George Gordon Meade. As the clarity of Meade's face sharpened, so did Jack's feelings of euphoria. *Holy crap! If this is Meade, Ulysses S. Grant can't be far away.*

At the dawn of 1864, Lincoln had not yet found a competent commander for his massive army. Before the war had officially begun, the job was offered to Robert E. Lee, who turned it down because his beloved home state of Virginia had seceded from the Union. Indeed, if the genius of Robert Edward Lee had commanded the extensive resources of the Union Army, the American Civil War might have been a quick and decisive battle. America could have avoided the bloody, prolonged calamity brought to you by the incredible incompetence of Union generals like Hooker, McClellan, and Burnside.

As Jack's dream continued to swim back to him, he realized that he was in Brandy Station on the cusp of the Wilderness battle. General Meade had been the Supreme Commander of the Army of the Potomac for nearly a year and he was beloved by his staff and troops. Meade was a conservative thinker who was detail-oriented and married to a prominent woman, but Lincoln was not satisfied with him. The Commander in Chief chose the informal, disheveled architect of his western forces, Ulysses S. Grant, instead. Lincoln looked to General Grant to unify the entire Army of the Potomac and lead the Union to victory.

The President promoted the hard-drinking Ulysses S. Grant to the rank of lieutenant general, last held by George Washington, and placed him in command of the entire 533,000 men of the Union Army. Except for a brief encounter during the Mexican War, Grant was unfamiliar with Meade but decided to trust his second-in-command to execute the Union's blood-spattering Overland Campaign. He would allow Meade to handle the details of the assault on the South and Grant would deal with "the big picture." During the very first day of the Wilderness battle, however, Grant quickly abandoned that plan and began to meddle in Meade's decisions.

Jack followed Meade's eyes as he looked up at his trusted headquarters guardsman. The formal guard was dressed in the baggy red trousers, blue tunic, and red cap of the 114th Pennsylvania Volunteers, who wore the uniform of the frequently photographed French Colonial Zouaves.

I wonder if Papa Smurf is related to any of these guys, Jack thought.

The guard saluted smartly and said, "Sergeants Bowler and Hoyle, sir."

"Show them in," Meade said.

The combined body odor of Matthew Bowler and Peyton Hoyle blended disagreeably with the smells of weathered canvas, cigar smoke, and stale whiskey in Meade's tent. The two men saluted almost comically, held their salutes, and remained at attention.

Meade finally looked up from the desk and said, "At ease. Help yourselves to a cigar."

"Thank you, sir," Matthew Bowler replied while both men groped for a cigar.

The cigars were lighted and Meade pointed at a large hanging map. "In the morning, I want you to travel south, cross the Rapidan River, and scout the Wilderness in this general area," he said. "You'll be looking for the eastern flank of Lee's troops and you'll report any sign of his forces directly to me. The whereabouts of J.E.B. Stuart's Cavalry would be invaluable as well. Return with your report as soon as you encounter either Stuart or Lee's main forces. Is that understood?"

"Yes, sir. We'll find 'em and report back real quick," Bowler said while nervously fumbling with his cigar and attempting to salute. Hoyle tried to follow Bowler's lead but clumsily saluted with his cigar still in hand.

Meade half-heartedly returned the salute and said, "Dismissed."

"Thank you, sir," Bowler said while both men continued to salute.

"Dismissed!" Meade said again with impatience.

He turned his back to the stink boys and the big guard quickly escorted them outside. Jack went along into the warm, tranquil night air, which was filled with the aroma of cooking food, sad violin music, and voices singing about a girl named Lenora.

I just drove through this town, Jack realized, although he could no longer remember when or why. He did remember that the settlement couldn't support a single traffic light, although such details were beginning to seem unimportant. He also recalled that the largest cavalry battle of the Civil War was fought in Brady Station. By May of 1864, it had become the home of thousands of Union soldiers and a mountain of supplies. Canvas-covered materials were stacked thirty feet high and hundreds of cannons were lined up in neat rows, along with huge pens holding horses and livestock. The encampment was massive; individual campfires seemed to stretch endlessly into the distance.

Jack floated along with Bowler and Hoyle as they shuffled past the staff officer tents that formed a semi-circle in front of General Meade's headquarters. Beyond that, officer's tents were connected with wooden-plank foot walks. A sea of smaller tents followed, some with stone chimneys and others with awnings made of evergreen boughs and bright green holly leaves.

This is incredible, Jack thought. *No wonder Amanda's father is concerned.*

When Bowler and Hoyle were alone, Hoyle said, "Hey Matthew, the old man didn't give us no whiskey this time."

"He still favors us though and you did good not talkin'," said Matthew.

"I keep my mouth shut like you said. You did good keepin' him fooled and that's all I care 'bout," Hoyle said.

Peyton was following one step behind Matthew, as usual, and he was producing a great deal of spittle on his cigar. He wiped his pug nose on his sleeve and said, "Hey Matthew. I can't wait to get out of here so how 'bout we leave before sunup?"

"Good enough. Wake me at four. My stomach is tight, so I ain't drinkin' no whiskey tonight. I want you to wake me up so you better not get drunk." He looked up at Peyton and said, "I'll leave you here to answer to the general if you're drunk."

"I ain't drinkin' and I'll be ready for sure."

"We'll have some damn fun in the Wilderness," Matthew said, changing the subject and slapping his friend's broad back. "Most cabins got women and all the men are gone. There's gonna be lots of ladies to call on and lots of other rewards for our trouble."

"I like how you think," Peyton said with a toothy grin.

Matthew, at five-seven, was much shorter than Peyton and he was both wary and afraid of the larger man. He didn't care what Peyton did, as long as he stole everything of value and shared the loot equally. Peyton was not good at sharing, however, and he didn't trust him. He figured he'd get rid of his dim-witted friend sooner or later, but he needed Peyton's excellent scouting skills to provide the general with reliable information. He didn't want to kill him while he was still useful, so he tolerated his companion's greed and went along with his little game.

Sergeants Matthew Bowler and Peyton Hoyle were believed to be seasoned scouts. They enjoyed doing whatever they damn well pleased without having to answer to a drill sergeant day after day. They had joined the army using false names and identities, which erased their criminal records. Their former illicit lives lived on only in their memories and souls.

Bowler, who was better-looking and certainly smarter than Hoyle, had presented the army with forged letters of commendation regarding their scouting skills. The army was pleased to welcome two such notable scouts and General McClellan enlisted their services early in the war.

General George B. McClellan was known as "Do-nothing McClellan" or "Little Napoleon." In 1862, his great army could have taken Richmond during his Peninsula Campaign as Amanda's father had feared. Instead, McClellan continually retreated and lost 16,000 men due to poor decisions and a lack of initiative.

McClellan wanted and needed scouting reports that described a formidable opponent in order to justify his stalling tactics, trepidation, and numerous retreats. He relied heavily upon Pinkerton Security for such reports, but their intelligence fell short of what he wanted, so he also used men like Bowler and Hoyle. Matthew understood McClellan's needs and satisfied him with exaggerated reports of strong Confederate resistance and substantial fortifications. The gamble paid off and McClellan showered the stink boys with favors. Matthew embellished his reports until his exaggerations bordered the absurd, but then the cunning scout found a delicate balance and fed McClellan's ego with just enough information to avoid being discovered. He also told Peyton to keep his mouth shut.

Matthew knew that McClellan was more of a politician than a soldier and he was sure the general had designs on the presidency. Lincoln's war would have been a great success if Richmond had fallen during the first year or two, although it seemed to Matthew that McClellan preferred a prolonged conflict. If the war dragged on, tens of thousands of men would die, but that wasn't Matthew's problem. Meanwhile, the war was a barrel of fun. Besides, if the good general *did* defeat Lincoln politically, Matthew would have it made.

"Hail to the Chief!" Matthew had said many times to Peyton, who laughed and slapped his knee having no idea what he meant.

While ordinary soldiers cleaned their muskets and dug ditches day after day, Bowler and Hoyle were free to launch a personal campaign of rape, murder, and looting. If the army had discovered their prison records, their day-to-day criminal activities, or their fabricated intelligence reports, they would have been hanged immediately.

When Lincoln finally fired McClellan, Matthew and Peyton jumped off their boss and buzzed around until landing on General Meade like flies on spoiled meat. As the war worsened, the stink boys became inspired and spearheaded an increasingly ruthless campaign of rape and pillage in the forward wake of the great crawling Union Army.

"They better stop changin' commanders, or we'll have to join the damn Rebels," Matthew declared while slapping the back of his senseless friend.

Yes, these were happy days for the stinkers. Matthew favored raping those feisty young women who put up a struggle or at least *tried* to run, although he would settle for those who were too old or too young to fight back. Once, a twelve-year-old girl, who had attempted to run from his tender intentions, managed to slam a rock into his face. He killed her, of course, cursing his own carelessness and broken nose.

Peyton, on the other hand, would rape anyone or anything, including farm animals from time to time. During scouting missions, Matthew felt uncomfortable while eating Peyton's raped sheep but always chose pragmatism over principles and dined heartily with his barbaric companion.

Each time they returned to camp they told tales of skirmishes with "Grayback soldiers" and encounters with wild animals while showing off their cuts and abrasions. Their stories increased their celebrity. Thanks to Peyton, they also managed to produce useful information for General Meade, who was not as easy to read as McClellan had been.

"What a great war! Smokin' the general's cigars and drinkin' his whiskey," Matthew said. "And, hot damn! Here we are on the second day of May, goin' for another romp in the woods in the name of God and Union."

They were being sent into the Wilderness forest to find the eastern flank of the Confederate Army. Soon, more than 100,000 Federal troops would move south, traveling at one mile per hour. The slow, lumbering army was preoccupied with the protection of its extensive supply line that would be especially vulnerable at river crossings.

"The general is desperate for Lee's where 'bouts and we're his two favorite scouts," Matthew declared.

They laughed aloud as they walked toward their tents and Jack floated along with them. The pilot slapped his face again but, instead of waking or changing the subject, he went to the latrine with Peyton and then to his tent. Hoyle packed his gear, puffed on his saturated cigar, and drank foul-smelling whiskey from a battered tin cup. He stripped down to his long underwear, gulped water from his canteen so that he would wake early, and stuffed himself into a small tent. Jack was forced to hover nose-to-nose with the foul man, whose horrendous breath desecrated his acute sense of smell and watered his eyes.

As he floated in the dark, wishing he had not retained his sense of smell, a lamp was lit. Hoyle was gone and the face of a young soldier named Elston Hobbs had replaced him.

20

Thank God! I've escaped the stink man all-nighter, Jack thought as he watched the boy write a letter to his mother.

Dear Mother,

I am still here at Brandy Station, Virginia and I am fine. The hot weather and the local people are not to my liking. Army food is not like your good cooking, but we have plenty to eat. I read my Bible every day and I don't drink no whiskey.

Rumor is we'll be marching south soon to chase the Rebels to Richmond and make them surrender. The war will be over real soon. Don't worry because the Rebs all ran home when we licked them in Gettysburg and Colonel Chamberlain says they might keep running. If they got a lick of sense, they will, all right.

Colonel Chamberlain is a good leader and the 20th Maine is hard-fighting and brave. We did good at Gettysburg and the colonel says we are heroes. I don't feel like a hero. I just want to come home. We watch out for each other. You can feel joy in that. I know I do.

I'll write more letters when I can and I got your letter last week. I'm glad everyone is doing fine. Please be sure to send news about my brother. I'm praying for him. Say hello to Dad and Grandma and all my friends. I miss my home. If it's God's will, I'll be home soon. Your loving son,

Elston

The young man had a boyish face, red hair, and freckles. He looked far too young to be a soldier in any army. He reached inside his nightshirt and pulled out a small silver angel, which was attached to a chain. Elston's thoughts turned to his last few days at home in Blue Hill, Maine and Jack went along.

They stood at sunset on a sheer rock cliff fifty feet above the crashing ocean while seagulls circled and cried sad songs. The waves collided with the rocks below, filling the chilly evening air with fine salt spray. Elston turned from the craggy edge and walked toward a beautiful saltbox house, which sat handsomely as if painted by a magician. He and Jack entered the house through the kitchen door and a dozen people greeted him with smiles all around.

"There you are, Elston," a man said with a thick down-east accent. "Thought you might'a fell off the cliff! Wouldn't want that to happen on your last night home. The Union would have a hard time without you for sure."

The others chuckled and made room for him at the table.

Another man said, "Oh yeah, Elston. Forgot to tell you 'bout army food. Thing is, it don't taste too good, but it'll push a turd, all right."

More laughter erupted and a glass of whiskey appeared in front of Elston.

The boy's father said, "Drink up! You're a man today and we're as proud as we can be."

Jack watched the party with a woman who was sitting quietly in the corner of the room. Elston's mother, Merriam Hobbs, listened with her head lowered in prayer. Her oldest son was already fighting and she was praying for his safe return. *Now, Abe Lincoln is taking my only other son into service and both boys will be fighting to free Negroes!* Few in Blue Hill had ever seen a Negro, much less owned one. Slavery was a repugnant concept, but most folks said they would like to "meet one first, then make up their own minds."

Oh, what a worry this war is, she thought. Merriam couldn't bear the loss one son, much less both of them. She wished that Elston would join the "Skedaddlers" and hide in the woods of Aroostook County or let a Portland dentists pull his front teeth out. She knew soldiers needed healthy teeth to bite cartridges before loading a musket. *That would do it, all right*, she thought, knowing she could never suggest such things to her son.

As Elston drank his first whiskey, a tear rolled down Merriam's face. She watched her son's Irish eyes crease with laughter and listened to him lie about wanting to be trained real fast, "so I can fight in the next big battle." Merriam knew better. Elston was a gentle boy and she was well aware of her son's terrible nightmares. She had held her son in her arms just last night to calm his soul after another of his violent dreams.

Jack didn't know why he was in Maine with Elston, but he too wished the boy would hit the road with the Skedaddlers up north. Elston was unusually short and Jack decided that he looked about thirteen. He was definitely not cut out for the business of war.

But then, who was? he thought.

In the morning, Elston kissed his sobbing mother goodbye. She hugged him fiercely and slipped a shiny chain over his head. Attached to the chain was a small silver angel, which had belonged to Merriam's mother. The boy accepted the gift, controlled his emotions, boarded his father's wagon, and waved his hat to the crowd. They left for Portland to report for service and, when Blue Hill was out of sight, Elston hung his head over the side of the wagon and vomited.

He was assigned to the 20th Maine and fought as a decorated hero under the command of Colonel Chamberlain at Little Round Top in Gettysburg. His only wish was to return to sleepy Blue Hill, though, where seagulls circled and everything made perfect sense.

Back in Brandy Station, Elston kissed his silver angel, extinguished his oil lamp, muttered a few prayers, and found sleep that rewards the innocent and comes quickly to those with a clear conscience. Floating with the peaceful boy in the dark, Jack recalled that twenty percent of Civil War soldiers were under eighteen and thousands of them perished in the war.

21

When the light returned, Jack was back with General Meade. The Union Army was about to move south and Meade was anxious and concerned about many things. He did not trust Bowler and Hoyle, but he had sent dozens of scouts into the Wilderness and was well aware of the Confederate headquarters in Orange Courthouse. The location of J.E.B. Stuart's Cavalry was a mystery to everyone, including General Lee. Variables like J.E.B. Stuart gave Grant and Meade insatiable appetites for good intelligence, but the sources had to be reliable and disloyalty could not be tolerated.

Meade and his staff disliked and resented the newly appointed General Grant and they strongly objected to the peculiar-looking General Phil Sheridan, who was the new Chief of the Cavalry. Meade's disdain for Sheridan was especially well-known but, in order to mitigate his personal lack of respect for Grant and his staff, he cunningly requested the help of several of Grant's loyal personnel. One such request was for Grant's most trusted scout, Henry Mueller.

Oh my God! Jack thought. *Uncle Henry! Who dreams like this?*

The Zouave guard escorted Henry into Meade's tent and the general said, "Sergeant Mueller, I've sent two scouts into the eastern quadrant of the Wilderness and, frankly, I do not trust them. Their names are Sergeants Matthew Bowler and Peyton Hoyle. Do you know these men?"

"I've heard of them, sir."

"Very well. They left camp early this morning. You will follow them and report any suspicious activity to me. I believe they're unreliable and traitorous. Please report back to me as soon as possible."

"Yes, sir."

"General Grant has every confidence in you as a trusted soldier and scout and you have done a stellar job for the Union. I understand this will be your final campaign and it should be an easy assignment for a man of your caliber. The Union thanks you for your service."

Henry had no words. Flooded with self-confidence and determination, he saluted and said, "Yes, sir. Thank you, sir."

After receiving a sincere salute in return, Henry packed quickly and wrote a brief letter to his wife. Jack was able to read Henry's letter and realized that, in the future, his mother would become obsessed with it—but why?

Jack and Henry left camp immediately knowing that Bowler and Hoyle had a head start. Henry was a smart, tough individual with keen tracking senses. He caught up with the stinkers quickly and discovered that their progress was delayed because Bowler was ill. He respected Sergeant Hoyle's skills, however, and allowed ample distance between his quarry and himself.

General Meade must have good reason to doubt them, Henry thought as he spied on the two men.

Sergeant Mueller understood Meade's concerns and he was determined to provide the general with everything he asked, although he was also anxious to leave the army and return to his family in Illinois. The massive Union Army was ready to deploy and Henry was eager to complete his last assignment before the slaughter began.

22

Peyton's bladder woke him shortly after 3:00 a.m. and Jack was forced to watch him urinate outside his tent. *We're getting the hell out of here, so I ain't walkin' all the way to the latrine,* Peyton thought, as he grunted, belched and pissed on the tent next to his.

He woke Matthew and they left Brady Station quietly.

The morning was warm and humid. Once they crossed the Rapidan River, Matthew developed a low-grade fever that continued to worsen toward mid-morning, forcing them to stop and make camp. Matthew was feverish all night, but his fever broke just before dawn and he was well enough to ride. He discovered an ugly canker lesion on his genitalia. He was not yet aware that he had contracted syphilis several months earlier at a Washington brothel, nor that his fever was a classic symptom of the secondary stage of his infection. He had raped several women since then and, before those unfortunate victims developed symptoms of their own, Matthew would be dead. Peyton would be dead as well, giving them the distinction of being the first of 25,000 to die as a result of the Wilderness campaign.

Makes sense to me, Jack thought. *The stink boys have a great deal to explain, so why not be first in line?*

Jack was forced to float along with Peyton; Matthew rode slowly and wasn't in the mood for rape and such. In fact, he was downright cranky most of the time, which greatly troubled Peyton. They passed up a young woman, who was working alone in a field, and Matthew never gave her a second look. Peyton had no confidence in himself and he was unable to accept changes in his friend's behavior. He liked it when Matthew talked about raping women because then his friend was happy and things were good. Whenever Matthew encountered a defenseless woman and said, "I want to be close to her skin," it was music to Peyton's ears. Then, things were good indeed.

It became apparent that things were not good as they continued south. Matthew's sour mood led to bickering and the exchange of nasty insults. They circumnavigated the Wilderness Tavern to the east and then rejoined the Orange Courthouse Turnpike until they spotted Rebel pickets patrolling the outermost perimeter of the Confederate Army. They turned back to the east and continued south on Brock Road until it intersected with the old railroad cut.

Jack was fascinated by the Wilderness Tavern and remembered that the Parker Store Road ran from the tavern, past the Higgerson and Chewning Farms and on to Parker Store near the old railroad cut. He wanted to float down the Parker Store Road rather than continue with the stink boys, but he had no choice.

Peyton had a marvelous sense of direction; he could find his way through impossible terrain. He was also familiar with the railroad cut and chose that hidden convenience to travel toward Bobby Lee's eastern flank near Orange Courthouse. On the evening of May 4th, the two men bedded down within the cover of the unfinished railroad bed, one-quarter mile from Luke and Amanda's meeting place.

Bowler and Hoyle fell asleep and dreamed hard dreams as Jack drifted away.

23

Jack was relieved to be rid of Bowler and Hoyle, even though Amanda was sobbing and Permelia was doing her best to console her niece. The sun had not yet risen and the women were hugging one another in the light of an oil lamp. Permelia welcomed Amanda's embrace, ignoring the pain that riddled her body every time her niece sobbed or blew her nose. Ironically, these last moments together were also the closest they had ever been. Amanda was crying, Permelia was praying and they were both frightened and filled with guilt.

Amanda's departure had been delayed by needs of the heart while they held one another in a desperate attempt to postpone the inevitable. The first and second times they broke their embrace were because of Permelia's coughing, but then a sense of urgency separated them for the last time—and forever.

Better get going, Jack thought. *It's May 5th and the Union Army is close—they've already crossed the Rapidan River and they're are almost here.*

Amanda mounted Star along with Jack and slowly rode away, sobbing like a child. She glanced back at her aunt, wishing she would wave and gesture for her to return. Permelia remained steadfast until her niece was out of sight. Then, she walked painfully back to her lonely cabin, drank peach brandy from a dusty old bottle, and flirted with suicide.

Because of the delay, dawn had erupted into brilliant sunshine as Amanda rode past Widow Tapp's small cabin on the Parker Store Road. Jack noticed Truitt, who was watching them through a telescope, and he was reluctantly drawn toward the boy. Truitt had bedded down in Tapp's field and became suspicious when he saw Amanda in Benjamin's clothing. He followed the peculiar little man because "somethin' don't look right."

Since striking out on his own, Truitt had been terrorizing the Northern army and killed and mutilated more than a dozen Yankee soldiers. Several unfortunate civilians were also maimed because he thought they were spies or Northern sympathizers. In Truitt's mind, the freelance slaughter of traitorous civilians would enhance Major Mosby's love for him. Therefore, soldiers and civilians, especially those who resembled his father, were torn apart with the imagination of a madman.

The gruesome remains of his victims were hung like scarecrows on the doorstep of the advancing Union Army. Truitt's inspired imagination found a bit of dear old dad in each of his quarries and, since each target resembled his father more than the previous one, no brutality was overlooked. He became more creative with each kill and the ferocity with which he gutted and mutilated his prey threatened his fragile emotional state of mind. Each slaughter cast him further into an eddy of despair. Butchering men and woman his own age had an especially profound effect on his mental stability, making the troubled assassin even more unstable and dangerous.

Amanda brought Star to a halt, patted her face with water from her canteen, and removed her hat. Her hastily pinned hair fell like silk and flowed gently over her shoulders. She looked up into the sky and saw a large black bird being intimidated by a much smaller, but determined sparrow. The smaller bird darted and pecked while the black bird ducked, weaved, and retreated to the north.

The airborne conflict was common in the spring season. Amanda had always thought of herself as the sparrow and cheered its efforts. As the birds flew overhead, she shielded her eyes from the sun and prayed urgently for the smaller bird. She was well aware that the Southern army was outnumbered by almost two to one, but what if they were able to drive the dark force away like the sparrow hounds the black bird? If so, Permelia would be alone and helpless in the dreadful Wilderness while she was far away in Richmond. She turned and watched the sparrow bully the larger bird until the pair disappeared into the distance.

She felt compelled to return to the safety and security of her aunt's home, but she couldn't go back; she had to honor her father's wishes. Permelia had sternly warned her about many things, with great emphasis on the threat of men who would not hesitate to violate and murder young women during the chaos of war. She couldn't fathom such behavior, although Permelia swore that the threat was real.

I must, therefore, remain disguised as a man and avoid contact with everyone—especially soldiers! she decided.

When she turned in her saddle to follow the birds, she also turned full-faced into Truitt's lens. The boy gasped, lowered the telescope and quickly raised it again.

The day was already warm and the pungent smell of the Wilderness wafted through the air. Amanda stretched, sighed, and tucked her hair back up under her floppy hat while thinking about her aunt and Luke with mixed emotions. She had to trust Luke in spite of her aunt's harsh warnings about men and she felt overwhelming guilt for abandoning her precious aunt. She could not return to the Higgerson Farm and she was becoming wary of traveling with Luke, as exciting as that prospect had once seemed. She was both confused and full of remorse but exhilarated by the unknown. Her confusion had elevated her trepidation and caused her to pause on the trail.

With her face still raised into the warm sun, she closed her eyes and prayed for her mother's guidance.

24

Truitt and Jack watched Amanda through a telescope and the boy was astonished when her gleaming hair fell to her shoulders. He had never seen anything more beautiful. As he squinted through his lens and watched the girl unpin her hair, he gasped when she turned her face into his lens. In spite of the psychopath's emotions, however, the predator within him sensed that something was wrong, not only because of her disguise, but because she seemed confused and preoccupied.

His insights regarding his prey were keen and he always scrutinized his targets before taking advantage of an apparent weakness. The girl turned and rode on with a peculiar lack of enthusiasm and the killer decided to follow. Her lack of conviction was a vulnerability that he could exploit, of course, but he didn't want to kill her—at least not yet. He wasn't sure what to do but, *bein' that she looks like an angel, I'll leave her be for now.*

He unconsciously rubbed his thigh with his free hand while his watery eyes darted and flashed over the entire area, returning to the girl every few seconds. He was looking for any additional threat and saw none. He studied the girl intently, searching for any likeness to his father. The evil in the old man's spirit could disguise itself as anything or anyone—even an angel. *Is she really an angel?* he thought as worms squirmed inside his brain. *Followin' her is excitin' and it feels good to watch her, but what would Major Mosby think? Would the major want me to kill this suspicious girl?* He was unable to settle on anything, so he and Jack followed and watched.

He pressed silently ahead so that he could watch her approach from a concealed position and waited in the brush by the roadside. He licked his lips, rubbed his pant leg, and tried to control the nervous twitch in his eye as Amanda passed within a few yards. As she rode by, the entire side of Truitt's pale face began to tremble while his clear assassin's eyes analyzed and recorded every detail of her face, clothing, supplies, and especially her weapons.

He patted sweat from his brow while the astounding image of the girl assailed his suppressed teenage imagination. He became enamored of the young beauty and his steadfast dedication to Mosby began to erode. The killer continued the pursuit and eventually decided that he would happily follow the girl through the gates of hell and beyond. Amanda quickly became his mother, Mosby, and Kuruk rolled into one. He became helplessly enchanted as his obsession with Mosby was precipitously transferred to the girl in his lens.

Jack was able to penetrate far enough into Truitt's mind to understand that the boy's hunger for human intimacy and his vicious nature had resulted in powerful obsessions at opposite ends of the human spectrum. Things were black or white, right or wrong, north or south. There was no middle ground and, luckily for Amanda, the monster living inside his unbalanced mind did not see her as an enemy or threat. Instead, his entire reason for living shifted quickly from Mosby to Amanda. As his infatuation grew, his whole purpose began to revolve around his newfound, breathtaking idol.

Amanda continued to ride on the narrow road and Jack wished he could join her. Being around Truitt was slowly exhausting his positive attitude like a drain on a battery. He was thankful that he couldn't penetrate too far into Truitt's head, knowing that if he did delve too deeply he might swim forever in a demonic pit of despair. Avoiding the diseased core of Truitt's mind seemed to be one of the only things he *could* control, however, and he was grateful for that.

All at once, Jack got his wish and rejoined Amanda. They rode past a few small buildings known as Parker's Store, which sat quietly within shouting distance of the railroad cut. With a nervous flutter in her stomach, she dismounted at the rendezvous point within the railroad bed and removed her hat. She felt dizzy in the warm morning sun and, when the feather in her belly overwhelmed her, she vomited into the thicket.

She splashed water on her face, sat in the shade, brushed her hair, and decided two things: First, her mother would have wanted her to comply with her father's wishes. Second, Permelia would be safe until she was able to return for her. Only then was the emptiness in her young heart filled with thoughts of the boy she loved and the excitement of the journey ahead.

She couldn't believe that she and Luke would be alone for the next several days. That frightened her, but her aunt trusted Luke and he was everything she had ever dreamed. Then, she thought of her father. *General McClellan's forces had never attacked Richmond as he feared and the capital city must have remained a safe stronghold for the South after all. The great Confederate Army will be stronger than ever and Richmond will be heavily fortified. I will be safe in Richmond and someday settle in Hampton Sydney with Permelia, Luke, and my father. The Union will be defeated and we will celebrate the independence of the great South.*

Close enough, Jack thought.

Still, as she looked into the dark thickets, she felt isolated and alone. She then became convinced that Luke would not show up at all.

Meanwhile, Amanda's clothing and curious behavior had confused Truitt. As he watched her dismount and throw up he thought, *she's doin' what she's got to do to survive.* He identified strongly with that as he climbed a tree as close as he dared, steadied his telescope on a tree branch, and watched his Wilderness angel carefully.

Jack hovered close to Truitt and thought, *this is one strange-looking dude.* Truitt's facial features seemed contrary to the laws of nature. His narrow chin and thin lips were dwarfed by his hooked nose that had been broken several times and left to heal on its own. But it was his disproportionate eyes that made him look so bizarre. His huge, inky-black, wet, protruding eyeballs were shadowed by impossibly thick "stage makeup" eyelashes. *If he shaved his long, greasy black hair, he'd look like and alien on the sci-fi channel,* Jack thought as he began to slip into Truitt's mind again.

To Truitt, Amanda was everything he could never have. The thought of actually facing her, however, terrified him and made him twitch with fear. No, he could never face her because she was heaven and he was hell. She was glowing and he was invisible. She was life and he was death.

Jack fought to free himself from Truitt's mind while the extra-terrestrial psychopath continued to twitch and salivate. As feelings of hopelessness and physical pain returned to Jack, he felt trapped and struggled desperately to free himself from Truitt's torment.

"LET ME OUT!" the desperate pilot yelled, although no one could hear him.

25

*...the Wilderness, a broad stretch of impenetrable
thickets and dense second growth that had replaced
forests cut down to fuel local iron and gold furnaces.*[10]

Jack did managed to free himself from Truitt but went from the fire to the frying pan. He was back with Matthew, who was winching in syphilitic pain as he urinated. Matthew had just woken on the morning of May 5th and he greeted the beautiful morning with disdain.

I'll kill him today, he thought as kicked Peyton to wake him.

Syphilis had infected Matthew's gut as well as his brain and he was full of foul-smelling gas. He began to break wind and Peyton laughed every time Matthew farted.

"Shut the hell up!" Matthew said.

Peyton held his nose, fanned his hat in Matthew's direction, and then stood and walked toward his horse, still chuckling. Matthew considered killing him then and there, but a gunshot would be too noisy. Besides, he still needed him. *Today is the day, all right. I'll kill him soon enough but not yet. I might still need him for a while. Besides, the longer I wait the more I'm gonna like it.*

Matthew continued to break wind as they walked cautiously leading their horses west within the cover of the railroad cut. Peyton's plan was to continue west until the railroad bed ended or they saw signs of the Confederates. Matthew had a different idea.

"Johnny Reb is gonna smell you comin'," Peyton said.

"I told you to shut the hell up, damn it!"

Peyton was relieved to see that Matthew was in better spirits; being told to "shut up" was more like it. Matthew's dark pockmarked face, big mustache, and dimpled chin were in contrast to Peyton's beady eyes, squat nose, and elephant ears. Peyton liked the way Mathew moved—smooth and liquid, like a fancy dancer. Peyton had given the lead to Matthew, knowing that his small friend couldn't get lost in the rail bed. Besides, he enjoyed watching the little guy's rear end and he was content to follow him in spite of his nasty gas.

As usual, Matthew ignored Peyton and continued to fantasize about creative ways to kill him. *I'd shoot him in the back of the head, but I can't risk no gun shot noise so I'll use my knife on him. Besides, he won't quit walking behind me. Maybe he's not as stupid as I thought.*

As the odd couple approached Amanda, she had an overwhelming urge to relieve herself and decided to squat before Luke arrived. Her hair fell to her shoulders again when she removed her hat. Jack wondered why she couldn't pee with her hat on while she lowered Benjamin's pants and squatted with her back to the approaching stink brothers. They stopped in their tracks when they saw her and exchanged nods of appreciation for their good fortune.

"Glory be and Hallelujah," Matthew whispered. "Just when the war was gettin' to be a bother, looks like I found me somethin' to cheer me up and warm my belly."

Peyton stood still, quietly picking his nose with his pinky finger; he always picked his nose when he became excited. He knew what Matthew was about to do and he was exhilarated.

Matthew whispered, "I want to be close to her skin."

Peyton was happy to have his friend back and smiled broadly. Then, Matthew's neighing horse alerted Amanda, who thought Luke had arrived on horseback. She reddened with embarrassment, thinking he might have seen her squatting, and quickly stood while pulling her uncle's ridiculous pants back up.

She gasped when she turned to face Matthew and Peyton.

Truitt blushed when Amanda lowered her trousers and the young killer diverted his eyes. Then, he heard Matthew's horse and assumed that the girl was waiting for the stink boys.

"Well, what we got here?" Matthew said maliciously.

"Looks like a little boy peeing like a girl," Peyton said, still picking away.

"Are you a boy or a girl?" Matthew sneered.

"I am a lady and you should turn your backs," Amanda said with surprising indignation.

The stink boys looked at each other and burst out laughing.

Matthew said, "How come a pretty little lady like you is way out here wearin' them trousers?"

"I'm waiting for my father and his men who will be here any moment," Amanda said, holding her head high and trying not to tremble.

She was becoming more and more frightened as they moved closer. She thought of the small derringer that Permelia had sewn into her long underwear, but Matthew's approach was too fast and both men were carrying huge revolvers. Besides, they would surely notice if she suddenly reached down into her pants.

You got that right, Jack thought.

"Well then," Matthew said. "Maybe we'll keep you company till your pappy gets here."

With each step, Matthew's yearning for the girl grew and he became more determined to violate the innocent fawn. Time was short though, and he would have to take her quickly and quietly "on account of the Rebels might be near."

Truitt couldn't hear the conversation but, based on the girl's reaction and body language, he knew his angel was in danger. He tried to find either man in his gun sights, but it was difficult because of his compromising position in the tree. He had chosen a thick stand of small trees that blocked most of his view but gave him good cover at close range. He found Matthew in his sights briefly, then Peyton, but he had no clear shot. *I can't risk shootin' my mother...I mean, my angel*, he thought.

Bowler and Hoyle positioned themselves on either side of Amanda and then Matthew lunged for her and cupped his hand over her mouth. Amanda bit him and screamed. Matthew slapped her with the back of his hand, knocking her to the ground, and she cried out again as she scrambled away. She cried out once more when Matthew grabbed her again and struggled with surprising strength until he hit her with his closed fist. His attempt to silence her opened her lower lip and blood burst from the seemingly unconscious rag doll.

Amanda's screams infuriated Truitt, but he could no longer see anyone from his position. He had been waiting for a clear shot but decided that he would reveal himself if need be. Slowly and quietly, he climbed down the tree.

The May morning sun shone brightly on the rape scene. The sun's frustrated rays could not penetrate the dense undergrowth adjacent to the railroad bed. Earthworms and slugs living in that moist darkness could easily watch as if spotlights were illuminating the lowest form of human behavior.

Matthew quickly tied his dirty neckerchief through Amanda's mouth and roughly pulled her pants down to her ankles, exposing Benjamin's long underwear. He smiled when he saw the underwear and Peyton became a more interested spectator while Amanda managed to lie still and play dead. Matthew loosened his gun belt, leaned over her, and hung his sidearm on a low branch of a small tree. Then, he lowered his own trousers and tore at Amanda's shirt, quickly tearing it open. Somehow, Amanda was able to control herself and remain still while Matthew's dirty underwear strained to contain his erection.

From deep within the woods to the south, Luke heard Amanda's screams and shouted her name in response.

"A-MAN-DA!"

Jack thought, *I've heard all of this before, but it wasn't here and it wasn't now.*

The thicket muffled Luke's voice, but Peyton had keen ears. He drew his sword and turned in Luke's direction, squinting into the thicket and picking his nose with his dirt-filled pinky finger.

Matthew sensed his partner's concern and said, "What is it?"

Peyton spit on the ground and said, "Go on, Matthew. It ain't probably nothin'. There's only one and he's still pretty far off. I can handle this."

Matthew smiled at his pitiful friend and then looked back at Amanda. He was so enamored of her that he decided to trust Peyton—at least for now. Peyton could handle a sword better than most and he would use his gun only as a last resort. As much as Matthew wanted to enjoy his good fortune, however, he knew he should wait before tearing into the helpless girl. Then again, he had never been happier than he was at this moment. Standing over the

vulnerable, unconscious child was rousing enough to dull his sense
of caution.

Little man in control of the big man, Jack mused.

"Okay," Matthew said. "This won't take long. Take'em with
your sword if need be—I got my revolver ready in case."

Peyton answered with a simple nod. Matthew looked back
down at the girl and smiled. He glanced toward Peyton again and saw
that his friend had drifted a few yards away and seemed to be
concentrating on the potential threat. Matthew had always been able
to depend on that kind of allegiance from his dim-witted companion.

Maybe I won't kill'em, after all, he thought.

26

What luck for rulers that men do not think.
                              ~ Adolf Hitler

Jack and Luke arrived at the Stewart Farm to give his mother the bad news.

"You expect us to leave our home and you're not coming with us?" Luke's mother, Margaret, said. "How could Mrs. Higgerson suggest such a thing...and why did you agree?"

It seemed like a good idea at the time, Luke thought.

He had anticipated resistance from his mother and rehearsed his position during his walk home from the Higgerson Farm. He had been the man of the house for more than two years and the family accepted him in that role. Luke was not stupid and planned to use his position of authority and a good helping of emotional appeal to convince his mother to leave without him.

"Adam is just as capable as me to lead you to safety and I gave my word to Mrs. Higgerson. Her farm is north of here and in greater danger than we are. Mrs. Higgerson is too ill to travel and her only concern is for her niece."

"She plans to remain there alone?"

"Yep. I offered to take them with us to Heathsville, but she can't travel so I promised to carry Amanda to Richmond. Her father is a surgeon and he wants his daughter to go to the capital where she'll be safe. We'll be riding a sturdy horse that Mrs. Higgerson is giving me for my trouble. I'll meet you in Heathsville in about one week and we'll all come back home after the Yankees are gone."

"How old is this girl, Amanda?"

"Oh, she's old enough to keep up. She looks strong enough too, but she can't travel alone, that's for sure."

At a boy, Luke, Jack thought. *I'd leave it at that.*

Like Permelia, Margaret did not want to leave her home to the Yankees or anyone else. She believed her son, however, and finally accepted the fact that the Union Army would be arriving soon. There was no time to lose and Luke was going to Richmond whether she liked it or not.

Adam comforted his mother by welcoming the responsibility and the family spent the rest of the night packing their two wagons with supplies and valuables. They used the smaller wagon to secure what little livestock they had and then Luke and Adam covered both wagons with canvas. The sun had risen by the time they finished. Luke's crying mother hugged him hard and let him go.

Luke, Jack, and Zeus hurried through the woods to meet Amanda. When Luke heard Amanda scream, he ran as fast as he could on the winding trail. "A-MAN-DA!" he hollered while saplings slashed his face and his old sword clanked against small trees. The blood and perspiration, which flowed over his face and stung his eyes, increased his rage as he charged recklessly.

Jack remembered that the reasoning lobe of the human brain doesn't fully develop until the age of about twenty-three. *That's why Luke is doing all this,* he thought. *And I guess that's why college was so much fun.*

Jack also knew that the lack of sound reasoning was why young adults took risks, wrecked cars, followed orders well, and became good fighter pilots. He was reminded of the waves of young soldiers, who had charged into a continuous barrage of bullets at Marye's Heights during The Battle of Fredericksburg. Some pulled the brims of their hats down as if to ward off heavy rain. *I wonder what would have happened if the enlistment age for Civil War soldiers had been twenty-three.*

The "brain-challenged" boy continued to run wildly toward Amanda's desperate screams until he saw a glimmer of sunlight reflecting from Peyton's sword. He ran directly at the flash of light, not knowing what was causing the reflection or what he would do once he reached it. He hoped Amanda was sending a signal and he shouted her name again.

"A-MAN-DA!"

When Zeus heard Amanda's screams, he was determined to protect his master. He ran in short spurts though, never allowing Luke to lag too far behind. Another sapling smacked Luke in the face and he lost sight of Zeus, who seemed to have vanished into thin air. He continued his desperate charge alone.

Like Homer's irresistible sirens calling Greek Argonauts, Luke, Jack, and Zeus, all responded to Amanda's desperate cries for help, although in different layers of time. When Zeus disappeared, he transcended time, tumbled into the future, and collided with Jack in 2014. Jack's consciousness was thrown into the past and Zeus began a bewildering journey back and forth through time.

27

Although he could see nothing in the thick brush, Sergeant Hoyle stood with his gleaming sword in hand, dutifully waiting for Luke to emerge from the woods. As Luke thrashed through the thickets and shouted Amanda's name at closer range, Peyton became increasingly excited. Then, Peyton removed his finger from his nose and moved slightly to his right. At the same time, Matthew leaned over Amanda within reach of his revolver.

Truitt was scrambling down the tree when he heard Luke shout Amanda's name for the last time. He quietly made his way through the snarled thicket, aiming his rifle in the general direction of Peyton. His target eluded him until Hoyle moved another yard to his right and turned his good ear to the threat. When he turned his head, he moved directly into the iron sights of Truitt's rifle and the boy touched the trigger.

The Hawken had double triggers. When the rear trigger was pulled, it merely "set" the front trigger transforming it into a "hair trigger." As soon as he touched the front trigger, the .50 caliber bullet, which was the size of a large marble, entered stink man's head directly behind his right ear. The slug tumbled ever so slightly as it passed through Peyton's limited brain matter. It exited below his left eye and produced a gaping exit wound, which removed most of his face. Bits of bone and gray matter exploded into the thicket like a water balloon slamming into a screen door.

A second later, Luke burst into view and Matthew shot him.

28

Amanda was terrified. Her attacker had roughly torn her shirt and pulled her pants down. The man stepped out of one leg of his trousers and moved forward, straddling Amanda's inert body. He was a small man and wanted his revolver to be within his reach, so he leaned over Amanda with his legs spread apart. He was looking at Peyton and concentrating on the impending threat.

Peyton will kill'em quick, then I'll get this over with, he thought.

Amanda's wild hair was full of dirt and leaves and she could see nothing but the repulsive underwear of the monster. She could taste the blood from her broken lip and she could smell Matthew's gas and diseased odor. She heard Luke calling her name and prayed for strength as she slowly moved her trembling hand toward the concealed derringer. When she finally held the pistol, she was overcome with an extraordinary sense of calm. She held her breath and opened her eyes as much as she dared, squinting up between Matthew's legs.

"A-MAN-DA!" Luke shouted again.

He was close now and both men heard the threat loud and clear. Matthew continued to look at his friend.

Lord help me, Amanda thought as she fully cocked the tiny hammer. The miniature pistol felt even smaller than she remembered, but she knew it would do some damage at close range and waited for the right moment.

"A-MAN-DA!" Luke screamed for the last time, just before he burst into view.

Faster than spit on a skillet and much more quickly than Amanda had expected, Matthew reached forward, snatched his revolver from the holster, and fired in Luke's direction.

An instant before Matthew fired, two things happened almost simultaneously: Truitt's rifle shot cracked the air and blew Peyton's head apart and Amanda quickly raised the derringer straight up pulled the trigger.

Pop! The small slug shattered Matthew's left testicle and continued upward through his colon with just enough velocity to sever his inferior vena cava. The immediate pain was excruciating and a torrent of blood flowed instantly.

Jack knew that Matthew would have been better off if the bullet had pierced an artery instead of a vein. Arteries pump blood *away* from the heart at a tremendous rate and would have ended his life quickly. Bleeding from a major vein that carries blood *to* the heart would be fatal as well, although it would take a longer time to do the trick.

Tick-tock, tick-tock, Jack thought.

Jack's dealings with evil were detached and dispassionate. As with Truitt, he was able to temper the vile nature of things that threatened his generally euphoric dreamscape. He had tried to do the same thing in the conscious world with the help of alcohol—without much success.

Matthew's shot almost missed Luke but not entirely because of Amanda's efforts. When he pointed his deadly .44-caliber Colt 1860 Army Revolver in Luke's direction, four things stabbed at his brain: the ear-splitting sound of Truitt's rifle shot, the sudden appearance of Zeus, who was galloping toward him, the image of Peyton's exploding head, and the excruciating pain in his groin. Matthew fired the big Colt inefficiently and then snapped his head back to look, with astonished outrage, into Amanda's terrified eyes.

Then, Zeus slammed into Matthew and embedded his teeth in his shoulder. He didn't feel the pain from the dog's jaws immediately because the pain in his groin was like passing a kidney stone the size of the slug that had ruined Peyton's day. His trousers were still tangled around one of his ankles and, as he toppled backward, his revolver flew from his hand. When Zeus and Matthew tumbled to the ground, they rolled and stopped several yards from Amanda.

Zeus vanished, once again.

Matthew curled into a helpless fetal position, holding his bloody crotch with both hands. He was in shock and moaning low guttural sounds as the bloodstain grew on his greasy underwear. Jack couldn't quite read Matthew's thoughts, probably because his mind had not yet caught up with his dire circumstances, although he knew Matthew's unpleasant day had only just begun.

29

The smell of spent gunpowder filled the railroad cut as Amanda scampered to a sitting position and wrapped her arms around her knees. She was still gagged with Matthew's neckerchief and the front of her torn shirt was stained with blood from her lip. Matthew's blood was splattered on the lower part of her underwear. She was looking at Matthew with a blank stare, swaying back and forth in unison with the dying man. The would-be rapist was looking at her and rocking involuntarily as if in agreement. When their eyes locked together, her frozen gaze met his tormented bewilderment.

After a moment of disorientation, Luke realized he had been shot while adrenalin rushed through his brain. When the bullet passed through his arm, he fell to the ground while searing pain moved up and down his shoulder. Clutching his bleeding right arm, he rose unsteadily; he saw what remained of Peyton and heard Matthew moaning in the otherwise silent landscape. Then, he saw Amanda sitting up against a tree under Matthew's dangling gun belt and staggered toward her. She was covered in blood.

Luke removed the neckerchief from her mouth and said, "Are you hurt, Amanda? Are you hurt?"

She buried her face in his chest when he touched her and remained silent. He held the trembling girl with his good arm and rocked back and forth with her while looking around the narrow clearing. The man on the ground was helpless and his near-death groans were fading into low guttural sounds. Luke saw the US Army belt buckle tangled within the soldier's trousers and realized they were in great danger. All of the gunshots seemed to have come at the same time. Luke assumed that one of the soldiers had mistakenly shot the other and he was caught in the crossfire. Amanda was clutching a mysterious derringer that she had used to protect herself. Luke didn't understand any of it, but he knew the gunshots would attract the attention of others.

He pulled Amanda's pants back up and helped her to her feet. She buried her face at his side while he untied Star but would not release the now useless derringer. She held the pistol tightly as they walked to the east and then turned abruptly into the tangled Wilderness. They had planned to continue east within the cover of the railroad's path until reaching Brock Road, but that was impossible now. Hiding in the thickets and bogs of the Wilderness was their only option and Luke prayed that the woods would swallow them and keep them hidden.

Travel was slow on the path because Amanda remained attached to Luke, who was weak and losing blood. He awkwardly pushed his way through the underbrush and held Amanda as best he could. Star followed the traumatized teenagers while Luke's old sword clanked along and his bleeding arm stained the ground. He was half-carrying Amanda, rather than guiding her, and straining to maintain consciousness. He was about to give up when they finally reached the same small clearing where they had fallen in love.

They stumbled into that once-beautiful place and Luke fell to the ground like a bag of dirt. Amanda remained standing over him, holding the derringer close to her breast and swaying slowly from side to side. Her eyes were closed and she was lost within herself, unaware of her surroundings. Luke's blood loss was severe and he made a clumsy attempt to apply a tourniquet, but the blood continued to flow. Desperate for help, he looked up at the despondent girl and said, "Please help me, Amanda."

The next moment, an agonizing cry erupted from Matthew in the railroad cut that hurled Amanda back into reality as if being jolted from a horrible dream.

"You're wounded!" she gasped.

She shoved the derringer into her pocket, ran to Star's packs, and returned with rolled bandages, liniment, and clean water. She quickly applied an efficient tourniquet and cleaned Luke's wound. Then, she applied Permelia's disinfecting ointment made from arnica, goldenseal, sweet gum root, thyme, and yarrow. The disinfecting qualities of the liniment were a mystery in 1864, although the same ingredients had been healing wounds for centuries. As Amanda worked, she silently thanked her aunt for carefully packing everything from bandages to the little pistol. She remembered everything her father had taught her about treating and wrapping wounds and dressed Luke's arm with incredible skill. She concentrated on the task and became completely absorbed in the process.

Luke raised his head and watched her work with the efficiency of a trained physician. Without her help, he would not have survived his blood loss. Without his bold response to her screams, she would have been raped and probably murdered. Still, he felt like a failure because he had promised to protect and care for Amanda, yet she was caring for him. He could do little more than watch her wrap his arm; as she worked, the magical forces of nature blossomed within the boy. He swore he would sacrifice his life to protect her.

Amanda was oblivious to Luke's state of mind as she continued to dress his wound. When she looked up at him, she blushed, diverted her eyes, smiled weakly, and gently kissed his bandaged arm. With that, Luke pulled her close and they lay together in silence.

There, in the belly of the monster, the young lovers found a few precious moments of peace.

30

Matthew was curled up on his side and moaning although less enthusiastically. Jack was looking at the brutal man's blood-filled ear dispassionately when a line from a country song popped into his head—"I've got tears in my ears from lying on my back and crying over you." He couldn't remember the rest of the song, so he thought of silly alliteration—*the bastard's balls are busted and the fiend's friend is finished.* He was wondering how long he would have to remain with stink man when movement in the brush drew his attention to Truitt. The delusional assassin was squatting and staring at Matthew like a predatory animal. He was watching intently as Matthew's impudent face morphed into the face of his dead father. The young lunatic scrutinized his unhappy pappy and became enraged because his old man had managed to attack his angel from the ashes of his fiery grave. *How could the old bastard try to rape my angel, just like he raped me? How come he won't die?* His father's demonic red eyes blazed back at the boy.

Truitt had heard the quick pop of Amanda's derringer, as well as the almost simultaneous report of Matthew's revolver. From within the cover of the nearby brush, he watched Luke struggle to his feet and approach the girl. He knew his angel had wounded his old man and Luke was no threat to her, so he waited until they left the killing zone before moving closer to the injured man.

Truitt was astonished to see that Matthew Bowler was actually his father. His angel had tried to kill the old bastard and, therefore, he felt a kinship toward her that was beyond love. Her attempt to kill the ogre had given them something in common and instantly elevated the girl to a deity in his twisted mind. He also felt overwhelmingly compelled to protect her from his father's evil spirit. Since he couldn't destroy the devil, he had to disable him as best he could. He digested those thoughts and then rapidly emerged from the brush and scampered on all fours like an enormous crab toward Matthew.

He unfolded a dull blade that also served as a spoon as he lunged out of the brush. With pure hatred, he gaped at Matthew's terrified face and quickly removed his father's eyes. The first eyeball burst like a raw egg, but his technique improved and the second eyeball popped out neatly with a small sucking sound and dangled a few inches above the ground. Truitt's clumsy ophthalmology resulted in Matthew's last earthly cry, which was the same shattering scream that snapped Amanda out of her trance and allowed her to save Luke's life.

While Truitt melted back into the quagmire and disappeared, Jack wondered if Matthew's dangling eyeball could see his broken one.

31

"Where's that dog?" Luke said, while peering into the twisted brush.

Amanda returned from the stream where she had quickly washed and changed into the spare set of Benjamin's clothing. She said, "He was probably scared off by all the shooting."

Matthew's hideous face flooded Amanda's mind and she fought to control her emotions. She moved away from Luke, peered into the underbrush, and continued to tremble. She looked back at Luke and said, "I'm scared."

Luke approached her and they sat down. "Even if we hide from them, we might still be crushed by the war," he mumbled, just above a whisper. "If the war keeps coming, these woods are gonna explode, but we can't run yet. First, we have to hide—then we'll run like hell."

Shock and stress had produced tremendous fatigue and Amanda allowed herself to be swept away by the comfort of Luke's melodious voice. For an instant, the serenity of the sleepy family garden in Hampden Sydney surrounded her and then she woke with a shudder. She felt Luke's large hand smoothing her hair and tried to pay attention to what he was saying—something about a swamp.

"We can't take Star into the marsh with us either," he said. "We have to leave him behind and hope the Yankees take him, instead of us. I'll lead Star into the woods and give them a good enough trail to follow. Then, I'll double back to you. When we get in the swamp, they can't track us and they won't want to 'cause it's so nasty in there. Besides, when they find Star with all our supplies and your daddy's Whitworth rifle, maybe they'll just quit and leave us alone."

He was gulping water and talking very fast. Before she could object, he rambled on about knowing his way through the swamp and how it would be slow going for a while. "We're gonna get stunk up some, but nobody will follow us and we'll be real safe in there till things calm down. The swamp is the only place to hide for now. When they give up hunting us, we'll hurry to Richmond before the war catches up." He looked into her captivating green eyes and said, "We can't get captured by either side, Amanda."

She dreaded the thought of entering a swamp and she hated snakes. When she protested, Luke comforted her by patting her back and telling her that they would be okay and it wouldn't be so bad, and so on.

Jack knew that Luke was worried about many other things, none of which he had mentioned. *Amanda has stopped my bleeding with amazing skill, but my injury is serious,* Luke thought. *Our desperate appearance would be suspicious. We might be shot on sight like some civilians were at Chancellorsville. The Yankees might even hang us as spies. Amanda would be discovered in no time and any woman dressed like a man would be in real bad trouble. We can't go back and the only sure place to hide is in the big swamp.*

He couldn't warn Amanda about the dangers of the marsh and had to act nonchalant about it, but he was plenty worried about that as well.

"Do we have to leave Star behind?" Amanda asked as she pulled herself away from Luke's embrace and looked into his eyes, hoping for a different answer.

"We've got to leave him. Like I said, they might keep Star and everything in his packs and be satisfied. Besides, a horse can't go where we're goin'." He looked around, squinted up at the sun and said, "I know a dry place in the swamp where we can put up for the night, but we've got to get there before dark. We should carry what we need and leave the rest. We've got to hurry."

That sense of urgency drove Luke to his feet, but the Wilderness spun around him and he fell back to his knees. He rose slowly when everything stopped sliding and realized that Amanda hadn't noticed his stumble. He remained still and pretended to be looking for Zeus. Amanda joined him and they both peered into the sticky woods, frustrated by the necessity to remain silent. There was no sign of the dog and the woods were quiet.

"Zeus will turn up," Amanda said. "He always does."

32

Luke, Amanda, Star, and Jack plodded along on the meandering trail that led to the largest and most foreboding swamp in the Wilderness. The vast bog was a half mile wide and stretched more than three miles to the south. The morning sun had covered them in sweat by the time they reached the edge of the steamy marshland and the very sight of the place upset Amanda. She didn't hear what Luke was saying because the thought of wading through the reptile-infested pool of black water was twisting her stomach into knots.

Luke could see that she was uneasy and preoccupied, so he held her shoulders, looked into her eyes and said, "Listen real close, Amanda. I'll lead Star to the west a piece like we talked about. I'll leave tracks for the Yankees to follow and then double back. They probably heard those gunshots back in the cut and they'll be looking for us. They'll likely take Star and leave us alone but, like I said, we'll be safe in the swamp."

He was repeating himself because she was traumatized. He looked around and said, "Why don't you wait over there in that dogwood grove? You best hide if anyone comes along. I'll be back real soon." Her eyes wandered away from his again, so he gently turned her face back to his and said, "Amanda, do you understand?"

"Yes, I understand," she said, with her eyes darting around the area. "Please hurry, Luke."

After a clumsy embrace, Luke led Star away and Amanda reluctantly walked into the dogwood grove. She found a dry log and sat with her back to the swampy hell. Resting her head on her raised knees, she considered that her quiet life in the Wilderness had been replaced with confusion, chaos, and death. The young virgin was terrified; she knew nothing of men like Matthew and visions of his bulging underwear and tormented face haunted her every time she closed her eyes. She fingered the spent derringer in her pocket as she thought of the horrible man suffering and bleeding out in a twisted pile of bloody rags.

She tried to block the whole thing from her mind and prayed that Luke would return quickly. Their romantic journey was ruined and Yankees were probably after them for killing two of their own. She and Luke were about to enter a swamp that horrified her and she had to find the courage to go with him. He was not aware of her tremendous loathing of snakes and she couldn't even tell him about her fears.

He doesn't know much about me at all, she realized.

She was sitting in a magnificent grove of dogwood trees in late bloom. Hundreds of dogwoods flourished here because most of the large trees were gone, allowing the sun to warm the delicate white flowers. The damp ground had filled the roots of the trees, along with all of the thirsty undergrowth that swelled throughout the snarled Wilderness. The ground was covered with white blossoms. As sunlight flickered through the canopy, thousands of stunning flowers looked like sticky snow in the twisted branches.

She stood and walked slowly toward the bog until water seeped through the soles of her boots. Shielding her eyes, she gazed at the soggy landscape that was filled with dead trees leaning at odd angles and various black-green blobs of vegetation. It smelled like death. Dozens of dragonflies darted above the surface of the murky water, each scurrying to deliver its own urgent message from hell. She noticed three huge vultures perched together in a dead tree and the despondency in their black eyes drained her remaining strength and will, leaving her weak-kneed and hopeless.

The patient scavengers would again enjoy the spoils of war. Soon, the birds would gorge themselves on tasty, human viscera as they had done in Chancellorsville and in Fredericksburg before that. For the third time in three years, the war would fill the bellies of the greedy birds. For now, however, the tenacious vultures patiently watched the curious human female and willed her into the swamp.

Amanda forced her eyes away from the scavengers and withdrew the derringer from her pocket. She looked at the small, deadly weapon and slowly ran her finger over her father's tiny engraved initials. *"J.M.P. ATKINSON,"* she murmured. She began to cry and said, "Father, Please! I need you. Please help me!"

Filled with sadness and a strange sense of gratitude, her thoughts drifted from her father to the horrible man who had attacked her. She didn't know why she felt dirty and ashamed and she couldn't erase stink man's stare from her mind. She looked at the derringer again and then threw the small pistol as far as she could.

Plop! The pistol splashed into a pool of inky water and disappeared. The distressed girl watched a cloud of water bugs bustle and rise in a frenzy and then her eyes settled on a blue heron standing still and alone. The heron mesmerized Amanda. Neither she nor the bird moved a muscle until the heron spread its huge wings and leaped into the air. It flew directly at her—so close that she could see the black plumes on its head, breast, and back. Amanda had studied these graceful birds and knew the ornate black plumes were visible only during the mating season, which drew her thoughts back to Luke. She shielded her eyes and watched the heron turn, effortlessly gain altitude, and disappear beyond a stand of rotting dead trees. She wished she could join the majestic bird and soar to safety, far above the miserable swamp and the inescapable war.

Then, she was attacked by a swarm of hungry mosquitoes. She swatted at them with her hat while hurrying back to her shady spot among the dogwoods. The beautiful bird had lifted her spirits and disposing of the nasty weapon eased her conscience some. She realized that the flowering dogwoods were like a string of pearls around the neck of a rotting corpse. The stunning trees were the last breath of beauty before all signs of natural splendor gave way to the sour, rotting decay of the marsh.

Dozens of white petals floated in the imperceptible breeze and she was reminded of the snow that had once blanketed her home in Hampden Sydney. She drifted back to a Christmas Eve when a rare snowstorm had transformed the city into a Nordic fairytale. She and her mother had carefully wrapped presents and Amanda ran excitedly from one house servant to another, offering satchels of candy and gifts with brightly colored bows.

We owned those people, she mused.

After living and surviving in the Wilderness and becoming close to Mr. Richard and Evaleen, the idea of owning another human being seemed absurd. *Once I return to Hampton Sydney and this horrible conflict has ended, I will never own another Negro. I know Father will agree.*

She looked up into the trees again and sighed. She could feel the weight of the inescapable swamp behind her and the threat of the ominous war bearing down from the north. The delicate girl was frightened, alone, and overwhelmed with guilt. During the previous few hours, she had abandoned her aunt and narrowly escaped being raped. She seriously wounded, or perhaps killed a Yankee soldier and managed to lose her dog, horse, and most of their supplies. She was terrified of swamps and Luke was wounded. *Maybe he's been captured!* Her tears fell again as her eyes drifted back to the beautiful white blossoms.

Truitt also saw the blossoms, but the only beauty he saw was Amanda. He and Jack watched her walk to the edge of the swamp and they were surprised when she threw the small pistol into the water. As the graceful heron circled his angel and then drifted off to the south, Truitt half-expected her to join the bird in flight. As wondrous as that would have been, he was greatly relieved when she stayed put. By the time she returned to the dogwood grove, she was no longer a girl dressed like a man. Instead, she had transformed into a beautiful angel walking upon white clouds.

When Amanda sat back down, Truitt's disturbed mind could not decide if she was real or some evil incarnation that was vomited up by his dead, liverless father. *Sure, she's real in my lens but that don't mean she's genuine close-up. In my scope she's pure and handsome, but she could be somethin' else. Maybe the old man sent a witch to trap me. What if she is a witch? What then?*

Kuruk's mother had told tales of spirits who "roam the land, haunting folks who done bad things." Truitt feared the spirit world and wondered if the spirits thought he was bad for trying to kill his father. *No, I did good by tryin' to kill the old bastard and Major Mosby told me to kill Yankees, so that can't be the thing neither.*

The Catawba woman said that spirits could change things in order to fool people. Then, they would fall off cliffs and drown in rivers. Truitt quickly became convinced that his father had summoned a witch to trick him and the old man, or the witch in the dogwood grove, would try to kill him for sure.

He grunted, removed his eye from the scope, peered at the girl, and quickly looked back through the lens again. He wiped the sweat from his eyes, pulled a tick from his neck, and repeated the process. Then, he thumbed through the semi-nude pictures in his fairytale book and imagined his angel in similar postures. *Is she an angel or a witch?* He twitched and rubbed his free hand on his pant leg. *No, she's real, all right, but I got to touch her to know for sure.*

Breathing deeply and drooling on himself, he lowered his telescope and wiped his mouth on his sleeve. Then, without realizing it, he assumed his crab-like posture as he and Jack moved silently toward Amanda.

33

Truitt wasn't making any more noise than Jack, who was reluctantly floating next to him. The drooling killer crept close enough to hear the angel sobbing and then stopped to examine her, the same way he had scrutinized Matthew.

Jack screamed, "NO!"

He was startled when the killer snapped his head in his direction as if he heard him, and then Truitt disappeared.

I'm getting good at this, Jack thought as he watched Luke slap Star's rump. The startled horse ran farther west leaving huge tracks in the soft ground and breaking small saplings and swamp reeds as he plowed along. Luke carefully covered his own tracks as he and Jack returned to Amanda and they were surprised to see that she was lying on the ground like a baby fawn. Alarm bells went off in Luke's head and he ran to her for the second time that day, risking exposure to whomever might be watching or waiting. His useless arm was on fire and he needed Amanda as much as she needed him.

Maybe more, he thought as he shook her gently.

Her smile shot through him like a lightning bolt and his relief instantly blossomed into confidence and self-reliance. They looked at each other in silence and then embraced hungrily—frozen in time and history.

When they separated, Amanda felt strong enough to enter the swamp. They hopped from hard clay mounds to not-so-solid hummocks until they were forced to step into the watery muck, which threatened to cover the tops of Amanda's boots. They held hands at first but quickly separated to maintain balance as they moved carefully over slippery logs and through scum covered water.

Dozens of startled frogs and turtles jumped into the black water ahead of them and Amanda was haunted by thoughts of snakes and leeches. Her aunt had told her about the leeches she used in the apothecary shop to remove bad blood from patients. That had given the young girl more than one nightmare. She thanked heaven for her uncle's sturdy trousers and for the knee-high riding boots her father had sent last Christmas.

She pictured her poor aunt trying to slosh through the swamp in her black dress. *The snakes would probably fear her.* She immediately scolded herself for having such thoughts. She missed Permelia terribly and prayed for her well-being. As she lumbered along, she talked aloud to her dear aunt telling her that she and Luke were fine and safely on their way to Richmond. She repeated her promise to return and prayed that her father had, once again, misjudged the Union Army.

Meanwhile, Luke was determined to hide their tracks and they plowed through the sticky water, even when dry land was available. Slimy submerged branches looked like snakes to Amanda, but she took shallow breaths and managed to control her fear of the slithering reptiles.

While studying Amanda, Truitt heard Luke approaching and melted back into the woods where he curled into a small ball and cursed his recklessness. He hadn't been seen but realized how vulnerable he had been and felt a deep shudder of fear. He had become reckless and let his guard down for the first time. That was his father's fault because only his old man could torment him enough to become careless. *Then again, maybe the witch tricked me. 'Till I kill the ogre for good, I can't trust nobody—not even the angel, 'cause she could be good or bad.*

His trepidation and self-doubt elevated his blood pressure and the pounding in his ears increased his smoldering headache. *No, the angel in my glass can't be evil like the old man, so why am I afraid of her?* The twitch in his eye returned and he pounded the side of his head as if doing so would calm his twitching eye and remove his headache. *Maybe she's evil up close but looks like an angel in my lens*, he reiterated as he squinted to keep sweat from fogging his view. *I got to be more careful. I know she's real and I'll prove it soon. Meantime, ain't nobody gonna hurt her–not my old man for sure.*

34

Henry Mueller was tracking the stink boys from a safe distance until he heard gunfire from the railroad cut, which drew him toward the sound. He discovered the bodies of Bowler and Hoyle and cautiously remained within the cover of the woods to watch and listen. When he examined the bodies, he was revolted by the mutilation of Bowler and the faceless body of Hoyle. The tired soldier was forced to leave his comrades unburied so that he could pursue the gruesome killer or killers.

Tracking the teens was not a challenge for the master scout, who followed Luke's trail of blood to the edge of the swamp like a road map. He quickly found Star and led the horse around the southern side of the bog, listening to every sound that came from his targets.

He was unaware that he too was being followed.

Mid-morning on the 5th of May, Luke and Amanda heard crackling gunfire that echoed through the woods. They glanced at each other and then picked up their pace, moving farther into the sour swamp. Jack realized that the gunfire had come from a brief cavalry skirmish near Parker's Store, which was actually the very first fighting of The Battle of the Wilderness.

The war is right on schedule, he thought.

The teens moved as fast as they could, sucking their boots from the mud and making sluggish but deliberate progress. Hundreds of insects swarmed in the stagnant air and fastened themselves to their exposed skin. Amanda hitched Benjamin's shirt collar up and pulled her hat down until she could barely see. That frustrated some of the hungry pests but it also upset her equilibrium; she reverted to her dance training and extended her arms to maintain balance. In spite of that, she stepped on a sunken log, which was hidden by a surface membrane of thick yellow pollen, stumbled, and almost fell into the oozing water. She paused, steadied herself, and loosened her collar because of the stifling heat and humidity.

Unaware of Amanda's problems, Luke had moved farther away from the exhausted girl, whose feet were settling into the green-black muck. Her strong will would not allow her to call for help as she struggled to pull her boots from the greedy ooze, releasing grunts of frustration. One particularly greasy and vindictive log, which had waited patiently for her approach, slid under her boot at just the right moment and spun in place. Amanda yelped and fell butt-first into the jelly water.

Splash!

Imaginary snakes and leeches slithered over her arms and neck and into her shirt and britches. She screamed and thrashed in the lumpy sludge. Luke hurried back to her, pulled her to her feet, and cupped his hand over her mouth. She slapped hysterically at her neck and rubbed her face to remove dozens of invisible leeches. When the wide-eyed girl stopped grunting into Luke's slippery hand, their muddy faces were inches apart. He removed his hand and she surprised him with a string of words that his mother would have considered "indelicate" for sure.

Luke burst out laughing and quickly covered *his* mouth, which made Amanda laugh. The overwhelmed teens carried on like two giggling children in church, laughing into their wet, muddy hands and making odd farting sounds that made them hysterical. In spite of being frightened, wounded, and desperate, the young lovers made faces at each other and laughed aloud.

Once they calmed down, they held one another in the middle of the swamp, in the middle of the afternoon, in the middle of the Civil War.

35

It was well past noon. The pair ended their embrace, reluctantly pulled away from one another, and giggled again when their clothes stuck together. Then, distant cannon fire shocked them back to reality.

That's the outbreak of fighting at Saunders Field, Jack realized. He assumed that his history books were allowing him to dream it as such. *Now The Battle of the Wilderness has indeed begun.*

The early-afternoon cannon fire startled the refugees and fear propelled them forward. They slashed through the quagmire at an exhausting pace, stopping briefly to rest and drink clean water. Their mud-covered faces protected them from some of the voracious mosquitoes, although the insects swarmed around them and continued to dart into their eyes and open mouths. As the sounds of war erupted behind them, they waded heavily through the cold dark water until they came to a small dry island. The sanctuary was forty yards from the southern border of the enormous swamp and it looked like heaven to Amanda.

Henry, who had been circling the swamp, stopped abruptly when Amanda fell into the water and screamed. *A female for sure and a young one at that,* he thought, trying to make sense of it. Then, he heard laughter. A young man and a woman laughing! *How can that be? The bodies in the railroad cut weren't brutally murdered and maimed by giggling youngsters.* Henry felt an adrenalin rush when he realized he was tracking the wrong targets. He quickly scanned the thickets behind him and then he too heard the deep rumble of cannon fire from Saunders Field. The scout looked with dread to the north and thought, *the fools are gonna fight in the Wilderness—what a mistake.*

He had made promises to both General Meade and his family and, although the battle was coming sooner than he had predicted, he still had a job to do. Assuming that his stalker was watching him, he casually led the horses farther south, pretending to be unaware of the threat. Since Truitt was too skilled to be spotted, the game continued until Henry reached the south-eastern end of the swamp. Towering piles of slippery, rotting debris and logs had been deposited there by violent storms; the only exit was a narrow point where the swamp emptied into a stream. The blameless pair would come to him soon, so he settled down to see if a real threat would present itself.

Luke and Amanda heaved themselves up on dry, hard ground and lay in silence for several minutes. The island was nothing more than a high clay knoll that guarded the eastern end of the swamp, but they were dry and safe. Debris was piled high to their left and right although their island was higher still and they were surrounded on all sides by slow-moving, black water. Scrub pines and brush covered the top of the island and would keep them hidden from anyone on shore. Dozens of flies were buzzing around the putrid remains of a small animal that lay with its head and shoulders in the water and its rotting hindquarters exposed. Luke threw the decomposing possum as far as he could and it splashed into the water leaving its horrendous odor behind.

"This stink will hide our scent," Luke said while Amanda wondered what had killed the possum. The débutante was tired, filthy, and slightly nauseous. Her uncle's woolen clothing was wet and itchy and she imagined that leeches were still attached to her back. She was grateful to be out of the water and fought to control her boiling stomach while Luke began to whisper.

"We'll stay here tonight 'cause no one can see us," Luke said softly. "Will you be all right?"

"I'll be fine as long as we're together," Amanda said, realizing that Luke was right. They couldn't be seen from the shore. Even if they were spotted, no one would traverse the deep water to reach them. It would be nearly impossible for anyone to climb the slippery walls of debris that surrounded them and the island provided protection from any would-be sniper. Besides, Luke still had the LaMat twin-barrel revolver. The hefty, nine-shot weapon had a second, sixteen-gauge buckshot barrel making it a formidable weapon.

No one can possibly smell us—of that I'm certain, she thought.

"If there are any soldiers nearby, they might wait around till morning but I don't think so," Luke whispered. "I think they'll leave before nightfall to join the war."

After a short rest, they used the remaining daylight to clean up and Amanda carefully changed Luke's dressing with damp but clean wrappings. He hadn't complained, although the gash in his arm was discolored and angry. They ate more dried meat and drank the last of their precious water as nightfall awakened the living swamp and the sounds of the crickets and frogs became deafening. Smoke from the burning Wilderness drifted in the air as they watched fireflies blinking in the hazy darkness. Amanda listened to Luke's rhythmic voice ramble on about the plan for the next day.

"I love your voice," she said.

Luke smiled and Amanda drifted off to sleep, thinking of Permelia.

36

> *Before you are the fields of the Higgerson Farm,*
> *one of only a few clearings in the Wilderness Battlefield.*
> *On the afternoon of May 5th, Union troops swept across*
> *this open space bound for bewildering combat in the*
> *thickets to the north and west. When Federals tramped*
> *her fence and garden, Permelia Higgerson emerged*
> *from her house, berated the Yankees and predicted their*
> *quick repulse. 'We didn't pay much attention to what she*
> *said,' admitted a Pennsylvania man, 'but the result*
> *proved that she was right.' After successions of bloody*
> *clashes in the distant woods, the Federals retreated*
> *back across this field. Mrs.Higgerson taunted them as*
> *they passed.[11]*
>
> ~*National Parks Exhibit*

Permelia swatted Yankee soldiers with her broom in a feeble attempt to slow the progress of the inexorable army. Jack watched as she cursed and scolded the resolute young soldiers from Pennsylvania, who sidestepped the crazy woman. The soldiers trampled her fence and garden as they marched on, ignoring Permelia's feeble resistance. When they were gone, she limped back into her cabin, drank the last of her ancient brandy, and crumpled into her rocking chair. The liquor soothed her throat and warmed her belly as she listened to the battle that had erupted in a swampy area a short distance from her home. She heard crackling gunfire and the odor of spent powder drifted in the thick air.

When the soldiers retreated, she gathered enough strength to confront the same men as they ran through her farm in withdrawal, just as she had prophesied. The brandy and hot sun caused Permelia's head to spin as she waved her broom wildly, still chastising the wide-eyed Pennsylvanians, one of whom lay severely wounded near her garden. One too many swats of the broom brought her to her knees, but she managed to crawl back into her cabin, giggling like a madwoman.

Exhausted, she lay on the floor, prayed for Amanda and Luke, and lost track of time. Eventually, tremendous thirst forced her to rise unsteadily and shuffle outside toward the well. When she felt the sun on her translucent face, she raised her chin to the sky while brilliant sunlight exploded into elaborate patterns and colors. She waited until her lightheadedness subsided, limped past her demolished garden, and moved one baby step at a time toward the well.

Water dribbled down her chin and soaked the front of her black dress as she struggled to drink from the bucket, which was left half-full by the Yankees. As the sun set in the Wilderness, she coughed up blood with a ferocity that exhausted her and left the sickly woman teetering with her head and shoulders hanging over the walls of the well. She remained balanced there for some time and then pulled herself from the well and crawled downhill toward her special place behind the house. Her progress was slowed by harsh coughing episodes and the delicate skin on her face and hands bled unmercifully.

After what seemed like hours, she reached the small clearing, which she and Benjamin had once cherished, and collapsed next to Benjamin's grave. She stared through tearless eyes into the warm darkening sky until a feeling of pleasant warmth replaced the bottomless pain within her body.

Permelia died thinking of the man she loved and Jack drifted away.

37

Jack was now face-to-face with his long-lost relative, Henry Mueller. Although the voices and laughter in the swamp had confused Henry, he would not be deceived. He would kill his enemy without hesitation, but he had to be sure who the enemy was and there could be no doubt about it. He hoped that the feigned attention he was giving to the youngsters in the swamp would cause the real threat to reveal itself, although sensible ideas like that were often annulled by nightfall in the Wilderness. Henry found cover behind a large dead oak tree that marked the swamp's exit point. When darkness fell, he felt great fatigue and greater self-doubt. *Should I report back to General Meade now or track these killers?* He was exhausted and decided to stay put, ahead of the war for now.

Sounds like the general is coming to me anyhow, he thought.

Meade had summoned him immediately following another one of the scout's week-long missions and three additional days of tracking Hoyle and Bowler with little sleep had drained him. Henry allowed himself to relax for the first time in more than a week, although his mind remained filled with the dread of the long war.

Too much life had been wasted and too many men were left with twisted bodies and minds. Many such scars were deep enough to damage the human spirit, yet men continued to slash and maim their brothers and kin. Thousands of teenagers threw themselves on the sword without questioning authority. Discovering the mutilated remains of his fellow scouts was the stuff of Henry's nightmares. Seeing such gruesome remains gave him reason to pray that his son would never go to war. He hoped that God had shown him enough war to spare his sons and grandsons from that gruesome business.

The dog-tired soldier wanted to carry his infant son through the fresh air of his apple orchard rather than tote his rifle through the broiling wastelands of Virginia. He yearned to place his son on his chest and feel his heartbeat instead of dreaming of heaven while knee-deep in hell.

Unfortunately, for Henry, the melodic swamp welcomed such dreamers and lulled its victims into deep, inviting sleep.

Like all good terrorists, however, Truitt had endless patience, especially when highly motivated. He was determined to protect his angel from his father—but how? *How could the ogre be stalking her after bein' stabbed, burned, shot, and having both eyes plucked out!* He had left his father in the railroad cut, yet here he was relentlessly following his goddess. He loved the angel in his scope and he had to stop the devil, so he inched toward Henry in the moonless night like a hungry praying mantis. He blended into a stand of laurels and listened carefully. *Why is the old man breathin' so quiet like 'stead of snorin' and snortin' like usual?*

Truitt was conflicted and his eye began its maddening twitch, but then Henry stirred and began to snore. The young killer quickly silenced the devil by sliding his razor-sharp blade into Henry's larynx and holding his hand over his victim's mouth. He quickly slashed his jugular veins and carotid arteries with one deep, powerful stroke. Little sound came from the soldier's brief thrashing and death came quickly.

Truitt thought he might have finally killed the evil spirit and he knew his angel would be pleased. He fit a noose into his father's neck wound and used Star to quietly hoist the corpse to a standing position against the oak tree.

My angel will be mighty pleased, he thought.

To further impress the girl he loved and make Major Mosby proud, he removed Henry's boots, put them in Star's packs, and cut his father's heart out.

38

Amanda dreamed that the red tongue of a huge snake broke the ground beneath her. She couldn't move and was forced to watch the snake rise from the earth as if being released from hell. Horrified, but unable to scream, she could do nothing but watch the behemoth emerge from the ground between her legs. The snake forced her to hug its three-foot girth like a child rides on the back of an enormous horse.

Jack went along as the snake slid into the murky water where darkness grew until nothing could be seen in the cold black void except a pinhole of light. As the circle of light grew, Amanda realized she was inside Permelia's well looking up at her aunt's face, which was dangling over the edge.

Blood was dripping from Permelia's mouth as she smiled down at Amanda and cheerfully said, "Hello, dear. Dinner is ready and Benjamin will help you out of the well if you like. You'll have to eat alone tonight because Benjamin and I have a lot to do."

That made perfect sense to Amanda. Before she could speak, however, the snake turned and plunged back down into the darkness. She shivered and held on with all her strength as a gigantic image of Matthew's repugnant face appeared, glowing and shimmering in the darkness like a hideous Wizard of Oz. The Viper slithered into Matthew's open mouth and the great reptile was pleased when the black water turned red. The demon twisted and rolled through the crimson liquid and climbed rapidly through the thinning scarlet water, breaking the surface like a German U-boat.

It landed on the island with a wet thump and Amanda and Jack were thrown from the hissing serpent. Jack was left face-to-face with Amanda and watched her REM sleep eyelids jump and flutter. Then, he began to rise and drift toward the shore where a dead oak stood like an enormous exclamation point in the thin, swirling fog. A hooded sentinel stood guard under the tree, but the soldier's bootless feet were dangling above the ground.

The human shape in the fog seemed to glow as Jack floated nearer. The new moon could illuminate little else and the surrounding colorless trees waited for something to stir their leaves. As he drifted closer, the rant of agitated flies began to echo in his head and the pervasive smell of death filled the stagnant air. He wanted to turn away but glided closer to the phantasm like a cloud of smoke on an infinitesimal breeze.

The gruesome figure was hanging by the neck from a towering dead oak tree and a threadbare blanket was draped over its head. Compelled by something beyond curiosity or reason, Jack raised the blanket with a single finger and gazed at the distorted face that lived only in the sticky sweat of nightmares.

Hungry flies crawled over the dead man's extended purple tongue and scurried in and out of his wide-open mouth. A noose had been inserted into a gaping neck wound, which tilted the head of the corpse unnaturally and raised its protruding eyes to the heavens. More flies filled the gash in his neck forming a moving black ribbon and his nearly decapitated body dangled beneath him as if on a thread.

I'm living...or dreaming my nightmare! Poor Henry has been waiting for me, Jack realized.

He placed his hand on the swollen cheek of the cadaver. The flies swarmed and then it's dead, upturned eyes shifted to meet Jack's stare! A smiled formed on Henry's hideous face and the animated horror bridged the gap between worlds. The pilot was catapulted back to the hospital like a bullet from a gun. He heaved for air as if drowning and convulsed while the electronic monitors in his hospital room surged.

39

Jack's coma had nearly shattered and he felt the pain and anguish of a world without dreams. In spite of that, he fought to escape his fantasy. He wanted to return to Jill, but could not emerge from his own oblivion. By the time the night nurse reached him, his stoic, comatose posture had returned.

Once again void of pain and emotion, he rejoined Amanda, who was lying on the island next to the great snake. The purple-black belly of the serpent was pulsating and expanding in the early dawn light, looking more like a pregnant eggplant than a reptile. Then, the belly of the eggplant tore open and hundreds of squirming newborns poured out like intestines pour from a gutted whale. The slimy infants slithered over and around each other until they enveloped the horrified girl.

Her scream woke Luke, who found a harmless black snake sliding over Amanda's arm. He threw the three-foot reptile into the water, quickly covered Amanda's mouth, and held her tightly. When she focused on him, he placed a finger on his lips and pleaded for her silence. The predawn light of May 6th had arrived and they were enveloped in fog.

Amanda hugged Luke and whispered, "I had a terrible nightmare."

"Rest easy now," he said. "Someone might have heard you, so I'm going up to take a look."

Luke crawled up the towering mound and peered into the gloom. Anyone on shore would have heard Amanda scream, but the morning fog had embraced the shoreline and it was stone silent. Amanda relieved herself and joined Luke on the rounded top of the island, which was above the blanket of fog. On the pregnant belly of the swamp, she relayed her dream in whispers as they watched the morning sun burn into the day.

"Look there," Luke whispered. "I can see a horse and it looks like Star!"

Amanda squinted, smiled, and nodded in agreement. "Maybe he heard us and followed," she said.

Luke thought that was possible, but if Star could find them the Yankees could as well. They continued to peer through the diminishing mist until the form of a soldier emerged. The man was facing them and standing at attention. Exasperated, they quietly backed down the steep slope.

Did I really think we could hide from real soldiers? Luke thought.

"I suppose they found Star and now they're waiting for us," Amanda whispered.

"We can't get caught," Luke murmured, ignoring her. "We killed two of them and they know we're here. We could go back, but the sun is rising and they might see us. We better stay put for now."

"I agree. We can't go back into the swamp," she said, thinking she would rather die than return to that version of hell.

"Maybe they'll give up soon and leave us alone because the war is coming."

Luke crawled back up the slope and studied the soldier. Something was wrong—the sentry hadn't moved. "No soldier would stand at attention like that, just staring into a foggy swamp," he whispered.

As the day brightened, they could see that the man's head was covered with a blanket and his feet were not touching the ground. "Looks like that man is dead," Luke whispered. He decided to throw something in the direction of the inert soldier to see if he would react and broke dried clay from the surface of a fist-sized rock. His throwing arm was infected and burning, but he had to ensure that the soldier was dead and decided to risk opening his wound to find out.

"Listen," Luke said. "I'm gonna throw this rock at him to see if he moves any. Watch him and let me know."

"How will you throw that rock with your injured arm?"

"Don't worry about that," he said.

Luke's wound opened when he heaved the rock that bounced off some debris and splattered on the wet ground near the dangling man.

"He didn't move at all!" Amanda said. She looked back at Luke and continued, "They left that man there to scare us."

Luke didn't answer because his teeth were clenched in pain.

"Why would they do that?" she whispered as she reapplied the tourniquet.

"Don't know, but if they left a dead man there I reckon they're gone and we should get out of here before they come back."

They gathered what little they had, quietly eased into the waist-high water, and lost sight of the hanging soldier as they waded toward the congested exit. As the watery gap tightened, they climbed over slippery branches and logs and made their way down the huge pile of debris to soggy but solid ground. They carefully walked over oily rubble and sidestepped the gruesome corpse, expecting the dead man to spring to life. Amanda kept her eyes lowered and stroked Star's head while Luke looked around for other soldiers.

None of this makes any sense, Luke thought. *Why would the Yankees go through all this trouble to scare us and then leave Star behind with full packs? Was it a trap? Were they being watched?*

Amanda looked around the clearing. She settled on the mutilated face of the cadaver for a long dreadful moment but saw only Matthew Bowler's haunting stare while her stomach boiled.

As a deep rumble of cannon fire echoed through the swamp, Amanda, Luke, Star, and Jack turned south and ambled farther into their living nightmare.

40

Later that day, as the miserable teens plodded along, General Burnside was enjoying the last of his leisurely champagne brunch near the Higgerson Farm. He and his massive Federal 9th Corps were seriously late but finally ready to engage the Confederates and support those who were already fighting and dying in the thickets ahead.

The Confederates had been anticipating the arrival of Burnside's troops:

> *...the brigadier feared that his left flank would be decimated by the Federal 9th Corps. Riding to the far left of his line, he found Oates's force ensconced behind a pile of logs. Nearby was a small Florida Brigade under Brigadier General Edward A. Perry. The Floridians, however, had neglected to conform with Oates. Instead, they had formed at right angles to the Alabamians. Their line projected a hundred yards past Oates's defenses toward Burnside.*[12]

Privates Simon Hayes and George "Rooster" Lipscomb were unfortunate enough to be fighting with that Florida Brigade. Instead of being parallel to their comrades from Alabama, they were at a ninety-degree angle to the main line. They stood at the northern tip of the fatal finger that stretched directly toward Burnside's vast advancing army. The Floridians were entirely unprotected and Simon and Rooster were first in line. The boys had heard that they would be facing Burnside and oozed bravado, directing their entire mental wrath toward "the bushy old bastard."

Rooster said, "When I see him runnin' I'm gonna hog-tie that old son of a bitch."

Not to be outdone, Simon said, "Shit-fire, I'm gonna shoot Burnside 'tween the eyes, sure enough."

They weren't "worried none, neither" partially because for the first time in months they were not barefoot. They had walked miles with nothing but rags and strips of leather tied to their feet but not anymore. Boots and everything of value had been taken from dead Yankees and what a glorious feeling it was to wear sturdy Union boots after being barefoot for so long. The boots they found were "made special for the left or right foot—hot damn." When Simon and Rooster found their new boots, they also discovered a full bottle of Irish whiskey, which was why they were invincible by noon. They were going to advance toward Burnside's army, by God, and "pity any Yankee who tried to stop'em."

When Rooster and Simon approached the Federal Army, they may not have been the only inebriated soldiers in the fray, but they were the first two drunkards to mount a charge. Without being ordered to do so, however, they were also the *only* men who attacked.

Jack went with Simon and Rooster on their mighty two-man assault and looked into their cow-stupid faces when they realized they were alone, facing hundreds of Yankee rifles. The boys gawked at Burnside's men, glanced at each other and then raised their rifles and hollered blood-curdling Rebel yells. Yankee bullets riddled their bodies as they quivered, shook, and fell. Silence filled the clearing while Burnside's men waited for more Rebels to charge. When none came, they shrugged their shoulders and laughed among themselves.

Jack was particularly interested in Rooster because he looked so familiar. He had seen him before, but how could that be? And why was he able to question the logic of his dream? Those thoughts filled Jack's head while lead filled Rooster's head. As the pair did the "funky chicken," Jack remembered where he had seen Rooster. He looked exactly like a local man named Darryl, who had worked on Ralph Burnside's basement! *Rooster is a dead ringer for Darryl—so to speak.*

He had seen Darryl working at the Burnside house on several occasions. He received a few uneasy waves from Darryl as the handyman walked back and forth from his truck. He even shared a couple of short conversations with the nervous man. Darryl was the "stupid hick" whom Ralph hired to do electrical wiring in his basement.

Darryl and Rooster could have been twins. "Burpee seeds" was printed on the threadbare ball cap perched on the back of Darryl's impossibly small head; Rooster's beat-up Rebel cap was balanced on his puny skull the same way. Both Darryl and Rooster looked as though they had soaked their faces in tobacco juice on a regular basis. *Spit and chew, spit and chew. Rooster and Darryl are definitely related.*

Meanwhile, the foolish drunkard's last thoughts were not of their sweethearts or mothers. They didn't think of their homes or their God. Instead, they imagined General Ambrose E. Burnside sitting tall in his saddle—laughing heartily at their folly.

41

Exactly 150 years later, the ghosts of Rooster Lipscomb and Simon Hayes, who had been haunting the Burnside's house, finally won their war. After months of practice, their spirits managed to use every ounce of their collective supernatural power to trap one of Charlotte's guinea hens in the basement microwave. Then, they pushed the "popcorn" button. The epidermis of the unfortunate bird couldn't contain its own rapidly agitating, internal molecules and the hen's "innards" exploded, slamming the oven door open. The microwave vomited superheated poultry parts, blood, and feathers throughout the Burnside's basement.

The device erupted into sparking flames because Darryl had failed to install circuit protection. Go-kart repair was his bread-and-butter, but he also offered his skills at basic home repair. He didn't mind listening to Ralph ramble on about General Burnside, in spite of the fact that Darryl Hayes was a modern-day Rebel, complete with Confederate flag mud flaps on his truck.

He proudly informed Ralph, "My own great-great-grand pappy was a brave Civil War fightin' man from Florida. Grandpa fought and died right here in the Wilderness."

Jack realized that Darryl and his great-great-grandfather had identical green-tooth grins, which were truly inspiring. "This is my brother Darryl and this is my other brother Darryl."

Darryl had wired Ralph's basement "like a hog reading a wristwatch" and overlooked details such as circuit protection from time to time. As he worked, he felt little chills that tightened his "tobacco juice scalp" and forced him to quicken his pace. The cold, skin-crawling puffs of breath on his neck were exactly what Charlotte had experienced, although she giggled after each ticklish episode. Darryl reacted by slapping the back of his neck and glancing over his shoulder repeatedly.

The jumpy man became increasingly nervous as the job progressed. By the time he attempted to install the last ground fault relay and circuit breaker, he was frightened, nervous and downright scared. In his haste, he wired the final outlet directly, thus bypassing all circuit protection. At that point, he was so terrified that he ran from the basement, spewing profanity and looking over his shoulder with real fear in his eyes. He left several tools behind rather than "go back down into that damn place." Ralph quickly claimed Darryl's tools, just as he had claimed golf balls and cold bottles of beer, which were not his.

Darryl scribbled the bill while sitting in the sanctuary of his truck, hoping no electrical inspector would examine his work. *I don't give a damn anyhow. I ain't goin' back down into that basement for nobody.*

Ralph had plugged his spirit-amusing microwave into Darryl's unprotected circuit and the exploding hen caused the unit to short circuit. The electricity kept right on flowing as the microwave sparked, sputtered and burst into flames, igniting dry packaging paper. A smoke alarm, together with the master-repeating unit on the main floor, sent ear-splitting warnings throughout the house.

Barefoot and terrified, Ralph responded by charging down into the smoke-filled basement where hundreds of floating feathers confused the frightened man. Several cardboard boxes had welcomed flying cinders and jumped into flame. By the time Ralph reached the bottom step, several fires had erupted.

Ralph fumbled with his hand-held Halon fire extinguisher, which he had installed for just such an occasion. He did his homework well and spared no expense; the volunteer fire department recommended this very type of in-home firefighting equipment, particularly for new construction. Hundreds of gallons of glue, caulking, and paint are used to hold new houses together. The oil and alcohol-based materials, together with gas furnaces and water heaters, can transform new dream homes into bombs that can actually explode.

Burnside was well-prepared because he had studied the instructions on his new extinguisher that read "Direct Stream at Top of Flames." Holding the impressive fire extinguisher empowered him and, since he knew better than the manufacturer, he planned to aim at the base of the flames instead. He turned toward the roaring fire, gritted his teeth, and pulled the pin on the device like a hand grenade, undaunted by the smoke and feather-filled air.

Burnside staged a mighty charge. The ghosts of Simon and Rooster knew that the smoke and floating feathers would hide the slippery blood and guts, which covered the slimy concrete floor—a gizzard here, a bloody liver there. When Ralph's bare feet met the cold blood-smeared cement, his feet flew out from under him. When his head hit the hard cement floor, his skull cracked open like a coconut and he was able to see his blood mix with Eggberta's before he died.

Meanwhile, Charlotte peered down the smoky basement stairs and had enough sense to slam the door and speed dial 911. Then, she returned to the basement door without any sense and burned her hand on the hot doorknob. The door flew open and she staggered backward while thick smoke billowed into her house. She screamed a mighty scream, stumbled through the living room, and burst through the front door coughing and gasping all the way. She couldn't believe how fast the fire was spreading and how slowly she was reacting. Driven by fear and terror, she ran to the back yard and peered into the windows of the walkout basement. She saw only smoke and flames and the basement door was tightly closed.

She shouted at the basement door, "Ralph! Ralph! Where are you, you son of a bitch! How could you let this happen? Come out! Come out right now you little peckerhead!"

No one heard her screams and babblings because Jill and Artie were at the hospital. Charlotte ran into Jill's unlocked house, still spewing uncharacteristic profanity, called Jill's name several times, and then dialed 911 from the kitchen phone. While the operator attempted to calm her, she watched helplessly in her smoke-filled muumuu as fire incinerated her husband and destroyed her haunted house.

"Ralph!" she shrieked after dropping the phone in mid-sentence. She didn't see him but she thought she did, so she ran outside again and stumbled around in circles in a desperate, although futile attempt to locate her husband. Then, she ran back into Jill's house and repeated her circling technique in the kitchen.

"Where is he? And where are the damn fire trucks?" she shouted into the phone.

When she heard no immediate response, she cried uncontrollably into one of Jill's dishtowels and then became aware of the terrific pain in her burned hand. She filled the towel with ice, wrapped her hand, and struggled to catch her slobbering breath.

As she paced around and waited, the poor woman became desperate for some form of comfort—large amounts of chocolate usually did the trick. She knew that Jill didn't keep chocolate in her house and nothing remained of her Godiva chocolate gift box because she had eaten every piece during her visit. Then, the 300-pound gorilla in her mind blocked everything except the story about a woman who insisted upon being served chocolate ice cream when there was none. Finally, the clerk asked the woman to spell chocolate with an "F". She said "there is no "F" in chocolate" and the clerk said, "That's what I've been trying to tell you, there is no Fin' chocolate!"

She became obsessed and desperately opened cupboard doors and drawers repeating, "There is no Fin' chocolate! There is no Fin' chocolate!" Then, her frantic, mascara-smeared gaze settled on Zeus, who was considering the strange woman through skeptical yellow eyes. Since there was no "Fin' chocolate," she craved physical contact and looked around for Samantha. Sam had always returned her hugs like a good therapy dog should, but the golden retriever was also at the hospital. That left only Zeus, who sat warily in the corner of the room staring at the crazed woman.

Charlotte decided that the unfriendly dog would have to do, so the puffy woman raised her smoky muumuu and approached the suspicious dog. When she lowered herself to her knees and awkwardly hugged the confused animal, she received a jolt that propelled her across the room. She slid heavily on her rear end and collided with Jill's refrigerator.

Charlotte gawked at the dog with wonder and dread and then rose slowly to her hands and knees, dazed and confused. Her hair was an electrically shocked mess and her raccoon mascara gave her the "stay away, I'm probably possessed" look. Suddenly, she knew that Zeus was truly mystical. Unlike her ghosts, however, the dog was also flesh and blood and that terrified her.

She suddenly understood everything.

Astounded, she looked at her burning house again and, as flames danced in her eyes, she realized that her ghosts were responsible for the fire; they had killed General Burnside's great-great-grandson. By doing so, they were free to move on. She also knew that Zeus had something to do with Jack's coma. The traumatized woman absently scribbled a note on Jill's kitchen message board next to the telephone. Then, she stumbled outside and staggered in circles as if trying to mimic the living dead. The fire trucks wailed and she continued her zombie routine in the back yard until a firefighter covered her with a blanket.

Zeus followed Charlotte outside and his ears perked up when he heard two Rebel yells fading into eternity. He barked, ran toward the sound, and vanished.

42

Luke led Amanda and Jack toward his farm, praying that his family was long gone, although part of him hoped that the security of his home and family had remained. The burning remnants of the battle stained the air and the sounds of war blossomed behind them as they walked toward the Stewart Farm. From within the woods, they saw that Luke's family had left home and Union Cavalry occupied the abandoned house.

They remained within the cover of the woods and continued their lonely journey. Amanda knew that Luke was disappointed and riddled with guilt, so she did her best to console him by talking continuously. As she walked and talked, she hoped her distraught boyfriend would say something or at least answer any one of her thousand questions with a simple yes or no. Luke didn't realize he wasn't saying anything, he was simply thinking and Jack understood completely. When he finished thinking, he said, "Don't worry none, I know a good place for us to settle in for the night—we'll be there soon. We'll need a couple of hours of daylight to make things right, so we've got to keep moving."

Amanda was greatly relieved when he finally said something and continued to talk nonstop about buying a wagon in Richmond and returning to the Wilderness for Permelia, and so forth and so on. Luke wasn't listening to her because he was thinking again.

"We've got to backtrack some, but we'll be safe where we're headed," he said.

And so, the one-sided, rambling conversation continued until dusk when they came upon a stone outcropping that was smothered in laurel and holly.

"Me and Adam found this place when we were young and we camped here a few times. It's more like an overhang than a cave, but the laurel and holly will hide us for now and we can light a small fire in there," he said. "We'll be safe and well-hidden, but we'll have to unload Star and let him graze. In case somebody finds him, they'll think he's a stray."

"All right. He won't wander too far," she said. "And he'll come to me in the morning when I call him."

Luke's temperature was climbing, although he was able to hide his discomfort as they unloaded Star and carried everything into the cave. They discovered that Star's packs had been rearranged, but nothing had been taken and the valuable Whitworth rifle was left alone. Amanda found a pair of sturdy army boots, which were carefully concealed within one of Star's packs. She kept that confusion to herself, although it increased her paranoia.

Who would do such a thing? Was someone trying to help them? she mused.

Amanda insisted on examining Luke's wound, which had become raw and inflamed. She dissolved a primitive form of aspirin known as willow bark powder into Luke's drinking water. Then, she patiently reapplied goldenseal to the wound and rewrapped his arm with clean bandages. Amanda was alarmed by the condition and odor of the bullet wound. She kept her concern to herself and hummed little tunes while concentrating on her father's technique and rewrapping his arm with great care.

The feverish boy fell asleep before Amanda completed the task and Jack was delighted to remain with her, thus avoiding Luke's fiery dreams. She removed his boots and covered his feet with dry woolen socks. The mysterious boots were slightly larger than Luke's old worn pair. They were relatively new and were high enough to cover his ankles. She cleaned them as best she could and set them aside knowing he would be pleased with his new footwear. She assumed that the boots had belonged to the poor man who was left hanging from the tree and that someone had removed them from the victim and concealed them among Star's provisions. She couldn't imagine why anyone would do such a thing or why Star was left behind. She thanked God, though, and prayed for the unfortunate man. The dangling corpse frightened her nearly as much as the monster who had attacked her and the two horrific images were beginning to coalesce.

As she struggled with her demons, she applied ointment to her swollen lip and gazed idly at her sleeping boyfriend's bare muscular chest and arms. Small, warm pangs of stirring pain returned when she placed her hand on Luke's chest and considered the mysteries of fornication. *Will we survive? Will Luke be the father of my children? Will I be able to please him or will he reject me because of my ignorance regarding such matters?*

Not to worry, Jack mused.

When Luke stirred, she pulled away quickly and her heart quickened. Although he didn't wake, Amanda blushed with embarrassment and quickly moved to the opposite side of the small fire where she sat and continued to stare in wonder.

As the fire crackled, Jack looked at himself for the first time expecting to see shorts, a golf shirt, and topsiders. Instead, his rear end was sticking out of a green hospital gown and he had little brown non-skid booties on his feet. He began to recall an elusive dream in which he was convulsing in a hospital bed during a maddening effort to return to Jill. As bits and pieces of reality returned to him, so did physical pain until Amanda swept him out of the cave to fill the canteens.

Truitt's heart skipped when he saw his angel emerge from the cave. He followed her through his scope and spotted his father again.

43

Truitt studied his father and another man who was "maybe real and maybe not." Jack realized that they were scouts patrolling well ahead of the Southern army. They had watched the teens unload Star and noticed the Whitworth rifle.

"Let's watch'em and see what else they got," said Truitt's father.

They were curious about the short man because "he just don't look right." Amanda could dress like a man but her gait was "just plain wrong." That confusion had caused the two Confederates, who lay side by side, to hesitate as the strange little man by the stream went about his business.

"We got to make our move soon so as to get back to our lines before dark," Truitt's father said. "When he goes back into the cave, we'll surprise'em. We'll take the rifle and the horse too. A horse will fetch a good price from an officer I know."

"Then, we'll tie'em up but loose so they can get free, right?" said the other man.

"Ain't no reason to hurt'em. Besides, they won't follow us 'cause we'll scare'em good."

The scouts were lying on their stomachs watching Truitt's angel return to the cave with full canteens. Daylight was nearly gone and Truitt's keen eyes welcomed the magical hunting hour. Scrubbed clean with no scent, he approached the men in complete silence, blending with his surroundings like an olfactory chameleon. Even if they heard him and turned to look in his direction, he would be invisible.

Sort of like me, Jack thought as he floated along with the killer, thinking of ways to escape.

Truitt planned to kill both men "in case the devil's friend is real." The boy was almost naked and carrying a small razor-sharp ax that Kuruk had given him as well as his huge Bowie knife. When he split the back of his father's skull with the ax, the other horrified man gasped and tried to scramble away. Truitt was on him like a cat and quickly shoved the nine-inch blade into the man's chest while covering his mouth "so his noise won't scare my angel none."

When the man stopped shuddering and died, Truitt studied him carefully and decided, *he's real, all right, and his dyin' is the old man's fault.* The young killer looked into the gloomy forest, then up at the sky, and felt the need to be close to his latest victim. His eye began to twitch and he struck the side of his head several times while looking past the dead man at the crumpled body of his father. The lethal ax remained buried in the back of his father's head, but his face was turned toward Truitt and the ogre began to speak. He lay down behind the body of his second kill and buried his face in the nape of the dead man's neck. He spooned with the corpse while rocking back and forth and listened to the horrifying voice of his father, who would not die.

44

In spite of the dark, smoky haze, Truitt could see well enough to sever his father's head with the deadly ax. *I reckon I got to shut you up good*, he thought as he hacked away. He picked the head up by its long hair and carried it downhill to softer ground where he dug a hole in the soggy earth. His father's freshly severed head continued to threaten him with eternal damnation while Truitt scooped dirt from the hole and tried to ignore the ogre's repartee.

"You can't hide from me you little shit! Your angel is on *my* side. If I don't get you, she will for sure. You ain't got no chance 'cause you can't hide from spirits—you'll see."

Jack, who had a headache of his own, watched as Truitt tossed his father's garrulous head into the hole. He couldn't seem to leave the grisly scene and his pain was returning. The ogre continued to talk to his psychotic son while Truitt filled the hole with soggy dirt and stamped it down with his bare feet. *I should've done it right from the start, but I killed him this time for sure.* The young lunatic was not really sure, however, because the muffled voice didn't stop—at least not entirely.

Truitt cleaned himself meticulously, hoping to wash away the devil's residue, but the voice continued and he could neither sleep nor eat. Anguish overcame his sense of time and his sharp headache returned, elevating his appetite for brutality. Later that night, without realizing it, the clean, drooling, nearly naked boy found himself in the teens' cave. He was silently squatting next to Amanda and his heart was pounding in his ears. The sleeping girl glowed when he gently placed a finger on her forehead and he almost cried out from the searing pain that passed through him like a sizzling-hot knife.

The young lunatic was light-headed, exhilarated, deeply aroused, and perspiring heavily as he backed out of the cave and melted into the night.

45

Luke was disoriented when he woke on the morning of May 7th. He had dreamed that someone was in the cave with them during the night and that he was too delirious to respond to the threat. He rose slowly and discovered that Amanda had already repacked everything and left biscuits and water for him, as well as a new pair of boots. His fever had lessened during the night, but he was weak and his body ached. He assumed that Amanda would tell him about the new boots as he laced them up and walked unsteadily out of the cave.

The teens were not aware that their temporary sanctuary lay between the paths of the two great armies. Soon, the refugees would be sandwiched between the Union Army to the east and the Confederates to the west. Two days of fighting in the Wilderness had snuffed out thousands of lives and a few short miles now separated the remaining 155,000 soldiers, who were about to move south toward Spotsylvania Courthouse.

The blue army would use the convenience of Brock Road and the chief of the Confederate Army's Artillery, General Pendleton, would be ordered to construct a shortcut directly through the thick woods to the west for General Lee. Both armies would depend upon scouts, pickets and skirmishers for vital information and those men would traverse the neutral zone between the two forces as they moved south. General Lee would quickly and efficiently fight his way through the forest. The hot-headed General Meade would feud with General Sheridan and the Union command would be riddled with miscommunication, which would slow their progress.

Amanda greeted Luke with a hug and he said, "We have to keep moving."

They could not ignore the muffled sounds of the armies that seemed to fill the woods in all directions.

"How are you feeling?" Amanda said hopefully.

"I'm alright," he lied. "We have to hurry."

Although they were distraught and frightened, their only thought was to continue to Richmond as they were told. Their soggy, mud encrusted clothes had not dried in the humid air, which added to their discomfort as random sounds of war and the smell of burning woods continued to blossom around them. After two hours, Luke began to stagger and sweat heavily.

Amanda said, "We have to stop and rest."

They found a stream, drank fresh water, and cleaned themselves as best they could. Amanda fashioned a burlap sling for Luke that rendered his right arm useless and would prevent any further "rock-throwing and such." After another hour of walking, Luke could no longer continue on foot and was forced to ride on Star. Amanda, who was now in charge of the exodus, led them with the help of her father's compass.

She was exhausted and terrified. Each random gunshot that echoed through the woods increased her sense of urgency as the smell of smoke worsened. She pictured Matthew's repugnant face blowing dead smoke through the trees overhead. As they rode the wave of the Wilderness battle, she became convinced that tiny bits of burned human remains were floating within the smoke.

She's right of course, Jack reflected.

The more she thought about that, the more horrified she became. As they left the gnarled Wilderness and entered a forest of larger trees, everything began to upset her. The unfamiliar towering pines and hardwoods made her feel small and she envisioned tiny specks of charred human remains floating within drops of dew on the leaves overhead. Then, she imagined drops of dew the size of jelly jars with the tiny faces of burned soldiers floating within them like the snowflakes in her French snow globe.

Instead of looking up into the haunting trees, she kept her eyes lowered and imagined that the ashen human remains were being crushed underfoot. The distressed teenager hummed to herself, concentrated on placing one foot in front of the other, and fought claustrophobia. Exhaustion, hunger, a fervid imagination, and ingesting unfamiliar water and berries became the recipe for mild hallucinations. Large trees became personified and the images she saw terrified her.

I can't do this. She felt dizzy, tripped on a snake, which was nothing more than a root, and admitted defeat while lying face up on the canopy floor, sobbing about...well, everything. *I can't lead us to Richmond alone. I'm lost and I don't know where I'm going. I just can't do this.*

She considered surrendering to the Southern army but how? *How can we approach any army without being shot?* Her father and her aunt had told her to avoid both armies and Permelia sternly warned her about the behavior of men at war. *Are all soldiers like the one who attacked me? Is everyone crazy? If we surrender to the wrong army or evil men in the right army, we could be attacked and molested. We could be taken prisoner and executed because of the men we killed. We could be robbed or raped, or...God help us!*

After her horrifying experience in the railroad cut, approaching anyone in uniform was out of the question, especially since she would have to deal with them without Luke's help. Her tears left tracks through the grime and bits of human beings that covered her face. Overwhelmed and anxious, she became convinced that the contaminated smoke was not the only evil thing following them.

Because Amanda had enthralled Truitt and because he wanted to get as close to her as possible, he had become careless again. Amanda heard him, turned quickly and looked back into the murky woods. She saw nothing, although she knew something or someone was there. *Is it an animal or a human?* A mountain lion might stalk them, but she was convinced that it was a human predator. She shuddered thinking that it might be both human and animal and conjured up ghastly images of a hooved beast scampering through the woods in search of tasty humans.

Close enough, Jack thought again.

Amanda got to her feet and splashed water on her face. She looked around, saw a raccoon scampering between the trees, and hoped she had merely imagined the stalker. With new determination, she retrieved her father's large revolver from Star's packs, slid it into her belt, and increased her pace.

It was spring, and the newborn leaves were a delicate green. Amanda loved that shade of green, although the spectacle was muted by hazy smoke as if war could foul the season. The contaminated smoke continued to spread among the branches and lay above them like a low-hanging cloud. Suddenly, she felt Matthew's warm mucus slap against the back of her neck and jumped before realizing it was only a juicy sneeze from Star.

Amanda continued to trudge along, stopping only to rest, soak her blistered feet in stream water and tend to Luke. His wound had worsened considerably and he was dripping with sweat, so she soothed his forehead with a damp cloth and forced him to swallow more bitter-tasting white willow bark.

The concept of infectious bacteria was widely unknown in 1864. Gunshot wounds are prone to anaerobic infection, especially tetanus and gas gangrene; sloshing through knee-high stagnant water is not recommended. Luke's immune system would either win the fight or a surgeon like Amanda's father would sever the limb. Bingo! Another crippled young man, like thousands of Luke's peers. Dying was the alternative, although many amputees perished from post-op infection anyway.

Still, Jack thought. *Countless numbers of broken, hobbling men, who survived the war, would live out their days with no easy access or special parking privileges for the handicapped. Well into the following century, their altered bodies would serve as tragic reminders of the American Civil War.*

In spite of her prayers, she continued to hallucinate and Luke became increasingly despondent. She said, "Luke, I think someone is following us,"

He surprised her by mumbling, "I know—got to keep moving."

Late morning cannon and gunfire erupted behind them as Lee and Grant continued their chess game. Each Commander was probing the other and hard skirmishes erupted between the armies. The Wilderness was behind them, but they were forced to avoid open farmland and to veer away from the sounds of firefights. Amanda froze when she saw individual soldiers and then chose more rugged terrain in the opposite direction, resulting in an agonizingly slow, zigzag route. Just as Truitt assumed that everyone was his father, Amanda imagined that every soldier was the man who attacked her.

By 4:00 p.m., Luke was bumping along in a half-conscious state and could barely remain in the saddle. Amanda was becoming desperate for a place to hide for the night when they came across an open field with a wide stream running through it. The stream flowed northeast and ran into a steep ravine before disappearing into the woods. The fast moving water ran under a substantial wooden bridge that looked big enough to accommodate two wagons side-by-side. She tied Star off in the woods near the stream and helped Luke traverse 100 yards of open ground to the bridge. Like the homeless, who huddle under highway bridges, they crawled up the dry bank under the structure and lay exhausted in the damp, sandy dirt. The bridge was forty feet long, fifteen feet wide, and made of heavy timbers; Amanda could stand straight up at the water's edge. She filled their canteens with stream water and made her feverish boyfriend as comfortable as she could.

Before dark, she ran back to Star to retrieve supplies, knowing they would have to remain in the cool shade under the bridge until Luke's fever broke. As she huddled under the bridge with Luke, she heard muffled commotion and sporadic gunfire, although the loud, echoing stream muted most sounds. Luke was moaning and burning up, so she cleaned his wound again, applied more salve, and rewrapped his arm with the last clean bandages. He was despondent and Amanda was exhausted, but she felt safe at last and the loud, babbling stream brought dreamless sleep.

Jack discovered "Spindle Farm" carved into the side of the bridge. The high ground of the Spindle Farm and the neighboring Perry Farm would become known as Laurel Hill and The Battle of Spotsylvania Courthouse would begin in these fields. *My great-great-grandparents have chosen the wrong place to rest because the fighting is going to start right here in the morning*, he thought.

Amanda slept well while Luke tossed, turned, and sweated his way through the long, sticky night. Jack didn't follow Amanda into her dreams and he was happy to avoid Luke's nightmares as well.

The following morning, on the 8th of May, the teens woke to the real nightmare.

46

The stuffy morning was already humid and unseasonably warm. Disturbing noises penetrated the sounds of the stream and woke Amanda from bottomless sleep. Luke was still burning up, so she slid down to the water to clean up and refill the canteens. She splashed water on her face and peeked out from under the bridge.

What she saw made her gasp.

Union lines had formed downhill to her distant left on Brock Road and the Confederate Army smothered the high ridgeline, a mere 200 yards to her right. Impressive rows of Yankee troops were in place with banners flying and, in the opposite direction, piles of sharpened earthworks stretched as far as she could see, protecting the South from an uphill attack. They were imprisoned at the northeastern edge of a rolling field—trapped between the two great armies at Laurel Hill.

Jack knew that the South had the advantage of the high ground because the Confederate Army was not only retreating into their own territory, but they also seemed to react more quickly than the North. Brock Road had given the Union an easy route to the south. The Confederates had actually cut a road through the woods and managed to arrive at Laurel Hill and Spotsylvania Courthouse first. The South quickly and efficiently "dug in" on high ground at Laurel Hill, while the Union leaders argued among themselves and lost their advantage. After a brief skirmish with Union forces, the Rebels also occupied the nearby town of Spotsylvania Courthouse and held it throughout the battle.

Amanda scrambled back under the bridge and pressed her trembling body against Luke, who was unaware and perspiring heavily. They would be cut down if they tried to run, even if Luke could to keep up. She realized that their only option was to remain huddled together in their wooden cocoon—and pray.

"I love you," she whispered into Luke's ear, although he didn't respond.

She examined the broad, thick planks overhead and willed strength into them before curling into a small ball next to Luke, clutching her Bible, and listening to the birth of The Battle of Laurel Hill.

At 8:30, the fighting began. The noise was deafening as Union Brigade Commander Peter Lyle led the first of many unsuccessful assaults against the Confederates. Rifle fire cracked the air in one continuous barrage that sounded like a gale-force wind vibrating cedar roof shingles. Heavy cannon fire shook the ground. Amanda squeezed her eyes shut and held her feverish boyfriend tightly under a blanket. She struggled to keep him still while dirt and grit fell from the underside of the bridge, which shook but held.

Although the bridge was on the far right flank of the Union assaults, stray bullets pinged and splintered the wood and thick acrid smoke filled the air. Some Union men were able to advance as far as the bridge until they were picked off or ordered to retreat. The teens remained hidden under their blankets during each siege and remained unnoticed.

A soldier fell into the stream near the bridge and the water ran red. Another fell, then another. Shrapnel from canister rained down on the wooden planks above them; a cannonball exploded in the stream nearby. Amanda's scream was lost in the tremendous explosion while their sanctuary was peppered with sand, dirt, and water. Amanda was temporarily deafened by the blast and welcomed the loss of that sense while the ground quaked.

They remained locked together all morning and into the endless afternoon. The fighting came in waves for hours. During each lull in the battle, Amanda was tempted to simply run to the protection of the woods. She imagined riding Star home to Permelia and then admonished herself for having such thoughts. She held her Bible tightly and read it when she could. Another huge explosion rocked the bridge and she covered her ears. The cannon fire then stopped abruptly and only sporadic gunfire remained. A long silence was broken by three cannon volleys, followed by another long pause.

At that point, Amanda risked sliding down to the stream to soak a rag in cool water for Luke's forehead.

Suddenly, a crazed woman appeared from nowhere and hurled herself into the muddy sand on the opposite side of the stream.

47

A single candle illuminated Sarah Spindle's hiding place and Jack studied her wide-eyed face. Sarah had squeezed into a small compartment beneath her staircase; she quickly removed a one-by-five-foot board and positioned it back in place from within. Many farmhouses had such partitions, which were used to hide valuables and firearms. She and Jack were hiding from the raging war that had engulfed her home.

Such a deeply lined face for a relatively young woman, Jack considered.

Like Permelia, Sarah Spindle had refused to leave her home. Unlike Permelia, however, Sarah was healthy enough to leave but refused to "allow a bunch of Yankees to ransack *her* home, by God." Sarah was infuriated because Yankee sharpshooters were using her two-and-a-half-story farmhouse to shoot at Confederates. She was helpless and frightened. When the cannon fire erupted the house shook and extinguished her candle. She prayed in the darkness for the oldest of her four children, who was fighting for General Lee.

To stop the sniper threat, J.E.B. Stuart ordered an assault on Sarah's house with three incendiary shells. When the house began to burn, Sarah kicked out the board and ran; she and Jack bolted across her fields toward the woods.

> *Sarah Spindle, her hair streaming behind her,*
> *darted from the flaming building and crossed*
> *the field between the armies toward the Po*
> *River to seek shelter.*[13]

To the astonishment of young soldiers on both sides, a frantic woman in a black dress had appeared on the battlefield! She was running toward the woods with her long hair flying everywhere. Shooting her would have been like killing your own mother, so no one fired a shot. Sarah's fifteen minutes of fame caused a brief ceasefire at Laurel Hill and allowed the hysterical woman to reach the wooden bridge, which was the only shelter between her house and the woods beyond. She jumped into the stained water and dove under the bridge, landing clumsily in the dirty sand.

The sudden appearance of the frantic, soot-covered witch startled Amanda. She gasped, dropped her soaking rag, and the two bewildered women locked eyes.

Did the violence and death raise this witch from hell? Amanda thought.

She and Jack scrambled back up the slope to Luke while the glassy-eyed woman looked frantically up and down the streambed. She ignored Luke and Amanda and bolted for the woods, splashing in the water and stumbling over several dead soldiers. As quickly as she had appeared, the apparition vanished into the smoky haze and was gone.

Amanda shivered and tried to control her breathing, although she was overcome with fear and confusion. *Who was that woman? Where did she come from and how had she avoided being shot?* After a moment, Amanda decided, *this must be her farm.* She fought the urge to simply get up and run after the crazy woman. *No, I can't leave Luke,* she thought, shaking her head from side to side.

The fighting flared up again and Amanda huddled close to Luke while hundreds of men died nearby. The dead and nearly-dead were strewn across Sarah's fields. Pitiful groans and whimpering swelled as night fell and the cries of human misery bellowed louder than any explosion. The deafening explosions had not spared Amanda from hearing the sounds of human agony that were far worse than the ear-splitting percussion of war. During the long, miserable night, the nearly-dead were picked off by long-rifle sniper shots that rang out at random.

The unfathomable battle raged on for three days. Although Luke ate little, their food was gone by May 10th. Cannon fire was not directed at the bridge because no one knew if the "phantom woman" was still hiding there. Every night, however, snipers continued to fire at any movement, which kept the teens trapped in their prison.

Amanda had filled three canteens with clean water before the dead and dying tainted the stream and she mixed willow bark into one of them. Every hour she dribbled the medicated water into Luke's mouth and prayed. She was determined to keep her boyfriend's fever down and removed Luke's shirt. In spite of the dire circumstances, his muscular arms and chest continued to fascinate the young virgin. She had never been this close to a man, much less a half-naked one, and infatuated teen passed the time by dripping water on the contours of his chest and watching it flow and collect. Luke remained feverish and despondent.

Please don't let him die, she prayed.

On the evening of May 11th, Luke's fever finally broke, although he remained hopelessly weak and delirious. It had been raining lightly all day and the rain fell more heavily toward evening. Because he was oblivious, Luke was spared the torment of the sounds of human misery that filled the killing fields. In spite of the rain and her partial hearing loss, however, Amanda could still hear the cries and pitiful moans of the wounded.

One soldier, who was surely a young boy, penetrated Amanda's soul with whimpers and agonizing pleas for his mother. She could not ignore him because he lay directly above her on the bridge. His sorrow, together with the rain that mixed with his blood, seeped from the spaces between the timbers. The coppery smell of blood filled the wet, dismal chasm and Amanda was haunted again by thoughts of the bleeding monster, who lay groaning and dying in the railroad cut. She shivered in the darkness and listened to the boy whimper. Every sniper shot and Rebel yell soured her stomach and increased her claustrophobic anguish.

"Mamma, please send me my angel," was spoken, or slurred, repeatedly from above. That singular phrase was interrupted by agonizing sobs and pleas for "Water! Please, water!" The pitiful cries blended into a gruesome chorus with dozens of other helpless men. Amanda covered her ringing ears and hummed little songs but she could still hear the boy. As the endless night crawled on, his cries weakened and Amanda's torment grew; she no longer wanted his moaning to end.

She and the helpless soldier were both prisoners of the war and they needed their mothers desperately. Amanda became convinced that if the young soldier died, all of *her* hopes and dreams would die as well. She turned face-up and strained to hear him, now thankful for each muffled whimper. When he fell silent, she held her breath to filter out all other cries of misery and listened only for the familiar voice of the fading soldier.

"Please, God! Please help him!" she repeated to herself.

When she could no longer endure the boy's silence, she decided to carry water to him not caring about his political motivations. The snipers had been silent for quite some time, so she turned the wet rag on Luke's forehead, slid down to the stream, and filled a canteen. She wondered if the swelling stream was still stained red and decided it didn't really matter as she slithered up the eastern side of the muddy embankment. Her heart was pounding as she hoisted herself up on the bridge. Through the smoke and fog, she could see dozens of bodies strewn like jackstraws in all directions. Fortunately, the rain, smoke, and poor visibility prevented her from seeing the other 1,400 dead and smoldering men who lay on Sarah Spindle's field.

She lay face down on the bridge in the rain and mud, which covered the slippery planks, and remained as close to the surface as possible. The rain couldn't wash the stale smoke and fog from the air and the pathetic chorus that rose from the wounded was horrifying. She fought her chronic nausea and strained to hear the boy.

Living a hard life in the Wilderness had toughened the débutante and hunting gave her the ability to concentrate. As she lay still, she pretended that the rain was the grass Luke had playfully sprinkled on her and the acrid smoke, which stung her nasal passages, became the scent of lilacs. When the boy called for his mother again, she was able to slither past the dead stare of a soldier and down the western slope of the bridge toward the helpless warrior.

The young Union soldier was crumpled half-way-down the side of the bridge that faced the Southern army. As she approached, she could see that his legs were extended at impossible angles and his midsection was horribly blood-stained. She slithered closer and dripped water into the open mouth of Elston Hobbs, of 20th Maine, who suckled like a baby and then greedily pleaded for more. The canteen slipped in Amanda's shaking hand and she clumsily *poured* water into Elston's mouth, causing him to cough, sputter, and open his eyes.

When he saw Amanda's face, he gasped and blurted out, "My angel! Mama! You sent my angel!"

He reached out like a drowning man and she instinctively pulled away—springing up to her knees.

Sniper shots rang out.

48

Truitt was concealed in the tree line and was confused when he saw Amanda crawl up on the bridge. Then, to his horror, her silhouette became a target of opportunity and she recoiled from the powerful shots that followed. As she fell back and rolled down the eastern side of the bridge, the enraged boy emerged from the woods with Jack. He charged the Confederate lines firing his Henry Repeater wildly.

"No!" he shouted. The furious assassin slipped on the muddy ground as he spat rapid but ineffective rounds from the Henry. Dozens of Rebels directed their fire at his muzzle flashes. Two fatal slugs found their mark and slammed the boy backward into the oozing ground. There, in the mud and rain, Truitt's blood saturated his backpack and seeped into his quilt, mixing with the bloodstains of his precious mother and brutal father.

As the ill-fated child lay dead and still, his blood slowly marinated his fairytales.

49

Amanda and Jack drifted to Luke and watched him toss and turn in restless sleep. "I love you," she whispered, knowing he could not hear her. Then, they went to Permelia and found her crumpled body lying in the little clearing behind the cabin. She sat with her precious aunt and placed her palm gently upon Permelia's peaceful face. Never before had Permelia looked so content and Amanda was grateful for that.

She felt her mother's familiar brush strokes and, when the brush brushed no more, she opened her eyes and saw her father sipping whiskey by a campfire. The flames illuminated his grave face. When she spoke to him, his tears sparkled and flickered in the firelight.

Then, Amanda, Truitt, Elston and Jack rose together and hovered above the killing fields, swirling and spinning slowly like dry leaves turning in the wind.

Jack was reminded of the salad spinner he had brought home from the mall with high expectations. A cute kiosk girl convinced him that his wife would love the device, so he bought three of the handy appliances because "they also make great gifts." He demonstrated for Jill by placing wet lettuce in the miracle device and turning the little crank until the unwanted water drained away. Jill never told him that she already owned one—and used it all the time.

Jack joined the trio in their cosmic salad spinner as they peered down at their bodies and began to spin like the lettuce in Jack's kitchen-tested device. Both Elston and Truitt were transfixed on Amanda's serene face, although for different reasons. Elston saw her as a messenger from God. His sweet mother had answered his prayers and sent an angel to deliver him to heaven. The blameless boy from Maine thought of the way his mother had kissed his forehead every night and of her trembling embrace when he left her in Blue Hill. With his silver angel held tightly in his hand and his contented face turned toward the heavens, he began to rise up the sides of the cyclone until he faded and disappeared.

Truitt's twitching gaze, on the other hand, was full of lust and desire. Amanda was an angel, all right, but she was no messenger from God. Instead, she *was* heaven and there was nothing more. The concepts of God, Paradise, or spending eternity with anyone other than his demonic father, were far beyond his expectations. The emptiness of hell was all he could imagine and the anguish of that place was certain.

Maybe heaven or hell is determined by our expectations, Jack considered.

Amanda would be Truitt's only glimpse of heaven before he joined his father in ceaseless damnation. As he began to fade, however, he smiled because he had actually touched one of his mother's fairy tales. As he dropped down and away, the walls of the whirlpool narrowed and his tremendous eyes remained fixed on Amanda. He was absorbed into the parapet of the vortex as his glimmering black eyes slowly disappeared.

There were many such death swirls in all directions, hovering above the rolling fields like small white tornados. Some had expanded and others tightened and shrank, while others combined to form a hurricane of the human spirit. The energy of death was captured in the many ghostly cyclones that spread north toward the Wilderness where individual whirlpools had evolved into one vast, slowly swirling mass.

Jack was reminded of a hurricane as seen from a satellite and wondered if so many unexpected deaths had thrown God a curve ball. *Were souls being suspended in some sort of purgatorial soup while God sorted things out? Since God is all-knowing, you'd think that all of this would be on autopilot. Perhaps the timeless and patient scrutiny of thousands would not be determined for hundreds of years to come. Maybe the human concept of time is irrelevant in the cosmos.*

The souls of Truitt, Matthew, and Peyton were dealt with quickly as if negative energy had an automatic default.

The morning wind played across the blazing, smoke-covered landscape while Amanda and Jack continued to rotate, now face-to-face. She looked directly into his eyes, hypnotizing him instantly, and then she began to melt into the walls of the vortex. When she disappeared, Jack began to feel great pain and realized that he was also liquefying and dissolving into the unknown.

The monitors in his hospital room erupted, once again.

50

Artie remained at the hospital with Jill during the day and Jill insisted upon sleeping in Jack's room at night. When Jill heard the alarms, she sprang from her chair and bolted out of Jack's room to find a nurse. She almost collided with the Donna at the door and quickly turned back to her husband. She held his face in her hands—tears streaming.

"Jack! Jack, darling! It's me, Jill. Please stay with me, Jack! I love you."

He was muttering nonsense and tossing, rather than convulsing, although his consciousness remained dormant. He felt himself swirling and boiling away in the vortex and, at the same time, being forcefully injected into his hospital bed. He fought again to return to his wife but could not. Jill placed her forehead on his and continued to plead with him while the nurse called for a doctor.

Jill's pull was strong, but her comatose husband could not emerge from his coma.

Part Three

~revelation~

1

Because I could not stop for death,
He kindly stopped for me.
The carriage held but just ourselves
And Immortality...
~ Emily Dickinson

It was simply not Amanda's time to die, nor was it the end of Jack's dreamscape. The death vortex had rejected her like a shark coughs up a surfboard. Instead of dying on the bridge, the wounded refugee ended up inside Sanford's Tavern in the town of Spotsylvania Courthouse. When she opened her eyes, her father was sitting by her side reading a Bible.

"Amanda! Thank God," John exclaimed.

He reached for her and his Bible fell from his hands. Amanda focused on him and managed a weak smile before closing her eyes again. John soothed the only part of his daughter's forehead that was not bandaged, buried his face by her side, and began to sob.

When the rain ended on the evening of May 12th, the Confederates retrieved both Southern and Union wounded from Sarah Spindle's Farm. In the aftermath of the battle, the South controlled the battlefield and claimed everything on it. The seriously injured were taken to a nearby field hospital where amputations were done to save the lives of those who would have otherwise bled to death.

Because of Jack's medical training, he had become interested in Civil War medical techniques. Surgeons in field hospitals were rushed and frequently forced to make hasty decisions regarding appendage removal. During the early months of the war, a number of ambitious young surgeons actually took advantage of the opportunity to amputate limbs needlessly.

As the war progressed, however, surgeons learned to confer with one another about the need for amputation if time allowed that luxury. Eventually, the pendulum swung too far and, to *avoid* severing limbs, some surgeons did more harm than good by attempting to remove all shrapnel from a wound, thus complicating the damage. In 1864, finding pus on a wound, which is an indication an infection, was thought to be a positive sign. In most cases, however, if the bone was shattered the appendage was removed.

Sawing human bone was demanding and stressful work and surgeons depended heavily upon assistant surgeons, stewards, nurses, and anyone else who could be recruited to help complete the gruesome task. Chloroform or narcotics were used during most amputations although, by 1864, sedatives were sometimes scarce in Confederate field hospitals. Many Confederate medical supplies, including sedatives, came from blockade-running ships and captured provisions. A small number of amputations were actually done without any form of sedation. In those rare cases, a leather strap or a wooden stick was placed in the jaws of the unfortunate patient before flesh was cut and bones were sawed

Those few regrettable men screamed, all right, Jack thought. *I bet the collective wailing of the 50,000 men, who were told that they would lose a limb, was louder still.*

On the 12th of May, Amanda's father completed his work in the Wilderness. Later that day, his hospital wagon arrived near

Laurel Hill to treat hundreds of additional torn and maimed bodies. Amputation may have been the only way to save lives, although removing legs and arms from the bodies of proud young men, many of whom were teenagers, had taken its toll on John. After the Wilderness battle, he was forced to remove the leg of a drummer boy who was younger than Amanda, which exhausted his will and left him depressed. Severing limbs from men as if they were tree limbs in the forest had made him weary of his appointed task and filled his heart with remorse. Concern for his daughter was also eating away at the surgeon and Amanda's safe journey was the only hope in his alcohol-soaked prayers.

Late that afternoon, Union prisoners were finally brought to Major Atkinson's amputation table. In spite of the gruesome amputations ranging from six to twenty minutes each, John insisted upon having his operating table doused with buckets of water and wiped clean between each heartbreaking procedure. Most educated medical men of the time knew that illnesses could be transferred from one human to another; they just weren't sure how or why. Inoculations for smallpox were used prior to the Civil War, but little was known about the spread of confounding bacterial infections such as cholera.

A large number of surgeons were actually dentists, who were untrained and totally unfamiliar with the concept of transmitting infection. Because John was a medical school professor, he was well aware of Anton van Leeuwenhoek's discovery of microorganisms in the 1670s. He was also familiar with Louis Pasteur 's discovery, in 1860, that living germs can cause disease. Unfortunately, the untimely American Civil War and the overwhelming medical urgency of the conflict had postponed any serious consideration of Pasteur's research in America.

Harvard University didn't even own a microscope until 1867, Jack remembered.

Although Dr. Atkinson kept his operating table and instruments as clean as possible, billions of invisible bacteria covered his operating table and crawled over his instruments.

The final patient of the day was an unusually tall prisoner, whose long legs dangled over the end of the surgeon's table. The younger and more virile they were, the more John regretted removing their limbs and Luke was no exception. The Confederates found Luke under the bridge and the feverish prisoner's wounded arm became his ticket to the amputation table. When they discovered the impassive young man curled up under the bridge like Zeus under Jill's deck, they also found his sword, LaMat revolver, and Whitworth rifle. He was labeled as a hostile and they ignored his babbling objections.

"Easy, son," John said to Luke, who protested groggily.

Most conscious men, who found themselves on his table, pleaded futilely for some alternative to amputation until they were sedated. Luke was weak and offered little resistance to the same procedure so many had endured during the four-year conflict. The skin and muscle would be severed and pulled back from the bone. The doctor would then saw the bone, leaving enough skin in place like the open end of a sock, so that it could be folded back over the stump and sewn together. Chloroform was the wonder drug that made the process tolerable. Rare and unfortunate sedative-free patients always passed out from the pain, which was a great relief to everyone.

Prisoner Luke was chosen as one of the unfortunate candidates for amputation without any sedition. A leather strap was placed in his mouth while John wiped his scalpel with a length of bandage. The surgeon glanced around at the dreary scene, cursed the war and his lack of supplies, and decided to remove the prisoner's arm swiftly, hoping the soldier would pass out quickly.

"We must boil additional horse hair," his nurse interrupted.

Ironically, even cotton thread made from the Southern cash crop was wearing thin. The alternative was the stiff hair from a horse's tail, which was softened by boiling. The primitive substitute was, therefore, unwittingly sterilized. Ironically, those who were stitched with "the cheap stuff" endured fewer infections and had a greater survival rate than those who were stitched with cotton thread.

Dr. Atkinson's supply of cotton thread was long gone.

"Very well," John said, glancing at the nurse. "I'll return shortly."

He washed his hands, went into his tent, and gulped whiskey from a bottle. He thought of Amanda while staring at a gory pile of severed limbs. Then, he rose unsteadily, walked through the mud and muck to a nearby stand of scrub pine trees, and threw up on the stained earth.

The nurse watched the doctor walk toward his tent, knowing what he was about to do. Becky Cole, who had dark, classic features and a kind face, had been assisting the man she loved ever since Gettysburg. The thirty-year-old, childless woman had been married to an officer in the Confederate Army, who was killed in The Battle of Fredericksburg.

Upper and middle-class grieving widows of the time were required to wear black clothing known as "widow's weeds." During the Civil War, few could afford long periods of mourning and many others did not have the means to adequately maintain a widow's wardrobe. Many dark-colored crepe widow's weeds became tattered and rust-colored over time.

Becky, who could not afford formal mourning, escaped that fate by earning a crisp Confederate nurse's uniform instead. After being trained by nuns in Gordonsville, she volunteered for hospital field service. She was sent to follow Lee's army to Gettysburg where she was assigned to Regimental Surgeon Major J.M.P. Atkinson. John's excellent skills and reputation were well known. His background as president of the Hampden-Sydney College, as well as his command of the "Hampden-Sydney Boys," was held in high regard. Because of his reputation, he was asked to join an elite group of doctors who cared for high-ranking officers. He ignored those inquiries and remained in field hospital service where he believed he could do the most for the cause of independence.

Becky was bright, dedicated, and hopelessly in love with John Atkinson. She quickly became invaluable to him as his anesthesiologist and he trusted her to screen his patients. Few female nurses traveled with hospital wagons and still fewer filled the role of physician's assistant, but Becky had impressed John with her intelligence and nurturing personality. He trained the bright young woman and kept her close. The disheartened doctor soon found a confidante as well as a lover. Without her, he would have surely fallen into a pit of despair.

I know how he feels, Jack thought, wondering how long his astounding dream would last and if he would ever be reunited with the woman he loved.

As the pace of the war and the number of amputations increased, Becky was able to ease the surgeon's troubled mind regarding his dead wife, precious daughter, and gruesome duty. Without her, his dependence on alcohol would have become more severe and he might not have had the strength to overcome his depression. Jack watched the doctor gulp whiskey, knowing that alcohol-induced demons had nearly consumed the surgeon.

As Dr. Atkinson began to dissolve, Jack's physical pain returned as though *his* inescapable demons had arisen. Finally, John vanished from his dream entirely and the comatose pilot was left with nothing but pain and cold darkness.

2

While Eggberta was exploding in the microwave, Artie was driving to the hospital to relieve Jill. She didn't want to leave Jack but Artie insisted, so she kissed her husband, drove home with Samantha, and found Charlotte's smoldering house. The dusty road was crowded with emergency vehicles and fire trucks were spraying water on both homes so that the fire wouldn't spread.

"Mrs. Burnside was taken to the hospital for observation and Mr. Burnside is still missing," a firefighter said.

The antithesis of Sarah Spindle, Jill ran *toward* her house and was soaked to the bone by the time she reached her front door. Like the soldiers at Laurel Hill, the startled firefighters stopped spraying when they saw the frantic woman. Because her cell phone was useless in the hospital, she had left it at home. Jill could think only of Charlotte as she ran into her kitchen to call the hospital. She followed various phone prompts and tried to decipher the barely legible message that her distressed friend had scribbled on the chalkboard.

Ralph is dead
My ghosts are free
Zeus can help Jack
There is no Fin' chocolate!

"What the hell?" Jill said as she lowered the phone and turned to Zeus. The peculiar dog with the unwavering stare had returned and he was sitting in the middle of the kitchen. Jill kept one eye on Zeus while trying to convince the operator that she was related to Charlotte, claiming to be her sister. The hospital finally relented and said that Charlotte Burnside had been treated for minor injuries and admitted for observation.

"She's been sedated and cannot receive visitors until tomorrow," said the monotone voice on the phone.

Frustrated and confused, she walked slowly past Zeus, who followed her into the living room. They sat and stared at one another.

"Is everyone going to end up in the hospital?" she said to Zeus, who cocked his head.

Is poor Ralph really dead? They said he was missing, not dead. Maybe when they say missing, they really mean dead. She looked absentmindedly at Zeus and thought, *what do Charlotte's ghosts have to do with anything and how are you supposed to help Jack?* She glanced out at the fairway and then back at Zeus, who seemed to be considering her thoughts. She gently held the dog's face, the same way she had held Jack's face in the hospital. She stared into the dog's bottomless eyes and suddenly knew what to do.

"Jack needs you, doesn't he, boy?"

With that, the hound became animated and chased his tail in tight circles. When Zeus began to dance, there was another huge spike in Jack's blood pressure monitor.

3

While the horsehair boiled and the good doctor threw up, Becky and Jack waited along with the lanky patient who was strapped to the amputation table. His knees were bent over the end of the slab and his ankles were attached to the table legs so that he wouldn't kick like a horse during the procedure.

Because of Major Atkinson's rank, his hospital wagon normally contained ample amounts of sedatives, although the overwhelming number of operations following the Wilderness battle had taxed his supplies. Both Union and Confederate surgeons were required to carry a sidearm to protect their narcotic stores. John had guarded and protected his diminishing provisions and used them sparingly, but little remained. Each army gave priority to their own and wounded prisoners were sometimes shortchanged.

Patients were sedated with chloroform, opium, ether, alcohol, or an improvised combination depending on availability. Jack knew that chloroform was the drug of choice for most surgeons. It was applied to a piece of cloth or sponge, placed inside a funnel, and held a few inches from the patient's nose and mouth. Following each exhalation, the funnel was moved closer until simple clinical signs ended the procedure. Lubricating cream was sometimes applied to the face of the patient to reduce the harsh blistering effects of the chloroform, although that was a rare luxury.

Like many prisoners, Luke was weak and repeatedly claimed, "I'm not a soldier." Soldier or not, prisoner or not, being strapped to the amputation table and forced to wait seemed inhumane to Becky. While she waited for the surgeon, she could not ignore the terror and pleading desperation in the handsome boy's eyes. She knew the delay would be substantial, so the compassionate nurse gave Luke whiskey laced with a generous amount of opium. By the time Dr. Atkinson returned, Luke's head was swirling.

"Doctor, because of the delay, I have given this man some sedation." Becky placed a leather strap in Luke's mouth and said, "I have also examined him and I'm impressed with the way his arm has been bandaged. This is no field dressing."

John looked at the bandage and recognized the same technique he had taught his medical students. The boy was wrapped with the careful and efficient method that had been lost in the rush of war. He looked at the youngster's face, which he rarely did with his amputation patients, and gently opened one of Luke's eyelids. He hesitated and decided to carefully examine the wound, directing his knife to the boy's remarkable bandage rather than his flesh. The wound was deep and in need of stitches, although it was covered with a generous amount of ointment and showed signs of healing. Luke moaned while John examined the underlying bone and the surgeon was pleased to discover that it was intact.

He looked at Becky and said, "This wound will be sutured."

The nurse smiled and prepared the horsehair. Once the lesion was sewn and bandaged, a courier handed a written communiqué to John.

> *May 12, 1864*
> *Major Atkinson,*
> *We have recovered a civilian named Amanda Atkinson and a letter signed by Major J.M.P. Atkinson asking for notification if she is discovered. She has been injured and taken to the headquarters of General Jubal A. Early at Sanford's Tavern, Spotsylvania Courthouse.*
> *Captain Alfred J. Morris*

John handed the letter to Becky, gave command of his operating table to an assistant surgeon, and commandeered a horse.

The Sanford Tavern was within a few miles of Laurel Hill. Once it had been determined that Amanda was Major Atkinson's daughter, she was taken to the general headquarters building and a messenger was sent to notify her father.

When John arrived, he cleaned and bandaged Amanda's wound, sat by her side, and prayed. He had not seen her for almost three years and marveled at her resemblance to her mother. Jack "showed up" just when Amanda woke and in time to witness the major's tears of joy. Amanda tightened her grip on her father's hand and then slipped off to sleep while John buried his face in his hands and wept.

The sniper's bullet had grazed the left side of Amanda's skull; she tumbled back down the south side of the bridge, out of the line of fire. She flirted with death and her spirit rose and swirled in the vortex with Elston and Truitt, but God rejected her like a dog coughs up a bone.

She reopened her eyes and weakly said, "Luke. Where is Luke?"

"It's me, Amanda. Your father," John said calmly.

She squeezed her father's hand again and began to cry.

"Amanda, you're safe now."

"Luke. Where is he?" she repeated.

"Who is Luke and where is Aunt Permelia?" he said, fearing his daughter was delusional.

Now fully awake, she reached out to hug her father and said, "Of course, Father, you couldn't know. Aunt Permelia sent me from the Wilderness with a boy named Luke Stewart. She was too weak and ill to travel and insisted that we leave for Richmond immediately!" She closed her eyes, trying to both remember and forget the terrifying experience and said, "Oh, Father, it was horrible." She coughed and sobbed, "Aunt Permelia said she would be safe in her home and Widow Tapp would stay with her. Then she sent Luke and me on our way because the war was coming and, and..."

"Rest easy, Amanda," John said, stroking her face with a damp cloth. "I know of no such man."

"You must find him! He's wounded and he has a terrible fever. Oh, Lord, we were trapped under a bridge in a battlefield and it was horrible." She paused and said, "I think I may have died."

The débutante had always been a drama queen and she was obviously traumatized.

"Nonsense, Amanda," he said. "We'll discover the truth after you have had time to rest."

She persisted, "Father, please find Luke. I owe him my life and I love him!"

That was disturbing news and John tried to ignore it. Like every other male on the planet, however, he could not refuse Amanda and agreed to look for the boy.

"Very well, Amanda, tell me what happened."

Through her sobs and tears, she told the entire story. John hugged her tenderly and said, "You poor dear. I've been praying for your safety and I am truly sorry."

"No, Father, you have done your best to protect me. Luke needs your help now. Please find him."

"Of course I will," he said, not knowing if that was possible. "You said he had a fever?"

"Yes, he was wounded in his right arm while trying to protect me from a horrible man who attacked me. I used Aunt Permelia's goldenseal salve to treat his wound and I bandaged his arm exactly as you taught me, and…"

"Wait! You used goldenseal ointment and my technique? Is Luke tall? Of course he is. I treated him earlier today. Good God! I almost amputated his arm. God help me. I sutured his wound instead and he'll be fine. He's being held as a prisoner and I will find him."

"Oh, Father, thank you!" Amanda said as tears flowed down her cheeks. "Please find him. Please hurry!"

John gave opiates to his daughter for the pain and arranged for a local volunteer to care for her. He made his way back to Laurel Hill and trudged through the prisoners' holding area, looking carefully at each miserable face. Luke was not among them because amputees and injured men had already been sent to Guinea Station.

Jack knew that wounded prisoners were a burden on the Southern army because they could hardly support their own. Most were sent to Richmond by rail. They were held at railway stations in pens like farm animals, waiting for space on the crowded trains. Able-bodied prisoners were escorted on foot to deplorable prisons like Brown's Island in Richmond.

Thousands of other unlucky men walked all the way to Andersonville Prison in Georgia, which had opened in February of 1864. In April of that year, in response to Lincoln's demand that black prisoners of war be treated the same as their white comrades, the Confederates massacred black Union soldiers at Fort Pillow, Tennessee. As a result, Lincoln suspended all prisoner exchanges. The prisoner population at Andersonville reached 20,000 by early June, twice the camp's intended capacity. Although Andersonville was only three months old in May of 1864, it quickly became the most inhumane disgrace of the Civil War. The population soon swelled to 45,000 starving inmates and 13,000 died in disease-infested squalor. The camp commandant, Henry Wirz, was eventually tried and executed for war crimes because of the deplorable conditions at Andersonville.

Guinea Station was a thirteen-mile journey from Spotsylvania Courthouse and it was the northern end of the Confederate railroad system. The Union controlled the railroad in Fredericksburg to the north and the tracks between the two stations had been destroyed.

Jack remembered that Stonewall Jackson had been taken to Guinea Station after his arm was amputated in 1863. Jackson's wound was sewn with sturdy cotton thread and packed with soggy lint in a misguided attempt to administer the finest medical care. A linen wick was attached to the lint and placed in a dish of water at his bedside to keep the injury moist. The damp lint became a perfect breeding ground for bacteria and Stonewall Jackson eventually died of pneumonia.

The great soldier's final battle was with a microscopic enemy, Jack lamented.

One year after Jackson's death, during the Spotsylvania battle, Guinea Station remained secure although tremendously inefficient. Commissary-General Luscious B. Northrop ran the railroad supply lines for the South and he was so incompetent that he was thought to be a Northern sympathizer. Rail cars were small compared to modern containers and space was extremely limited. Once the single locomotive train reached Guinea Station, there was no way to turn around, so the engine was reversed and the overloaded cars were actually pushed backward toward Richmond.

John dressed in his full uniform. He said to Becky, "Permelia was too ill to travel, so Amanda was dressed in men's clothing and sent to Richmond with a young man named Luke Stewart. Luke was wounded when Union soldiers attacked them and they were forced to hide in the swamps of the Wilderness. They managed to find their way to the battlefield at Laurel Hill where Amanda was wounded and Luke was taken prisoner. I sutured Luke's injury, but all wounded prisoners have been taken to Guinea Station. I will treat Amanda's head injury and then escort her to the rail station where I hope to secure her passage to Richmond. I hope to find Luke Stewart there and arrange for his release."

"What of Permelia?" Becky said.

"I've hired a local man, who is familiar with the Higgerson Farm, to look in on her. I fear the worst."

"I'm sure Permelia will survive and I remember treating Luke. I've heard that Guinea Station is well behind schedule and hundreds of prisoners are being held there. If that's true, you'll find him." Becky wanted to go with John for many reasons. She paused before saying, "John, I can assist you when you treat Amanda and a woman's hand will be needed to prepare her for her journey. I have a dress she can wear and..."

"Of course, Becky. Thank you," John interrupted, wondering why he hadn't considered those details. "Please pack everything Amanda will need and come with me. Please hurry."

Becky quickly packed the wagon with food, clothing, and medical supplies and they pressed into the murky night. Major Atkinson was anxious and frustrated by the need to travel slowly on the mud-covered trail and he became impatient at various security check points. When they arrived at the tavern, the nurse cleaned Amanda's head wound again and administered narcotics while John prepared the sutures, regretting the use of boiled horsehair.

The surgeon was thankful that the bullet had merely grazed his daughter's skull and that most of the ugly scar would eventually be hidden within her hairline. She seemed to be uninjured otherwise, except for the unknown mental effects of the ordeal. He wanted nothing more than to go to Richmond with her, but the Confederacy needed him now more than ever, so he was compelled to send his unchaperoned daughter to the protection of that fortified city.

Becky bathed and dressed the groggy girl and administered additional opiates for the pain. John examined Amanda's filthy clothing, assuming that Permelia had hidden gold coins within them. He found five gold coins that were cleverly sewn into Benjamin's worn leather belt and the jar of goldenseal that Amanda had used to treat Luke's wound. He blessed his sister-in-law for her brilliance and vowed to someday learn the uses of healing herbs.

Perhaps Permelia has weathered the storm, after all, he thought as he studied her potion, unaware that the cancer had consumed his sister-in-law. He was impressed with the healing effects of Permelia's medicine and applied a small amount of goldenseal to Amanda's wound. Amanda was dressed in a crisp white dress, blue sash, and clean underclothes, which Becky had unfolded from her oilcloth. She had been waiting for the opportunity to wear her dress for John, but never had the chance because of the unfathomable pace and severity of war. Becky's ankle-high shoes fit Amanda well, although the dress was a bit snug at the bosom and recklessly short, reaching only to Amanda's mid-calf. The spaced-out débutante was unaware of her humiliating fashion statement and found humor in her new-found ankle-high shoes and bare legs.

Twenty hours of brutal fighting had just taken place at what would become known as "Bloody Angle." It was the longest hand-to-hand combat of the Civil War and Doctor Atkinson was sorely needed, but his daughter was a greater priority. General Early sympathized with him and granted the respected surgeon emergency leave. John purchased a wagon from a civilian for twenty times its value and readied a horse while Becky gently brushed Amanda's hair, wondering to what extent the lovely girl resembled her mother.

War can't erase human emotions, Jack realized.

As the brush moved through the euphoric teenager's long hair, she too thought of her mother. Amanda dreamily hummed "Amazing Grace" and Becky sang along with her. The nurse carefully placing a bonnet on Amanda's head and adjusted it to cover her bandage. Becky mentioned that the uncomfortable wagon ride to Guinea

Station would be painful for Amanda and recommended a steady stream of additional narcotics.

"Very well," John said. "But please use them sparingly. She must have her wits about her when we put her on the train."

John trusted Becky to administer all sedatives and she had mastered the use of drugs that were generally misused and abused. Misuse of ether gas had sometimes knocked everyone out, including the operating surgeon.

John placed his inebriated daughter on a blanket of hay in the bed of the wagon and covered her with a rubberized gum blanket to keep her dry. Amanda's transformation from Benjamin's muddy clothes to Becky's dress was dramatic and the clean white dress was both innocent and provocative. Except for a small part of her bandaged head and a slightly swollen lip, Amanda appeared to be uninjured and she sang happy little drug-laced songs as the pretty green trees passed overhead.

Alice in Wonderland, Jack thought, realizing that Becky may have been a bit liberal with the opium after all.

Clueless, John looked back at his dreamy teenage daughter and said, "I believe Amanda will recover. Thank you, Becky."

"She will be safe in Richmond and you will be able to join her soon," Becky said, hoping to be part of that future.

The nurse had done all she could for Amanda. As they bumped along in the drizzling rain, she snuggled close to John and rested her head on his shoulder. Although they had allowed ample time for the scheduled 2:00 p.m. train departure, the muddy road was clogged with artillery, supply wagons, and exhausted soldiers. Progress was agonizingly slow and they arrived with little time to spare.

4

The wagon ride had taken longer than anticipated, forcing Becky to give Amanda additional opiates. When they finally arrived at Guinea Station, the rain had almost stopped and Amanda had one foot in Wonderland. John was determined to secure passage for his daughter. He had told Amanda that Luke might be at the rail station and, somewhere deep within Amanda's drug-laced mind, she was determined to find her boyfriend. Her eyes darted through the impenetrable crowd while John realized there would be no time to deal with bureaucracy. He hoped that respect for his uniform and rank would secure Amanda's passage, but he was ignored and all eyes followed Amanda.

Gone with the Wind, Jack realized. *This is a scene from that movie.* Jack still believed that the images in his dream had been manufactured in his mind. Indeed, the chaotic scene in *Gone with the Wind*, in which Scarlett O'Hara walked among hundreds of disabled men, was an unforgettable panorama. The scene at Guinea Station was similar and the muddy fields on both sides of the tracks were filled with wounded men. There was a desperate flurry of movement near the overloaded train and soldiers bustled everywhere.

The crowd parted as Major Atkinson approached with Amanda and Becky. News of the beautiful young lady in the short, tight dress spread rapidly. Most of the soldiers had not seen a lovely woman for months; each man was sure that Amanda was looking only at him. Scores of silent soldiers tipped their hats, poked their friends, and pointed at her while John led the charge toward the train. Amanda exacerbated the situation by making eye contact with as many of them as possible, trying desperately to spot Luke in the crowd.

During the closing chapters of the war, tens of thousands of demoralized soldiers had suffered extended periods of separation from their homes, families, and sweethearts. When the exhausted men at Guinea Station saw Amanda, their thoughts of home blossomed and every heartsick eye followed her as she passed by.

The steam engine was stoked and the whistle shattered the air while John reached for Amanda's hand and guided her up the station platform and to the front of the locomotive. John climbed the ladder into the engineer's compartment, ignoring verbal protests from both the engineer and fireman. He held two 1862 three-dollar gold eagle coins in front of the bulbous nose of the engineer, who glanced at his fireman and then focused on the coins and grinned.

"Just my daughter," John said.

The greasy engineer hesitated, then smiled broadly revealing a gold tooth of his own and said, "Whatever you say, major."

Major Atkinson took another step forward so that he was nose-to-nose with the soot-covered man and said, "You will deliver her to Richmond and if there is any report of misconduct—I'll find you and kill you myself."

"No, sir! I mean, yes, sir! I reckon she'll be fine right here."

He pointed to a limber trunk sitting in the back of the cab and explained that Amanda could "Sit right here all the way to Richmond and not be bothered none."

Becky helped Amanda climb the narrow metal ladder. John kissed his daughter on the cheek and she hugged him fiercely. She knew her father would never consider leaving her here at the rail station to search for Luke and returning to Permelia was now impossible. He couldn't allow her to remain with him, so her only option was to go to Richmond.

With tears in her eyes, Amanda said, "Please find him, Father."

"I promise I will," he said as he backed out of the crowded compartment and stepped down the ladder.

Amanda stood in the open door of the engineer's compartment. Her tears were streaming and her hands were folded in prayer. The vision of the angelic young girl wearing the provocative dress continued to captivate dozens of war-sick men. Some saw their wives, sweethearts or daughters while others saw Elston Hobbs' angel. Amanda symbolized what the soldiers were fighting for—she *was* the South and they were willing to sacrifice their lives to protect her.

Knowing his daughter was still under the influence of narcotics, John bellowed instructions from the platform, "Don't forget! Go to the Stillwell home. They're waiting for you. The letter in your satchel should be presented to our army if necessary. It will identify you as my daughter. I will find Luke and join you in Richmond soon—I promise!"

The whistle blew again, steam bellowed, and the train spun its wheels until it was able to push the massive load with positive traction. Many Confederate soldiers felt as though they too were spinning their wheels and backing up, just like the Confederate Army had been doing since the South's disastrous defeat at Gettysburg. Since then, both armies had suffered tremendous losses while the South attempted to hold the blue tide at bay. The South was usually outnumbered and out-gunned and now the underdogs were being forced to retreat back to their capital city while Northern Virginia burned. Lee's beloved home was devastated by a war that had left farms and homesteads destroyed. Tens of thousands of bodies littered the scorched landscape.

John and Jack knew that the blue horde would continue to come. Dr. Atkinson couldn't have known that the Union Army would take possession of Guinea Station on May 21st, a mere eight days hence, or that the Federals would eventually take Richmond. Worse, as was the case in most wars, shock and awe was inevitable and General Sherman's march to the sea would become the Nagasaki of the nineteenth century.

For more than three years, John had kept Amanda from harm's way. *Am I making another mistake? Would the capital city of Richmond fall?* At this point, he had no choice. Amanda had to go to Richmond immediately. *Luke must be here and I'll find him. Permelia trusted the boy with Amanda's life and he has protected her. I am indebted to him,* he thought.

John glanced at the prisoner holding area. "I'll do my best to find Luke, but at least Amanda is leaving and that is a blessing," he said to Becky as they watched the train struggle backward. When the train cleared the station building, many more men saw Amanda standing in the engineer's compartment with her hands folded in prayer. Then, as the train chugged past the over-crowded prisoner holding area, a familiar voice shouted, "A-MAN-DA!"

Amanda spotted Luke and waved her arms. "LUKE! LUKE!" she shouted above the noise of the steam engine.

"A-MAN-DA!" Luke shouted again.

John followed Amanda's eyes and saw the tall boy pushing through a crowd of prisoners.

"LUKE!" the light-headed girl shouted again, just before she jumped.

The train was moving at ten miles an hour and a collective gasp rose from Guinea Station when the girl leaped. Thankfully, she jumped far enough to reach the saturated, grassy embankment and rolled like a rag doll.

When Luke saw Amanda hurl herself from the train, he bolted from the confines of the holding area and a young prison guard raised his musket.

5

Boom!

Hundreds of Civil War reenactors had filled the open farmland for a re-enactment of the May, 1863 Battle of Chancellorsville, and the first cannon volley rang out as Jill drove by. Desperate but inspired, she was speeding down Germanna Highway toward the hospital in Fredericksburg when the percussion of the cannon startled her and launched Zeus into the front seat of the SUV. The terrified dog forced his head behind Jill's back, pressing her against the steering wheel. The car swerved on the gravel shoulder, but Jill maintained control and floored the big engine to gain distance from the sounds of war.

"Damn it! Damn it!" she said, as she passed cars and raced east on the divided highway known as Route Three.

Earlier that morning, Jill had rummaged through a kitchen drawer and found Samantha's therapy dog vest. She managed to put the jacket on Zeus and loaded the reluctant hound into the back of the SUV.

Zeus had dislodged his head from behind Jill's back and curled up on the passenger's seat by the time they roared up to the main entrance of the hospital and double-parked. She dragged the mysterious dog toward the entrance and the hound freaked out when the automatic doors began to move. He comically spun his wheels on the slick marble floor of the lobby like Bambi on ice.

She fought to control Zeus, who could not pretend to be a therapy dog. Samantha deserved her title because she had taken the required classes. She was gentle with juvenile patients and old folks alike. She didn't mind slick hospital floors and she loved elevators. Everyone, from delicate senior citizens to children in the cancer ward, loved to greet Samantha when she padded up to them and rested her head in their laps. The hospital staff had always welcomed Jill and Wonder Dog with open arms and knew them well.

Zeus, however, frantically skated across the slippery lobby, never taking an actual step on the polished marble floor. His huge tongue was hanging out and his toenails were searching for traction as Jill pulled the frenzied dog past the reception desk.

She repeated, "Therapy dog in training! Therapy dog in training!" and everyone seemed to be more amused than upset. She and Zeus were able to slide through the lobby and into the elevator. Zeus curled into the corner of the cab and shivered but remained quiet until the elevator began to move. Then, the hound raised his head and howled as if they were headed straight for the moon and Jill was thankful they were alone. The elevator stopped on the third floor, however, and two candy stripers glanced nervously at the yellow-eyed monster before squeezing into the opposite side of the cab.

Jill held her breath when the doors closed and Zeus let out another set of blood-curdling howls. The two girls joined him in the screaming contest, adding to the anxiety of the dog and helping him to reach a more blood-curdling octave. The girls bolted as soon as the doors opened on the floor for unresponsive patients and so did Zeus. Convinced that the dog was chasing them, the girls continued to run while Jill's leather-soled shoes proved more useless than dog claws on the polished floor. Zeus and Jill slipped, skidded, and almost collided with a disgruntled nurse.

Jill spoke first, "I'm *so* sorry! He's a therapy dog in training and I guess he needs a little more preparation."

Lisa recognized Jill and said, "Oh, Jill. That's all right, but please keep him under control. The patients on this floor don't need this kind of commotion."

Zeus looked toward the end of the corridor and saw Jack in his bed. He whimpered once and then pumped his legs like the train at Guinea Station. His claws slipped and spun and then the leash flew from Jill's hand.

Zeus galloped toward Jack's room.

6

Jack realized that the young prison guard had little chance of hitting a moving target with his antique smoothbore flintlock musket. He had just arrived at Guinea Station as a new recruit and brought his ancient musket with him, all the way from Tennessee.

His first orders were, "Guard them prisoners and if any of'em try to run, shoot'em."

The bore, or inside of the boy's musket barrel, was smooth. Modern rifle-muskets had spiral grooves that spun the projectile like a tight spiraling football, making them far more accurate. His musket would launch its deadly slug with high velocity but more like a paintball gun than a modern rifle.

The tremendous casualty rate of the Civil War was due, in part, to the widespread use of modern "grooved" rifles. Early on, the commanders of both Civil War armies used Napoleonic tactics that were taught at West Point at the time. Both sides discovered that soldiers could no longer stand in neat lines and blast away at each other; modern rifle-muskets were far too accurate. Early in the war, thousands of good men died because of the obsolete tactics.

The ambitious young guard at Guinea Station was taking his first tour of duty seriously and he was eager to please. He was intimately familiar with his weapon, as most Southerners were, and he had primed his musket's ignition system using great care to keep his powder dry. In preparation for his first assignment, he poured black powder down the muzzle of his flintlock and carefully crammed a metal ball on top of the powder with his ramrod. He used the empty cartridge paper as a plug so that the ball wouldn't roll back out of the barrel, making him look foolish. He was a soldier, by God, and refused to look foolish!

Statistically, his weapon could hit a stationary, one-square-foot target at forty yards. That's how far Luke had run before the excited recruit raised his antique musket and quickly fired his first shot of the war. When the shot rang out, the big slug slammed through Luke's mud-encrusted shirt. Luke dove into the long, matted grass and covered his head with his good arm. The pain in his injured shoulder erupted, but he was otherwise unharmed as he looked up to see Amanda stirring.

"Cease fire! Cease fire!" Major Atkinson shouted. He was running down the railroad tracks with his arms raised and his gray cape flying. To Jack, he looked like the blue heron that had flown past Amanda in the swamp.

All other "would-be shooters" hesitated when they saw the frantic officer. Meanwhile, narcotics and a severe lack of reasoning-lobe brain development had made Amanda somewhat fearless and more pliable than she would have been. When she plummeted down the embankment, the lingering effects of the drugs softened her landing and prevented serious injury, like a drunk who trips on a curb and rolls. She remained unbroken, although the fall from the train and the effects of the drugs left her disoriented and she struggled to regain her bearings. If she had risen more quickly, she would have been directly in the line of fire. Instead, the deadly slug sailed over her head and thumped into the muddy embankment.

My great-great-grandmother has cheated death once again, Jack thought. *I guess I knew she would—otherwise I wouldn't be here...if I am here.*

While Jack thought about that, Major Atkinson approached Luke, who stood and held his hands up in surrender. John ran past him shouting, "Luke, stay down!" When he reached his daughter, he quickly pulled her to the ground and covered her with his body and cape.

Luke was tired, dirty, hungry, and confused. Nothing made sense to him—certainly not the officer who knew his name. He lowered his hands and walked tentatively toward the officer and his crumpled girlfriend. The officer gestured and said, "Down Luke, stay down! Keep your head down!"

The confused boy fell to his knees and crawled toward Amanda and John; no more shots were fired.

To the soldiers and prisoners at the train station, it appeared as though the Confederate angel had fallen from the train and perished. At that moment, the hopes and dreams of many dejected men died along with the young beauty. Some removed their hats while others fell to their knees to pray. Others mumbled among themselves and strained to see the fallen angel, who was covered with the officer's cape. Many of the disconsolate soldiers suddenly felt as though the war itself would surely and inevitably be lost.

"Luke. Where is Luke?" Amanda asked as she regained her senses.

When Luke approached, she flew into his arms. The mud-covered prisoner didn't know how to react and held Amanda clumsily while John stood and blended into the crowd of cheering men who had gathered around them. Amanda's father looked up to see the engineer smiling and waving to him as the train backed away.

The thankful surgeon smiled for the first time in months.

Luke was released to Major Atkinson's custody and Becky assured John that both Amanda and Luke were still "definitely virgins." John accepted her insight, wondering why he hadn't considered such a thing. He greeted Luke with a warm handshake and sincere thanks for having protected his daughter with his life.

7

Zeus bolted down the hospital hall, jumped up on Jack's bed, and straddled the comatose pilot. Jill and the Lisa clamored into the room and found the slobbering hound licking Jack's face with great enthusiasm.

Captain Stewart opened his eyes and smiled at Zeus.

8

One year later

"You'll never guess who I heard from today," Jill said.

"Hmm...let's see. The punk rock teenager at Starbucks with the metal studs in her tongue?" Jack guessed.

"In addition to her."

"Okay. I give up. Who?"

"I received a written letter from Charlotte. She bought a farm near the old Guinea Station."

"Really."

"Yep. And guess what she's raising on her farm."

"Muumuus?"

"No...guess again."

"Chickens?"

"No! Guinea hens, of course. She's also thinking about breeding golden retrievers."

"That's great. She's a terrific woman. I'm glad Charlotte is okay," Jack said sincerely.

"She seems to be fine, except that she does miss Ralph."

"Me too," Jack said.

Jill gave him "the look."

"Speaking of okay, how are you doing today?" she asked, just as she had asked every day of the previous year.

Jack was still on medical leave while the Federal Aviation Administration decided his fate. Once that strange agency's peculiar attorneys considered a case like Jack's, they seemed to enjoy passing it around and playing with it like cats play with a mice.

When Jack was released from the hospital, he convalesced for a month before claiming that he was "just fine." The FAA did not agree, however, so he continued to glide along in limbo receiving full pay as the months ate up his sick leave. Remarkably, the airline had been granted Chapter 11 bankruptcy protection once again and management was methodically destroying union contracts and compensation as if the employees had caused the problem.

He was spared that day-by-day misery and he was thankful to have only four years remaining before mandatory retirement at age sixty. While he was "recovering," however, the Feds proclaimed that airline pilots could retire at age sixty-five, as long as they flew with a copilot who was *under* sixty-five. Go figure. Once his sick leave was exhausted, disability benefits would carry him to "normal" retirement age. The FAA was actually doing him a favor by dragging their feet.

Still, he resented the FAA's staggering lack of empathy and it had been a long, laborious year. Neurologists and psychiatrists had examined him, although he never discussed his "dream" for fear of being "asked to leave permanently." Jill and Artie were his only confidants and they were enthralled with the tale he told.

Jill knew that her husband was still haunted by his "dream world experiences" and his dream was almost as real to him as reality itself. As the months passed, however, Jack seemed to accept the here and now more and more. In his heart, however, he still believed that, in some unexplainable cosmic sense, he had actually experienced the past.

The coma had changed Jack for the better. His experience strengthened his belief in God and the afterlife and reinforced his certainty that good is much more powerful than evil. He stopped drinking completely and became seriously involved with Samantha's visits to the sick and elderly.

He became even more obsessed with genealogy, however, and spent most of his time researching the characters in his dream. Luke and Amanda were, indeed, his great-great-grandparents. He was also proud to be an extended member of the Higgerson/Chewing family. Unfortunately, there was simply no record of Amanda Atkinson's life. Elston Hobbs and Henry Mueller appeared on regimental rosters, but there was no record of Matthew Bowler, Peyton Hoyle, or Truitt Simms.

He tried to follow the same path he had taken with Amanda and Luke, but housing developments, utilities, and farmland had replaced most of the uninhabited 1864 Wilderness. He finally gave up the search and began to accept his dream. Meanwhile, with the help of his Civil War research and the permission of private landowners, he roamed the Wilderness in search of artifacts. He and Zeus spent many hours with a sophisticated metal detector, carefully exploring "legal" areas that were not owned by the Park Service.

"So, you're doing well today?" Jill asked again.

"Say again?"

"I asked how you're feeling and you haven't answered me."

"Oh, I'm unbelievable. More unbelievable than yesterday and far more than two days ago," he said, regretting his sarcasm before he finished answering. It wasn't fair to Jill, who had given him nothing but support.

"I'm sorry, honey," he said. "I'm just frustrated with the Feds dragging their feet and all."

"I know, baby. It will all be sorted out soon. You know I love you," she said with a pout.

"I know," he said.

She rubbed the top of his head, kissed him, and then Zeus barked. After Zeus had awakened Jack in his hospital bed, the mysterious dog would not leave the pilot's side and the bond between them was strong. The hot pink collar seemed to suit Zeus and the original collar ended up in the Smithsonian with Doc Weaver's help and Jack's blessing. In Jack's mind, the leather collar belonged to Zeus in the past—good riddance.

He sold his Porsche and bought a used Dodge Dakota four-wheel drive pickup truck. Zeus would not ride inside the cab, although he was happy to ride in the open bed. How Zeus had appeared in his dream was one of many mysteries that had gnawed away at the sober pilot for months.

Zeus went everywhere with him in the back of the truck. Every time the truck stopped, Zeus would stick his snout through the little sliding window and try to lick Jack's ear. Sometimes, he would succumb to the hound's affections and toss a dog biscuit through the small window. Rain or shine, the window was left open just enough to accommodate Zeus' snout.

Rain, however, did not present a problem during that spring because Central Virginia was suffering through a terrible drought; everything had dried up, including the shallow swamps. Flowering trees blossomed weakly and dust filled the air.

While exploring yet another desolate area of the Wilderness, Jack stopped to eat lunch under a few anemic dogwood trees. Zeus ran to him, chased his tail around and around, and repeatedly ran a few feet away and back to him in a frenzy.

Jack laughed and said, "Okay, boy. What's up?"

He followed Zeus into the dry swamp where the hound began to dig in the hardened mud. Zeus dug furiously in the same spot until Jack bent over and looked at the shallow depression.

"What is it, boy?"

Zeus whimpered, ran in circles, and dug again while Jack passed his metal detector over the spot. It registered a significant return and Jack carefully burrowed into the dry clay until his small shovel clanked into something. He struggled to dig around the object, not wanting to damage it, and excavated a six-inch-wide chunk of red clay. His metal detector confirmed that there was a metal object buried within the hard clay and he carefully scraped dirt away with his knife. Zeus, who was dog curious, sniffed and poked his nose at the thing while Jack gently pushed his head away and concentrated on removing dry, crumbling dirt. He rubbed the remaining mud from the barrel of a small pistol with a wet rag.

What he saw astounded him. The tiny scripted letters *J.M.P. ATKINSON* were meticulously engraved on the barrel of the small pistol! It was the derringer that Amanda had thrown into the swamp more than 150 years ago and he was holding it in his hand. His entire "dream" flooded him and he was astonished as he excitedly cleaned and polished the small pistol, examining it from every angle.

"How can this be?" he repeated aloud.

Finally, he said, "Look, Zeus, it's Amanda's derringer!"

He looked around and didn't see Zeus, so he stood and called him.

"Zeus! Here, Zeus!"

Zeus always came when he called, but not this time. He called again and again with no response and looked in all directions. There was no sign of the hound. Then, he spotted something in the swamp grass and walked toward it. His heart skipped when he found Zeus' hot pink collar and his eyes filled when he realized that his friend was gone.

9

Jack sat down slowly and his tears splattered on the derringer and collar in his trembling hands. He remained for a long while, looking up every time a squirrel or bird made a rustling sound. He would have gladly traded the pistol for Zeus, but it was not to be. His amazing friend had given him the answers he so desperately needed and then returned to his own time.

Finally, he walked to his truck and sat with his head on the steering wheel. His tears would not stop and he couldn't go home. He drove slowly through the Wilderness for hours, hoping Zeus would jump into the back of the truck and stick his snout through the sliding window.

He swore he would never close that window again.

At sunset, he finally drove home and, as soon as Jill saw him, she knew something was terribly wrong. Without a word, she hugged him tenderly and he broke down in her arms. When he calmed down he told her what had happened.

"How is this possible?" Jill said while they sat at the kitchen table and examined the tiny weapon.

"It's not possible but here it is. Amanda threw this pistol into the swamp and her father's initials are right here," he said, peering at the scripted name with a magnifying glass.

"And poor Zeus has simply vanished?"

Jack choked up and couldn't answer. He excused himself and prepared a glass of ice water. He said, "Next to you, Zeus is the best friend I've ever had. He took me along on a fantastic journey. I don't pretend to know how, but I think I know why. I was in pretty bad shape before he came along and, because of that little guy, I have a new lease on life. I owe him a lot."

They both sat staring at the derringer and then Jack said, "I don't understand any of this, but the one thing I do know is that my contact with Henry Mueller allowed him to move on. He was one of the many soldiers whose spirits were imprisoned in the Wilderness all these years like the ghosts in Charlotte's basement. It was Henry I saw while driving home from the airport and again on the fairway later that night. He was asking for help. I relived my entire nightmare when I found him hanging from that tree. I know it sounds crazy, but Henry may have tried contact my poor mother as well. He meant no harm, but she just couldn't help him. They are both in my prayers."

Jack picked up the pistol and examined it. "We don't have any control over things like this and wish it could be different, but Zeus is back where he belongs and I'm with you where I belong. Losing Mom and Zeus is heartbreaking, but it's not our call and it had to end this way."

Jill wondered, for a part of an instant, if her husband was capable of planting the derringer to verify his dream. She examined the faded letters, looked into her husband's sober eyes, and knew it was the real thing. Losing Jack's mother was a tragedy and the larger cosmic meaning was beyond her. She also accepted the fact that Zeus had disappeared, which was also bizarre although easier to accept. She realized that no one would believe Jack's story because he had told only Artie and her about the initials on Major Atkinson's gun collection.

They sat in silence for a long time, staring at the small pistol. Finally, Jill said, "I guess no one will ever believe this...I mean if you ever told anyone else."

"That's true. We should probably keep it to ourselves anyway. It doesn't matter because now...I know."

Jill said nothing.

Real or not, she could see the peace in her husband's eyes. She had him back and that was all that really mattered.

"I love you," she said.

"I know," he said with a weak smile. "I love you too."

She rubbed the top on his head, hugged him, and led him into the bedroom where they tumbled before falling into peaceful, dreamless sleep.

The End

Epilogue

When the thirty-six-year-old hysterical witch named Sarah Spindle dashed across the Laurel Hill Battlefield and stumbled into the woods, she came across Star and thanked the good Lord for providing such a sturdy horse. She left her farm along with everything she owned and rode off with Star to join her family. After the war passed by, the Spindles returned to their farm and Star helped to rebuild Sarah's farmhouse and remove the ugly war from her fields. Sarah spent many long, haunting nights thinking about her encounter with Amanda. She became convinced that Star belonged to the mysterious girl and felt great guilt for having taken the teenager's horse.

I was hysterical and couldn't think right, she thought.

She made many inquiries about Amanda with no results. The grateful woman put Star out to pasture and treated the old horse like one of her own children. Star could always be found grazing near the old battered wooden bridge.

John arranged for Luke's release at Guinea Station, purchased a horse for him, and sent him in search of his family. Amanda was sent to live at the Stillwell home in Richmond and, in the fall of 1864, John and Becky joined her there. They cared for the sick and wounded at the huge Chimborazo Hospital until Richmond fell and the hospital was surrendered on April 3, 1865.

John, Becky and Amanda then returned to the scorched Wilderness. The damage to Luke's home had been repaired and their losses were minimal, thanks to Luke's warning and their timely exodus. Luke's father had returned from the war missing most of his left foot, but the family was safe and uninjured otherwise. Amanda and Luke were finally reunited and John expressed his deepest gratitude to the Stewarts.

"I would be honored to finance Luke's medical education," he said.

The family agreed. When Luke completed his training, he and Amanda were married and returned to the Wilderness where Luke served as a much-needed medical doctor.

After Amanda's reunion with Luke, she and her father returned to the Higgerson Farm. The man John had hired to look in on Permelia wrapped her remains in canvas and buried her in the soft earth of her garden, as instructed. John exhumed her remains and dug a proper grave next to Benjamin. The site was marked with a gravestone, which had been designed by Amanda.

Benjamin and Permelia Higgerson
At Peace Together
In the Wilderness

John also exhumed the family fortune that had been cleverly buried next to Benjamin. They were relieved when the gruesome chore was completed and Amanda cried softly while her father read from the Bible. They hugged each other for a long time, then loaded the valuables into the wagon and walked arm-in-arm back up to Permelia's house.

Suddenly, Zeus appeared from thin air and playfully knocked Amanda to the ground! They were astounded. The collarless dog ran circles around them like an excited puppy with a new toy.

Amanda said, "Zeus! I knew you would find your way home. You always do."

She fell into the grass and covered her head. She and John laughed while Zeus attacked her with his tongue and licked every exposed inch of her face.

Two years later, Amanda gave birth to a beautiful baby girl named Permelia.

Historical Note

The plight of the brave men who fought in our Civil War is well documented. Countless civilian tales, however, have faded from our memories. Permelia Higgerson's fifteen minutes of fame has survived the test of time. The story of the courageous widow is immortalized on a wayside exhibit at the site of her home on the Hill-Ewell Drive in Spotsylvania/Orange, Virginia.

On May 5th, 1864, when the Union Army swarmed through the Wilderness like hungry locusts, Permelia refused to abandon her home. She chose to face the massive army armed with nothing more than a broom. When the young soldiers from Pennsylvania marched across her farm and trampled her garden, Permelia berated and scolded them. They ignored her reprimands as well as her predictions of doom and continued to advance toward a swampy area within a mile of the Higgerson Farm. The Rebels picked them off like ducks in a pond and the Union troops were forced to retreat. During the hasty withdrawal, there were wounded men within several yards of Permelia's house and the air was filled with gunfire and the odor of black powder. Undaunted, Permelia left the safety of her home and continued to rebuke the same terrified soldiers.

The wayside exhibit describes the experience; there is a photograph of Permelia and her home on the exhibit as well. She appears to be a poor dirt farmer who could easily skin a hog while balancing a toddler on her hip. Nothing, however, could be further from the truth.

I became fascinated by Permelia and wanted to know more about the audacious civilian. I was able to find some information among in the archives at Chatham Manor in Fredericksburg. There, I uncovered historical facts about the Higgerson Farm, as well as a description of the nearby Chewning Plantation where Permelia's parents lived. The story of Permelia's personal life, however, remained a mystery.

On May 4th, 2009, The Friends of the Wilderness Battlefield celebrated the civilians of Wilderness battle and eighteen members of Permelia's extended family arrived to honor the Chewning/Higgerson family. Accounts of Permelia and her post-war life varied wildly among them, but Permelia's great-great-granddaughter was able to set the record straight.

Jacquelina, (Permelia's daughter) lived for nearly100 years and passed down Permelia's real story to *her* great-granddaughter, Mary Jane Fieser.

Permelia and her husband, Benjamin Higgerson, (related to the Elly family, who operated a local gold mine) lived on their 157-acre farm in the Wilderness. They had four children and owned two slaves. Because of the domestic help, however, "Princess Permelia" may not have known how to cook for her own family.

Permelia's parents lived next door on the large, productive Chewning Plantation and owned 23 slaves. Permelia's mother shared her first name. Early in the Civil War, the Higgerson's "took in" a sick Confederate soldier; Benjamin contracted typhoid fever from the man and died on Christmas day, 1862.

The Higgerson widow had, most likely, sent her children to safety before the Union onslaught. Civilians had learned that, in the wake of the Union Army, abandoned homes were sometimes ransacked or burned to the ground. Therefore, some determined residents remained at home to protect their property as the Union Army approached. Because of Permelia's astounding courage, her home stood until 1938 when it was finally destroyed by fire.

Before the war, many of the trees in the Wilderness were cut down and used as fuel in the hungry iron and gold furnaces. With no thought given to conservation, the Wilderness spawned scrub pines, tangled, thorn-covered underbrush, and swamps. During the two-day battle, nineteenth-century weaponry set the Wilderness ablaze, destroying most of what remained. After the Civil War, the entire area was a scorched wasteland.

Once the Civil War had ended, displaced Southern soldiers wandered throughout the South. Permelia met one such man named William Wallace "Daniel" Porter. She married the smooth talking William and they had children of their own. Perhaps because the scorched, high-iron content soil was not ideal for farming or because the family had grown, they decided to relocate. They packed everything they owned into a wagon, rented their home the Dempsey family and headed for St. Louis, Missouri (where one of Permelia's brothers may have settled). Heavily laden with numerous children, livestock, and all of their possessions, they traveled west and made slow progress.

Somewhere in route, William abandoned the family and returned to Virginia with Permelia's attractive, sixteen-year-old daughter, Jacquelina. She became William's common law wife and they had children of *their* own. Porter was, in effect, married to both mother and daughter simultaneously. Jacquelina did not have any contact with her mother for nine years. William and Jacquelina then returned to William's home state of Louisiana and eventually settled in Montana. There, William did it again—he abandoned Jacquelina for another woman and, no doubt, continued to spread his seed elsewhere.

Meanwhile, the incredibly resilient Permelia continued her journey with the remainder of her family, floated down the river on a raft, and made it as far as New Madrid, Missouri. She settled on the banks of the Mississippi River and managed to open Higgerson's Store, which catered to river folks.

(In 1811-12, many years before Permelia's arrival, New Madrid experienced the largest earthquake in American history, measuring 8.0 on the Richter scale. The force of the tremors rang church bells as far away as Boston and the Mississippi ran backward for nearly a week).

New Madrid was a precarious place to live and Higgerson's Store was flooded frequently. The store was moved to the higher ground several times and Permelia's descendants claim that Permelia's Bible is stained with the watermarks of each flood.

Permelia suffered many hardships, but found happiness in New Madrid and lived a long life surrounded by her children and many grandchildren.

Nearly 200 members of the Higgerson/Porter extended families meet in New Madrid for family reunions. These good people respect history and are thankful for Permelia's astounding fortitude and gut-wrenching determination.

In 2009, the Chewning/Higgerson family donated Permelia's water-stained Bible and other artifacts to the National Park Service in Fredericksburg. An exhibit honoring Permelia Higgerson is on display at Ellwood Manor, which is where Stonewall Jackson's amputated arm was once buried. Ellwood Manor served as a hospital as well as the headquarters for both armies during the four-year conflict. Ellwood has been beautifully restored with the help of The Friends of the Wilderness Battlefield and is located near the site of the Higgerson Farm on Route 20 in Orange, Virginia.

Permelia and William Chewning

Permelia's parents, William and Permelia Chewning, had nine children and about twenty slaves. William died in a mill accident, before the Wilderness battle, in 1863. Permelia Chewning died in 1875.

After the war, one of their children actually filed a claim against the United States for damages to the Chewning property. Plaintiffs were required to provide a detailed appraisal of the damages as well as witnesses, who were willing to testify that the members of the Chewning family were *Northern* sympathizers. The claim for $3,560.90 was finally refused in 1898.

Visiting the Higgerson Farm

If you live nearby or decide to visit the Wilderness, take a walk up to the peaceful ruins of Permelia Higgerson's home on Hill-Ewell Drive. Or, perhaps, hike through the unfinished railroad bed.

Close your eyes and let your imagination fly.

Endnotes

[1] https://www.facebook.com/HampdenSydneyCollege/.../1015174226442.

[2] Donald A. Bowers, Fawn Lake "Links to History"(Cardinal Press, Inc., 2008) 11

[3] Gordon C. Rhea, The Battle of the Wilderness May 5-6, 1864 (Louisiana State University Press, 1994) 359

[4] Hampden-Sydney College, available at: http://www2.hsc.edu/hschistory

[5] James John A. Ramage, Gray Ghost-The Life of Col. John Singleton Mosby (The University Press of   Kentucky, 1999) 23

[6] Ramage, 77

[7] Ramage, 81

[8] Ramage, 82

[9] Ramage. 77

[10] Rhea, 51

[11] Fredericksburg and Spotsylvania National Military Park, Permelia Higgerson Wayside Exhibit, Hill-Ewell Parkway

[12] Rhea, 384

[13] Gordon C. Rhea, The Battles for Spotsylvania Court House and the Road to Yellow Tavern May 7-12, 1864

Made in the USA
Middletown, DE
21 September 2015